THE CROOKED
HINGE

THE GREAT DETECTIVES

JOHN DICKSON CARR
THE CROOKED HINGE

Xanadu

To
DOROTHY L. SAYERS
IN FRIENDSHIP AND ESTEEM

British Library Cataloguing in Publication Data
The crooked hinge
I. Title
823'.52 [F]
ISBN 0-85480-015-9

First published 1938
This edition published 1989 by Xanadu Publications Ltd
Copyright © 1938 by Clarice M. Carr

Printed and bound in Great Britain by Cox & Wyman Ltd, Reading

PART I

Wednesday, July 29th

THE DEATH OF A MAN

The first rule to be borne in mind by the aspirant is this: Never tell your audience beforehand what you are going to do. If you do so, you at once give their vigilance the direction which it is most necessary to avoid, and increase tenfold the chances of detection. We will give an illustration.

PROFESSOR HOFFMANN, *Modern Magic.*

CHAPTER I

A T a window overlooking a garden in Kent, Brian Page
sat amid a clutter of open books at the writing-table,
and felt a strong distaste for work. Through both
windows the late July sunlight turned the floor of the
room to gold. The somnolent heat brought out an odour
of old wood and old books. A wasp hovered in from
the apple-orchard behind the garden; and Page waved
it out without much animation.

Beyond his garden wall, past the inn of the Bull and
Butcher, the road wound for some quarter of a mile
between orchards. It passed the gates of Farnleigh
Close, whose thin clusters of chimneys Page could see
above rifts in the trees, and then ascended past the wood
poetically known as Hanging Chart.

The pale green and brown of the flat Kentish lands,
which rarely acquired a harsh colour, now blazed. Page
imagined that there was even colour in the brick chimneys
of the Close. And along the road from the Close Mr
Nathaniel Burrows's car was moving with a noise audible
for some distance, even if it was not moving fast.

There was, Brian Page thought lazily, almost too much
excitement in Mallingford village. If the statement
sounded too wild for belief, it could be proved. Only
last summer there had been the murder of buxom Miss
Daly, strangled by a tramp who had been dramatically
killed while trying to get away across the railway-line.
Then, in this last week of July, there had been two
strangers putting up at the Bull and Butcher on successive
days: one stranger who was an artist and the other who
might be—nobody knew how this whisper got started—
a detective.

Finally, there had been to-day the mysterious running
to and fro of Page's friend Nathaniel Burrows, the
solicitor from Maidstone. There seemed to be some
general excitement or uneasiness at Farnleigh Close

7

though nobody knew what it meant. It was Brian Page's custom to knock off work at noon, and go over to the Bull and Butcher for a pint of beer before lunch; but it was an ominous sign that there had been no gossip at the inn that morning.

Yawning, Page pushed a few books aside. He wondered idly what could stir up Farnleigh Close, which had seldom been stirred up since Inigo Jones built it for the first baronet in the reign of James the First. It had known a long line of Farnleighs: a stringy, hardy line still. Sir John Farnleigh, the present holder of the baronetcy of- Mallingford and Soane, had inherited a substantial fortune as well as a sound demesne.

Page liked both the dark, rather jumpy John Farnleigh and his forthright wife, Molly. The life here suited Farnleigh well; he fitted; he was a born squire, in spite of having been so long away from his home. For Farnleigh's story was another of those romantic tales which interested Page and which now seemed so difficult to reconcile with the solid, almost commonplace baronet at Farnleigh Close. From his first voyage out to his marriage to Molly Sutton little more than a year ago, it was (thought Page) another advertisement for the excitements of Mallingford village.

Grinning and yawning again, Page took up his pen. Got to get to work.

Oh, Lord.

He considered the pamphlet at his elbow. His *Lives of the Chief Justices of England*—which he was trying to make both scholarly and popular—was going as well as might be expected. He was now dealing with Sir Matthew Hale. All sorts of external matters were always creeping in, because they had to creep in and because Brian Page had no wish to keep them out.

To tell the truth, he never really expected to finish the *Lives of the Chief Justices*, any more than he had finished his original law-studies. He was too indolent for real scholarship, yet too restless-minded and intellectually alert to let it alone. It did not matter whether he ever finished the Chief Justices. But he could tell himself sternly that he ought to be working, and then with a sense of relief go wandering down all sorts of fascinating bypaths of the subject.

The pamphlet beside him read, *A Tryal of Witches at the Assizes Held at Bury St Edmonds for the County of Suffolk, on the Tenth Day of March, 1664, before Sir Matthew Hale, Kt., then Lord Chief Baron of his Majesty's Court of Exchequer: printed for D. Brown, J. Walthoe, and M. Wotton, 1718.*

There was a bypath down which he had wandered before. Sir Matthew Hale's connection with witches, of course, was of the slightest. But it would not prevent Brian Page from writing a superfluous half-chapter on any subject which happened to interest him. With a breath of pleasure he took down a well-worn Glanville from one of the shelves. He was just beginning to muse over it when he heard footsteps in the garden, and somebody ' oi'd ' at him from outside the window.

It was Nathaniel Burrows, swinging a brief-case with unsolicitor-like gestures.

" Busy? " demanded Burrows.

" We-el," Page admitted, and yawned. He put down Glanville. " Come in and have a cigarette."

Burrows opened the glass door giving on the garden and stepped into the dim, comfortable room. Though he held himself well in hand, he was excited enough to look chilly and rather pale on a hot afternoon. His father, grandfather, and great-grandfather had handled the legal affairs of the Farnleighs. Sometimes it might have been doubted whether Nathaniel Burrows, with his enthusiasm and occasional explosive speech, was the proper person for a family lawyer. Also, he was young. But as a rule he had all these things under control; and managed, Page thought, to look more frozen-faced than a halibut on a slab.

Burrows's dark hair had a wide parting, and was smoothed round his head with great nicety. He wore shell-rimmed spectacles on a long nose; he was peering over the spectacles, and his face at the moment seemed to have more than the usual number of muscles. He was dressed in black with great nicety and discomfort; his gloved hands were clasped on the brief-case.

" Brian," he said, " are you dining in to-night? "

9

" Yes. I— "

" Don't," said Burrows abruptly.

Page blinked.

" You're dining with the Farnleighs," Burrows went on. " At least, I don't care whether you dine there; but I should prefer that you were there when a certain thing happens." Something of his official manner came back to him, and swelled his thin chest. " I am authorised to tell you what I am going to tell you. Fortunately. Tell me: did you ever have reason to think that Sir John Farnleigh was not what he seemed? "

" Not what he seemed? "

" That Sir John Farnleigh," explained Burrows carefully, " was an impostor and a masquerader, not Sir John Farnleigh at all? "

" Have you got sunstroke? " asked the other, sitting up. He felt startled and irritated and unwarrantably stirred up. It was not the sort of thing to spring on a person at the laziest period of a hot day. " Certainly I never had reason to think any such thing. Why should I? What the devil are you getting at? "

Nathaniel Burrows got up from the chair, depositing the brief-case there.

" I say that," he answered, " because a man has turned up who claims to be the real John Farnleigh. This isn't a new thing. It's been going on for several months, and now it's come to a head. Er— " He hesitated, and looked round. " Is there anybody else here? Mrs What's-her-name—you know, the woman who does for you —or anyone? "

" No."

Burrows spoke as though entirely through the front of his mouth and teeth. " I shouldn't be telling you this. But I know I can trust you; and (between ourselves) I am in a delicate position. This is going to make trouble. The Tichborne case won't be a patch on it. Of course— er—officially, as yet, I have no reason to believe that the man whose affairs I administer isn't Sir John Farnleigh. I am supposed to serve Sir John Farnleigh: the proper one. But that is the point. Here are two men. One is the real baronet and the other is a masquerading fraud. The two men are not alike; they don't even *look* alike.

And yet may I be damned if I can decide which is which." He paused, and then added: " Fortunately, though, the affair may be settled tonight."

Page had to adjust his thoughts. Pushing the cigarette-box across to his guest, he lit a cigarette for himself and studied Burrows.

"This is one clap of thunder after another," he said. "What started it, anyhow? When has there been any reason to suppose that an impostor stepped in? Has the question ever come up before now? "

"Never. And you'll see why." Burrows got out a handkerchief, mopped his face all over with great care, and settled down calmly. "I only hope it's a mare's nest. I like John and Molly—sorry, Sir John and Lady Farnleigh—I like them enormously. If this claimant is an impostor, I'll dance on the village green—well, maybe not that, perhaps—but I shall make it my business to see that he gets a prison sentence for perjury longer than Arthur Orton's was. ¯In the meantime, since you're going to hear about it to-night, you'd better know the back-ground of the whole thing, and why the infernal mess has come up. Do you know Sir John's story? "

" In a vague general way."

" You should know nothing in a vague general way," retorted Burrows, shaking his head disapprovingly. " Is that the way you write your history? I hope not. Listen to me; and keep these simple facts firmly fixed in your mind.

" We are going back twenty-five years, when the present Sir John Farnleigh was fifteen. He was born in 1898, the second son of old Sir Dudley and Lady Farnleigh. There was no question then of his inheriting the title: the elder son, Dudley, was his parents' pride and joy.

" And they required something noble in the way of sons. Old Sir Dudley (I knew him all my life) was a late-Victorian of the most rigid sort. He wasn't as bad as the romances paint such types nowadays; but I remember as a kid that it always surprised me when he gave me sixpence.

" Young Dudley was a good boy. John wasn't. He was a dark, quiet, wild sort of boy, but with so much sullenness that nobody could pardon the least offensive things he did. There was no real harm in him; it was merely that he didn't fit and wanted to be treated as a grown-up before he had grown up. In nineteen-twelve, when he was fifteen, he had a fully grown-up affair with a barmaid in Maidstone— "

Page whistled. He glanced out of the window, as though he expected to see Farnleigh himself.

" At fifteen? " Page said. " Here, he must have been a lad! "

" He was."

Page hesitated. " And yet, you know, I'd always thought from what I've seen of him that Farnleigh was— "

" A bit of a Puritan? " supplied Burrows. " Yes. Anyhow, we're talking about a boy aged fifteen. His studying occult matters, including witchcraft and Satanism, was bad enough. His being expelled from Eton was worse. But the public scandal with the barmaid, who thought she was going to have a child, finished it. Sir Dudley Farnleigh simply decided that the boy was bad clean through, some throwback to the Satanist Farnleighs: that nothing would ever change him: and that he did not care to see him again. The usual course was adopted. Lady Farnleigh had a cousin in America, who was doing well there, and John was packed off to the States.

" The only person who seemed able to manage him at all was a tutor named Kennet Murray. The tutor, then a young fellow of twenty-two or three, had come to Farnleigh Close after John left school. Kennet Murray's hobby, it is important to mention, was scientific criminology: which was what drew the boy to Murray from the beginning. It wasn't a genteel hobby in those days; but Sir Dudley liked and approved of Murray, so not much more was said.

" Now at this time, it happened, Murray had just been offered a good position as assistant headmaster of a school in Hamilton, Bermuda—provided he cared to go so far away from home. He accepted; his services were no longer required at the Close, anyway. It was arranged that Murray should travel out with the boy to New York, to see that he kept out of trouble. He should hand over the boy to Lady Farnleigh's cousin, and then take another ship down to Bermuda."

Nathaniel Burrows paused, considering the past.

"I don't remember much about those days, speaking personally," he added. "We younger children were kept away from the wicked John. But little Molly Sutton, who was then only six or seven years old, was frantically devoted to him. She wouldn't hear a word against him; and it may be significant that she has since married him. It seems to me I vaguely remember the day John was driven to the railway-station, in a phaeton, wearing a flat straw hat, with Kennet Murray beside him. They were sailing next day, which was a gala day for more reasons than one. I don't need to tell you that the ship they took was the *Titanic*."

Both Burrows and Page now looked at the past. The latter remembered it as a confused time of shoutings, and newspaper-bills at the corners, and legends without foundation.

"The unsinkable *Titanic* rammed an iceberg and sank on the night of April 15th, nineteen-twelve," Burrows went on. "In the confusion Murray and the boy were separated. Murray drifted for eighteen hours, in icy water, holding to a wooden grating with two or three others. They were presently picked up by a cargo-boat, the *Colophon*—bound for Bermuda. Murray was taken to the place he meant to go. But he did not worry any longer when he heard by wireless that John Farnleigh was safe, and later got a letter confirming it.

"John Farnleigh, or a boy purporting to be John, was picked up by the *Etrusca*, bound for New York. There Lady Farnleigh's cousin, a Westerner, met him. The situation was exactly as it had been before. Beyond making sure the boy was alive, Sir Dudley was still quit of him. And old Sir Dudley wasn't any more bitter than the boy himself.

"He grew up in America, and lived there for nearly twenty-five years. He wouldn't write a line to his people; he would see them dead before he sent a photograph or a birthday message. Fortunately he took an immediate liking to the American cousin, a man named Renwick, and that supplied the need of parents. He—er

13

—seemed to change. He lived quietly as a farmer on broad acres, just as he might háve lived here. During the latter years of the war he served with the American army, but he never once set foot in England or met any of the people he had known. He never even saw Murray again. Murray was existing, though not prospering, in Bermuda. Neither could afford a journey to visit the other, especially as John Farnleigh lived in Colorado.

"Back here at home nothing was disturbed. The boy had been practically forgotten; and, after his mother died in 1926, he was completely forgotten. The father followed her four years later. Young Dudley—he was not so young now—inherited the title and all the estate. He had never married; he said there was time enough for that. But there wasn't. The new Sir Dudley died of ptomaine poisoning in August, 1935."

Brian Page reflected.

"That was just before I came here," Page observed. "But look here! Didn't Dudley try to get in touch with his brother at any time?"

"Yes. The letters were returned unopened. Dudley had been—well, rather a prig in the old days. By this time they had grown so far apart that apparently John didn't feel any family relationship. However, when it became a question of John's inheriting the title and the estate at Dudley's death—"

"John accepted."

"He accepted. Yes. That's the point," said Burrows explosively. "You know him and you understand. Nothing seemed so *right* as his coming back here. It didn't even seem strange to him, though he'd been away for nearly twenty-five years. He didn't seem strange: he still thought and acted and to a certain extent talked like the heir of Farnleigh. He came here at the beginning of 1936. As an additional romantic touch, he met a grown-up Molly Sutton and married her in May of the same year. He settles in for a little over a year; and now this happens. This happens."

"I suppose the suggestion is," said Page with some uncertainty, "that there was a substitution of identities at the time of the *Titanic* disaster? That the wrong boy was picked up at sea, and for some reason pretended to be John Farnleigh? "

Burrows had been walking up and down with measured slowness, wagging his finger at any piece of furniture he passed. But he did not look comic. There was about him an intellectual strength which soothed or even hypnotised clients. He had a trick of turning his head sideways and peering at a companion past the sides of his big spectacles, as he did now.

"That's exactly it. Exactly. If the present John Farnleigh has been playing an imposture, don't you see, he has been playing it since 1912—while the real heir lay low? He has grown into it. When he was rescued from the lifeboat after the wreck he wore Farnleigh's clothes and ring; he carried Farnleigh's diary. He has been exposed to the reminiscences of his Uncle Renwick in America. He has come back and settled into old ways. And, twenty-five years! Handwritings change; faces and marks alter; even memories become uncertain. Do you see the difficulty? If sometimes he makes a slip, if there are gaps or clouds anywhere, that's only natural. Isn't it? "

Page shook his head.

"All the same, my lad, this claimant has got to have a thundering good case to gain any credence. You know what the courts are like. What sort of case *has* he got? "

"The claimant," answered Burrows, folding his arms, "offers absolute proof that he is the real Sir John Farnleigh."

"Have you seen this proof? "

"We are to see it—or not to see it—to-night. The claimant asks for an opportunity to meet the present holder. No, Brian: I am not in the least simple-minded, although I have nearly gone mad over this affair. It is not merely that the claimant's story is convincing, and that he offers all the minor proofs. It is not merely that he walked into my office (with, I regret to tell you, a bounder who is his legal representative) and told me things which only John Farnleigh could have known. *Only* John Farnleigh, I say. But he has proposed that he and the present holder shall submit to a certain test, which should be conclusive."

15

"What test?"

"You will see. Oh, yes. You will see." Nathaniel Burrows picked up his brief-case. "There has been only one gleam of comfort in the whole cursed mess. That is, so far there has been no publicity. The claimant is at least a gentleman—both of 'em are—bah—and he isn't anxious for a row. But there is going to be a remarkable row when I get my fingers on the truth. I'm glad my father isn't alive to see this. In the meantime, you be at Farnleigh Close at seven o'clock. Don't bother to dress for dinner. Nobody else will. It's only a pretext and there probably won't even be any dinner."

"And how is Sir John taking all this?"

"Which Sir John?"

"For the sake of clearness and convenience," retorted Page, "the man we have always known as Sir John Farnleigh. But this is interesting. Does it mean you believe the claimant is the real thing?"

"No. Not actually. Certainly not!" said Burrows. He caught himself up and spoke with dignity. "Farnleigh is only—spluttering. And I think that's a good sign."

"Does Molly know?"

"Yes; he told her to-day. Well, there you are. I've talked to you as no solicitor should and few ever do; but if I can't trust you I can't trust anybody, and I've been a bit uneasy about my conduct of things since my father died. Now get into the swim. Try my spiritual difficulties for yourself. Come up to Farnleigh Close at seven o'clock; we want you as a witness. Inspect the two candidates. Exercise your intelligence. And then, before we get down to business," said Burrows, banging the edge of his brief-case on the desk, "kindly tell me which is which."

CHAPTER II

SHADOWS were gathering on the lower slopes of the wood called Hanging Chart, but the flat lands to the left of it were still clear and warm. Set back from the road behind a wall and a screen of trees, the house had those colours of dark-red brick which seem to come from an old painting. It was as smoothed, as arranged, as its own clipped lawns. The windows were tall and narrow, with panes set into a pattern of stone oblongs; and a straight gravel drive led up to the door. Its chimneys stood up thin and close-set against the last light.

No ivy had been allowed to grow against its face. But there was a line of beech-trees set close against the house at the rear. Here a newer wing had been built out from the centre—like the body of an inverted letter T—and it divided the Dutch garden into two gardens. On one side of the house the garden was overlooked by the back windows of the room in which Sir John Farnleigh and Molly Farnleigh were waiting now.

A clock ticked in this room. It was what might have been called in the eighteenth century a Music Room or Ladies' Withdrawing Room, and it seemed to indicate the place of the house in this world. A pianoforte stood here, of that wood which in old age seems to resemble polished tortoise-shell. There was silver of age and grace, and a view of the Hanging Chart from its north windows; Molly Farnleigh used it as a sitting-room. It was very warm and quiet here, except for the ticking of the clock.

Molly Farnleigh sat by the window in the shadow of a great 'octopus' beech-tree. She was what is called an outdoor girl, with a sturdy and well-shaped body, and a square but very attractive face. Her dark brown hair was uncompromisingly bobbed. She had light hazel eyes in a tanned, earnest face, and a directness of look which was as good as a handclasp. Her mouth might have been too broad, but she showed fine teeth when she laughed. If she was not exactly pretty, health and vigour gave her a strong attractiveness which was better than that.

But she was not laughing now. Her eyes never left her husband, who was pacing the room with short, sharp steps.

"You're not worried?" she asked.

Sir John Farnleigh stopped short. Then he fiddled with his dark wrists, and resumed his pacing.

"Worried? No. Oh, no. It's not that. It's only— oh, damn it all!"

17

He seemed an ideal partner for her. It would convey the wrong impression to say that he looked in his element as a country squire, for the word has come to be associated with beefy roisterers of a hundred years ago. Yet there is a truer type. Farnleigh was of middle height, of a stingy, active leanness which somehow suggested the lines of a plough: the bright metal, the compactness, the crisp blade that cuts the furrow.

His age might have been forty. He was of darkish complexion, with a thick but close-cropped moustache. He had dark hair in which there were thin lines of grey, and sharp dark eyes with growing wrinkles at the corners. You would have said that at the moment he was at the top of his mental and physical form, a man of enormous repressed energies. Striding back and forth in the little room, he seemed less angry or upset than uncomfortable and embarrassed.

Molly started to rise. She cried:

" Oh, my dear, why didn't you *tell* me? "

" No use worrying you with it," the other said. " It's my affair. I'll manage."

" How long have you known about it? "

" A month or so. Thereabouts."

" And that's what's been worrying you all this time? " she asked, with a shade of different worry in her eyes.

" Partly," he grunted, and looked at her quickly.

" Partly? What do you mean by that? "

" What I say, my dear: partly."

" John . . . it hasn't got anything to do with Madeline Dane, has it? "

He stopped. " Good God, no! Certainly not. I don't know why you ask questions like that. You don't like Madeline, really, do you? "

" I don't like her eyes. They're queer eyes," said Molly, and checked herself out of a certain pride or another feeling she refused to name. " I'm sorry. I shouldn't have said anything like that, with all these other things coming up. It's not very pleasant; but there's nothing to it, is there? Of course the man hasn't got a case? "

" He hasn't got a right. I don't know whether he's got a case."

He spoke brusquely, and she studied him.

"But why is there so much fuss and mystery? If he's an impostor, couldn't you sling him out and let the matter drop?"

"Burrows says it wouldn't be wise. Not yet, anyway, until we've—er—heard what he has to say. Then we can take action. And real action. Besides—"

Molly Farnleigh's face grew expressionless.

"I wish you'd let me help you," she said. "Not that I could do anything, I suppose, but I should just like to know what it's all *about*. I know this man challenges you to let him prove he's really you. Of course that's all nonsense. I knew you years ago; and I knew you when I saw you again; you would be surprised how easily I knew. But I know you're having this fellow here at the house, with Nat Burrows and another solicitor, and being horribly mysterious. What are you going to do?"

"Do you remember my old tutor, Kennet Murray?"

"Faintly," said Molly, wrinkling her forehead. "Largish, pleasant man with a little cropped beard like a naval man or an artist. I suppose he was really young then, but he seemed ages old. Told wonderful stories—"

"His ambition was always to be a great detective," answered the other curtly. "Well, the Opposition have brought him from Bermuda. He says he can absolutely identify the real John Farnleigh. He's at the Bull and Butcher now."

"Wait a bit!" said Molly. "There's a man staying there who 'looks like an artist'. The village is full of it. Is that Murray?"

"That's old Murray. I wanted to go down and see him; but it wouldn't be—well, it wouldn't be sporting," said her husband, with a kind of inner struggle and writhing. "It might look as though I were trying to influence him. Or something. He's coming up here to see us both, and identify—me."

"How?"

"He's the one person in the world who really knew me well. The family has pretty well died out; you know that. The old servants have died out with my parents: except Nannie, and she's in New Zealand. Even Knowles has been here for only ten years. There

19

are plenty of people that I knew vaguely, but you know I was an unsociable cuss and I didn't make friends. Poor old criminal-investigating Murray is undoubtedly it. He's remaining neutral and not having anything to do with either side; but, if he wants to have the one shot of his life at playing the great detective—"

Molly drew a deep breath. The health of her tanned face, the health of her whole body, animated the directness with which she spoke.

"John, I don't understand this. I do not understand it. You talk as though this were a wager or a game of some kind. 'Wouldn't be sporting.' 'Not having anything to do with either side.' Do you realise that this man—whoever he is—has coolly announced that he owns everything you own? That he's John Farnleigh? That he's the heir to a baronetcy and thirty thousand pounds a year? And that he means to have it from you? "

"Yes, I realise that."

"But doesn't it mean anything to you? " cried Molly. "You're treating him with as great care and consideration as though it didn't."

"It means everything to me."

"Well, then! If anybody had come to you and said, 'I am John Farnleigh,' I should have thought you would have said, 'Oh, really?' and merely kicked him out without thinking anything more about it, unless you sent for the police. That's what I should have done."

"You don't understand these things, my dear. And Burrows says— "

He looked slowly round the room. He seemed to be listening to the quiet ticking of the clock, to be savouring the odours of scrubbed floors and fresh curtains, to be reaching out in the sunlight over all the rich and quiet acres he now owned. At that moment, oddly enough, he looked most like a Puritan; and also he looked dangerous.

"It would be rather rotten," he said slowly, "to lose all this now."

He caught himself up, altering the quiet violence of his manner, as the door opened. Knowles, the old and bald-headed butler, ushered in Nathaniel Burrows and Brian Page.

Burrows, as Page had observed during their walk up here, wore now his most buttoned-up and halibut-like look. Page would not have known him for the human being of that afternoon. But Page supposed it was necessary because of the awkward atmosphere: he felt it at its worst. Glancing at his host and hostess, he began to wish he hadn't come.

The solicitor greeted his host and hostess with almost painful formality; and Farnleigh had drawn himself up stiffly, as though he were going to fight a duel.

"I think," Burrows added, "we shall be able to proceed to business soon. Mr Page has kindly consented to act as the witness we desired—"

"Oh, look here," protested Page, with an effort. "We're not being besieged in a citadel, you know. You're one of the largest and most respected land-owners in Kent. To hear what I've just heard from Burrows," he looked at Farnleigh, and could not discuss the matter, "is like hearing that grass is red or water runs uphill. It's about as reasonable, in the eyes of most people. Have you got to be so much on the defensive?"

Farnleigh spoke slowly.

"That's true," he admitted. "I suppose I'm being a fool."

"You are," agreed Molly. "Thanks, Brian."

"Old Murray—" said Farnleigh, with a far-away look. "Have you seen him, Burrows?"

"Only for a short time, Sir John. Not officially. Neither have the Other Side. His position is, plainly, that he has a test to apply; and in the meantime he says nothing."

"Has he changed much?"

Burrows became more human. "Not much. He's older and stiffer and sourer, and his beard is grey. Old days—"

"Old days," said Farnleigh. "Of course!" He turned something over in his mind. "There's just one question I want to ask you. Have you got any reason to suspect that Murray isn't straight? Wait! I know it's a rotten thing to say. Old Murray always was too honest: transparently. But we haven't seen him for twenty-five years.

21

It's a long time. *I've* changed. No possibility of crooked work, is there? "

"You can rest assured there is not," said Burrows grimly. "I think we have discussed that before. It was the first thing that occurred to me, of course; and, considering the steps we have taken, you yourself have been satisfied of Mr Murray's *bona fides*. Have you not?"[1]

"Yes, I suppose so."

"Then may I ask why you bring it up now? "

"You will oblige me," retorted Farnleigh, suddenly freezing up in a very passable imitation of Burrows's own manner, "by not looking as though you thought I were the impostor and the crook. You're all doing it. Don't deny it! That's exactly what you're doing. Peace, peace, peace: I've been looking all over the world for peace, and where am I going to get it? But I'll tell you why I ask about Murray. If you don't think there is anything crooked about Murray, why have you got a private detective watching him? "

Behind the big spectacles Burrows's eyes opened in obvious astonishment.

"I beg your pardon, Sir John. I have no private detective watching Mr Murray or anybody else."

Farnleigh pulled himself up. "Then who's the other fellow down at the Bull and Butcher? You know: youngish, hard-faced chap with all the sly asides and questions? Everybody in the village says he's a private detective. He says he's interested in 'folklore' and writing a book. Folklore my foot. He's sticking to Murray like a limpet."

They all looked at each other.

"Yes," Burrows observed thoughtfully. "I have heard of the folklorist and his interest in people. He may have been sent by Welkyn— "

[1] Newspaper-readers may remember, in the bitter debate which followed tragedy in the Farnleigh case, that this point was often brought up by amateurs. Having myself once wasted time on many futile theories in an attempt to solve the mystery, I feel that I had better clear it up here. The honesty and good faith of Kennet Murray may be accepted as a fact. The evidence he possessed, with regard to establishing the identity of the real heir, was genuine evidence; and it may be recalled, was later used to establish the truth.—J. D. C.

" Welkyn? "

" The claimant's solicitor. Or he may have nothing to do with the case, as is most probable."

" I doubt it," said Farnleigh, and the blood seemed to come up under his eyes, making his face darker. " Not all he's interested in. The private detective chap, I mean. He's been asking all kinds of questions, from what I hear, about poor Victoria Daly."

To Brian Page it seemed that values had shifted slightly, and all familiar things were becoming unfamiliar. In the midst of a debate about his right to an estate worth thirty thousand pounds a year, Farnleigh seemed more preoccupied with the commonplace—if sordid—tragedy of the previous summer. Well? Victoria Daly, an inoffensive spinster of thirty-five, strangled in her cottage by a tramp who professed to sell boot-laces and collar-studs? Strangled, curiously enough, with a boot-lace; and her purse found in the tramp's pocket when he was killed on the railway line?

In the midst of a silence, while Page and Molly Farnleigh looked at each other, the door of the room opened. Knowles came in with an air of equal uncertainty.

" There are two gentlemen to see you, sir," Knowles said. " One is a Mr Welkyn, a solicitor. The other—."

" Well? The other? "

" The other asks me to say that he is Sir John Farnleigh."

" Does he? Oh. Well—"

Molly got up quietly, but muscles had tightened at the corners of her jaws.

" Take back this message from Sir John Farnleigh," she instructed Knowles. " Sir John Farnleigh presents his compliments; and, if the caller has no name to give other than that, he may go round and wait in the servants' hall until Sir John finds time to see him."

" No, come, come! " stuttered Burrows, in a kind of legal agony. " Trying circumstances—necessary to be tactful—freeze him all you like, but don't— "

The shadow of a smile crossed Farnleigh's dark face.

" Very well, Knowles. Take that message."

" Impudence," said Molly, breathing hard.

When Knowles returned he had less the air of a courier

than of a sensitive tennis-ball being driven to different corners of the court.

"The gentleman says, sir, that he deeply apologises for his message, which was premature, and hopes there will be no ill-feeling in the matter. He says he has chosen for some years to be known as Mr Patrick Gore."

"I see," said Farnleigh. "Show Mr Gore and Mr Welkyn into the library."

CHAPTER III

THE claimant got up from his chair. Despite the fact that one wall of the library was built of windows, multitudinous panes set in a pattern of stone oblongs, the daylight was going; and the trees threw heavy shadows. On the stone-flagged floor there was insufficient carpeting. The heavy book-shelves were built up like tiers in a crypt, scrolled along the top. Green-shadowed light through the windows drew across the floor a silhouette of a hundred panes, stretching almost to the man who rose to his feet beside the table.

Molly has since confessed that her heart was in her mouth when the door opened, and that she wondered whether a living counterpart of her husband might not appear from behind it, as in a mirror. Yet there was no great resemblance between these two.

The man in the library was no heavier than Farnleigh in spite of very powerful arms and shoulders. His dark, fine hair had no grey in it, but he was going a little thin on top. Though dark of complexion, he was clean-shaven and his face was comparatively unfurrowed. Any wrinkles in his forehead or round his eyes were those of amusement rather than doggedness. For the claimant's whole expression was one of ease, irony, and amusement, with very dark grey eyes, and eyebrows wisped up a little at the outer corners. He was well dressed, in town clothes as opposed to Farnleigh's old tweeds.

"I beg your pardon," he said.

Even his voice was a baritone, in contrast to Farnleigh's harsh and rasping tenor. His walk was not exactly limping, but a bit clumsy.

"I beg your pardon," he said with grave courtesy, but with a certain oblique look of amusement, "for seeming so insistent about returning to my old home. But you will, I hope, appreciate my motives. Er—let me present my legal representative, Mr Welkyn."

A fat man with somewhat protuberant eyes had got up from a chair at the other side of the table. But they hardly saw him. The claimant was not only studying them with interest; he was glancing round the room as though he were recognising and drinking in every detail.

"Let's get down to business," said Farnleigh abruptly. "I think you've met Burrows. This is Mr. Page. This is my wife."

"I have met," said the claimant, hesitating and then looking full at Molly, "your wife. Forgive me if I do not know quite how to address her. I can't call her Lady Farnleigh. And I can't call her Molly, as I used to do when she wore hair-ribbons."

Neither of the Farnleighs commented. Molly was calm but flushed, and there was a dry strain about her eyes.

"Also," went on the claimant, "I should like to thank you for taking this very awkward and unpleasant business in such good part—"

"I don't," snapped Farnleigh. "I take it in devilish damned bad part, and you might as well understand that. The only reason why I don't throw you out of the house is because my own solicitor seems to think we ought to be tactful. All right: speak up. What have you got to say?"

Mr Welkyn moved out from the table, clearing his throat.

"My client, Sir John Farnleigh—" he began.

"One moment," interposed Burrows, with equal suavity. Page seemed to hear a faint hiss as legal axes began to grind; as forensic sleeves were rolled up; as the conversation was being geared to the pace these gentlemen would have it take. "May I request, for the sake of convenience, that we refer to your client by some other

25

name? He chose to give the name of 'Patrick Gore'."

"I should prefer," said Welkyn, "to refer to him simply as 'my client'. Will that be satisfactory?"

"Perfectly."

"Thank you. I have here," pursued Welkyn, opening his brief-case, "a proposal which my client is prepared to submit. My client wishes to be fair. While under the necessity of pointing out that the present holder has no claim to the title and estates, nevertheless my client remembers the circumstances under which the imposture was begun. He also recognises the present holder's able stewardship and the fact that nothing but credit has been reflected on the family name.

"Therefore, if the present holder will at once withdraw without making it necessary to take the matter into the courts, there will be, of course, no question of prosecution. To the contrary, my client is willing to make some financial compensation to the present holder: let us say an annuity of one thousand pounds a year for life. My client has ascertained that the present holder's wife—*née* Miss Mary Sutton—has inherited a fortune in her own right; and the question of straitened finances should not, therefore, arise. Of course, I confess that should the present holder's wife care to question the validity of the marriage on the grounds of fraudulent—"

Again the blood had come up under Farnleigh's eyes.

"God!" he said. "Of all the brazen, bare-faced—"

Nathaniel Burrows made a noise which was too polite to be called shushing, but it restrained Farnleigh.

"May I suggest, Mr Welkyn," Burrows replied, "that we are here at the moment to determine whether your client has a claim? Until that is determined, any other considerations do not arise."

"As you please. My client," said Welkyn, with a disdainful movement of his shoulders, "merely wished to avoid unpleasantness. Mr Kennet Murray should be with us in a few minutes. After that I fear the result will be no longer in doubt. If the present holder persists in his attitude, then I am afraid the consequences will be—"

"Look here," Farnleigh interposed again, "let's cut the cackle and get down to the horses."

The claimant smiled, which seemed to turn his eyes inwards with some secret joke. "You see?" he remarked. "His pseudo-gentility is so grafted on him that he cannot bring himself to say 'osses."

"It doesn't bring him to giving cheap insults, in any case," said Molly and now it was the claimant who showed a slight flush.

"I beg your pardon. I should not have said that. But you must remember," said the claimant, his tone again changing a little, "that I have dwelt among wicked ways, and hardly by the springs of Dove. Have I leave to present my own case in my own way?"

"Yes," said Farnleigh. "Shut up," he added to both lawyers. "This is a personal matter now."

As though by common consent they all moved towards the table and took chairs. The claimant sat with his back to the great window. For a time he remained thoughtful, absently patting the slight thinning patch that showed in the crown of his dark hair. Then he looked up, with the edge of mockery showing in the wrinkles round his eyes.

"I am John Farnleigh," he began with great simplicity and apparent earnestness. "Kindly do not interrupt me with legal quibbles at this time; I am presenting my case, and am entitled to call myself the Cham of Tartary if I feel so inclined. However, I really do happen to be John Farnleigh, and I will tell you what happened to me.

"As a boy I may have been something of a young swine; though even now I am not certain I did not have the right attitude. My late father, Dudley Farnleigh, would put up my hackles just as much if he were alive now. No, I cannot say I was wrong, except that I should have learned more give-and-take. I quarrelled with my elders for pointing out that I was young, I quarrelled with my tutors because I despised every subject in which I was not interested.

"To get down to business, you know why I left here. I sailed with Murray in the *Titanic*. And, from the first, I spent as much time as I could with the steerage passengers. Not, you understand, because I felt any particular liking for the steerage passengers, but simply because I hated my own crowd in first-class. This is not a defence, you know: it is a psychological account which I think you will find convincing.

"In the steerage I met a Rumanian-English boy, about my own age, who was going out alone to the States. He interested me. His father—who could never afterwards be found—he said was an English gentleman. His mother was a Rumanian girl, a snake-dancer at a travelling circus in England during the times when she was not drinking. There came a time when real snakes would not mix with imaginary ones, and the woman was reduced to the position of part-time cook in the circus mess-tent. The boy became a nuisance. An old admirer of hers was doing well in a small way with a circus in America, and so she was sending the boy out to him.

"He would be taught to ride a bicycle on the tight-rope, he would be taught—and how I envied him. Lord of saints and snakes, HOW I envied him! Will any right-minded boy or man blame me?"

The claimant shifted a little in his chair. He seemed to be looking back cynically, yet with a certain satisfaction; and none of the others moved. The suave Mr Welkyn, who seemed about to interpose with a comment or suggestion, looked quickly round at the group of faces and remained silent.

"The odd part of it," continued the speaker, examining his finger-nails, "was that this boy envied me. His name (which was something unpronounceable) he had changed to 'Patrick Gore' because he liked the sound of it. He disliked circus life. He disliked the movement and the change and the din and the upset. He hated stakes driven in overnight to be pulled up in the morning, and elbows in your face at the soup-kitchen. I don't know where he got it: he was a reserved, cold-faced, well-mannered little bounder. The first time we met we flew at each other and fought until half the steerage had to drag us apart. I am afraid that I was so enraged I wanted to go at him afterwards with my clasp-knife. He simply bowed to me and walked away; I can see him yet.—I am referring, my friend, to you."

He glanced up at Farnleigh.

"This can't be real," Farnleigh said suddenly, and

28

passed his hand across his forehead, " I don't believe it. It's a nightmare. Are you seriously suggesting—? "

" Yes," agreed the other, with a decisive snap. " We discussed how pleasant it would be if we could swap identities. Only as a wild dream of let's pretend, of course: at that moment. You said it would never work, though you looked as though you would like to murder me to get it. I don't suppose I ever really meant to carry out any such thing; the interesting point is that you did mean it. I used to give you information about myself. I used to tell you. ' Now if you met my Aunt So-and-So or my Cousin This-and-That, this is what you must say to them,' and lord it over you in a way that I do not like to remember: for this is no justification of my behaviour there. I thought you were a prig and I still think so. I also showed you my diary. I always kept a diary, for the simple reason that there was nobody on earth I could talk to. I still keep one." Here the claimant glanced up almost whimsically. " Do you remember me, Patrick? Do you remember the night the *Titanic* went down? "

There was a pause.

On Farnleigh's face there was no expression of anger: only of bewilderment.

" I keep telling you," he said, " that you're mad."

" When we struck that iceberg," the other went on carefully, " I will tell you exactly what I was doing. I was down in the cabin I shared with poor old Murray, while he was in the smoking-room playing bridge. Murray kept a flask of brandy in one of his coats; and I was sampling it because they would not serve me in the bar.

" I scarcely felt it when we struck; I question if anybody did. There was a very slight bump, hardly enough to spill a filled cocktail-glass on a table; and then the stopping of the engines. I only went out into the alley-way because I wondered why the engines had stopped. The first I knew of it came from the noise of voices getting louder and closer; and then a woman suddenly running past screaming with a blue quilt wrapped round her shoulders."

For the first time the claimant hesitated.

" I am not going to bring back old tragedies by saying anything more about that part of it," he said, opening and shutting his hands. "I will say only this, for which God forgive me, even as a boy: I rather enjoyed it. I was not in the least frightened. I was exhilarated. It was something out of the common, something to take away the ordinary sameness of everyday life; and I had always been looking for things like that. And I was so wild with excitement that I agreed to change identities with Patrick Gore. The determination seemed to come to me all at once, though I am wondering if he had thought about it for a long time.

"I met Gore—I met you," amplified the speaker, looking at his host steadily, "on B Deck. You had all your possessions in a little straw suitcase. You told me quite coolly that the ship was going down, and going down fast: if I really wanted to change identities, it might be managed in the confusion, or if either of us survived. I said, what about Murray? You lied, saying that Murray was overboard and dead already. And I was willing enough to become a great circus-performer, so we changed: clothes, papers, rings, everything. You even got my diary."

Farnleigh said nothing.

"Afterwards," added the claimant, without altering the tone of his voice, "you were very neat. We were ready to run for the boats. You waited until my back was turned; then you fished out the steward's wooden mallet you had stolen, you caught me on the back of the skull with it, and you tried with three blows to finish the work."

Farnleigh still said nothing. Molly got up from her chair; but, at a gesture from him, she sat down again.

"Mind you," insisted the claimant, with a movement as though he were flicking dust from the table, "I am not here to bring that up against you. Twenty-five years is a long time, and you were a boy then, though I am wondering into what sort of man you have grown. I was considered a bad lot myself. It is possible that you despised me and believed you had justification. You need not have been so thorough because I should have assumed your identity in any case. Still—even if I was the black sheep of the family, I was never quite so black as that.

"The rest of it will be clear to you. By what I must

30

insist was a stroke of luck I was found, damaged but alive, and pushed into the last surviving boat. The casualty lists were at first uncertain, and America is a large country, and I was for some time in the world of shadows. Both the names of John Farnleigh and Patrick Gore appeared as missing. I thought you were dead, as you thought I was. When my possessions and papers identified me as Patrick Gore to Mr Boris Yeldritch, the circus-proprietor—who had never seen you—I was entirely content.

"If I did not like the life, I thought, I could always reveal myself. Perhaps I should have better treatment, I thought, if I miraculously returned from the dead. The prospect pleased me; it was a dramatic card in reserve; and, believe me, it gave me many comforting nights."

"And," said Molly as though with elaborate interest, "did you become the trick bicycle-rider of the circus?"

The claimant turned his head sideways. His dark grey eye was kindled with such strong inner amusement that he resembled a craftly small boy. Again he lifted his hand and rubbed the thinning patch on the crown of his head.

"No. No, although I had my first sensational success with the circus, I became something else. For the moment I should prefer not to tell you what it was. In addition to the fact that it is an excellent secret, I do not wish to bore you with details of my subsequent life.

"Believe me, I had always intended one day to return to my old home and astonish them with the baaing of a black sheep from the grave. For I *have* been successful; by all the prophets I have—and I felt that this would make my brother Dudley writhe. But this dramatic plum I reserved. I even visited England without being too much tempted. For, mind you, I had no reason to suspect that 'John Farnleigh' was alive. I thought he was supposed to be dead, instead of flourishing in Colorado.

"You will therefore understand my surprise, some six months ago, when quite by chance I picked up an illustrated paper and saw the picture of Sir John and Lady Farnleigh. My brother Dudley, I noted, was dead of a surfeit of lampreys. His 'younger brother' had inherited.

31

At first I thought this must be a mistake of the paper for some distant connection. But a few inquiries uncovered the truth; and after all, you know, I *am* the heir. Still a young man—still vigorous—but not revengeful.

"Such things grow exceedingly dim. A generation has grown up; there are a thousand good memories between me and the small whelp who tried to alter the succession with a seaman's mallet and who, I hear, has become a useful citizen since. All the trees look the same; but my eyes have changed. I feel strange and raw in my own home. I am not sure that I shall make the best possible patron for the local cricket-club or the local Boy Scouts. But I have (as you observe) a strong weakness for making speeches, and I daresay I shall get on well enough. Now, Patrick Gore, you have heard my proposal. It is generous enough. If I take you to court, I warn you I will have your hide. In the meantime, gentlemen, I am open to answer questions from anyone who has ever known me. I have a few questions to put myself, and I will defy Gore to answer them."

For a time after he had spoken, it was quiet in the darkening room. He had an almost hypnotic voice. But they were looking at Farnleigh, who had risen and stood with his knuckles on the table. In Farnleigh's dark face there was quiet, and relief, and a certain curiosity as he examined his guest. He brushed a hand under his cropped moustache; he almost smiled.

Molly saw that smile, and drew a deep breath.

"You have something to say, John?" she prompted.

"Yes. I don't know why he's come here with this story, or what he hopes to get out of it. But what this man says is absolutely false from beginning to end."

"You intend to fight?" asked the claimant with interest.

"Of course I mean to fight, you ass. Or rather, I'll let you do the fighting."

Mr Welkyn seemed about to intervene, with a vast throat-clearing, but the claimant stopped him.

"No, no," he said comfortably. "Please stay out of this, Welkyn. You brethren of the law are all very well to put in the 'whereases' and the 'proceed with caution', but you are out of place in a personal skirmish like this. To tell the truth, I shall enjoy this. Well, let us apply a few tests. I wonder if you would mind calling your butler in here?"

Farnleigh frowned. "But look here : Knowles wasn't—"

"Why not do as he asks, John?" suggested Molly sweetly.

Farnleigh caught her look; and, if there is a paradox which can be called humourless humour, his sharp features showed it. He rang for Knowles, who entered in the same uncertain way. The claimant regarded him musingly.

"I thought I recognised you when we came in here," the claimant said. "You were here in my father's time, were you not?"

"Sir?"

"You were here in my father's, Sir Dudley Farnleigh's time. Weren't you?"

An expression of disgust went over Farnleigh's face.

"You will do your case no good by this," interposed Nathaniel Burrows sharply. "The butler in Sir Dudley Farnleigh's time was Stenson, who has been dead—"

"Yes. I was aware of that," said the claimant, turning his eyes sideways. Then he contemplated the butler, sitting back and crossing his legs with some effort. "Your name is Knowles. In my father's time you were the butler at old Colonel Mardale's place, over in Frettenden. You used to keep two rabbits that the colonel knew nothing about. You kept them in a corner of the coach-house nearest the orchard. One of the rabbits was named Billy." He looked up. "Ask this gentleman the name of the other."

Knowles had gone slightly pink.

"Ask him, will you?"

"Rot!" snapped Farnleigh, and drew himself back into his dignity again.

"Oh," said the claimant. "You mean you cannot answer?"

"I mean I don't choose to answer." Yet six pairs of eyes were fastened on him, and he seemed to feel the pressure; he shifted and almost stuttered. "Who can be expected to remember the name of a rabbit after twenty-five years? All right, all right: stop a bit! There

33

was some nonsense about their names, I remember. Let me think. Billy and W—no, that's not it. Billy and Silly, that's it? Or was it? I'm not sure."

"That is correct, sir," Knowles told him with an air of relief.

The claimant was not out of countenance.

"Well, let us try again. Now, Knowles. One evening in summer—it was the year before I went away—you were going through that same orchard to take a message to a certain neighbour. You were surprised and rather shocked to find me making love to a certain young lady of twelve or thirteen. Ask your employer the name of that young lady."

Farnleigh was dark and heavy-looking.

"I don't remember any such incident."

"Are you trying to convey the impression," said the claimant, "that your natural chivalry restrains you? No, my friend, that will not do. It was a long time ago and I give you my solemn word that nothing of a compromising nature passed. Knowles, *you* remember what went on in the apple-orchard, don't you?"

"Sir," said the bedevilled butler, "I—"

"You do. But I thought this man would not remember it, because I do not think I entered the fact in my valuable diary. What was the name of the young lady?"

Farnleigh nodded. "All right," he answered with an attempt at lightness. "It was Miss Dane, Madeline Dane."

"Madeline Dane—" began Molly.

For the first time the claimant seemed a little taken aback. His quick eyes moved round the group, and his quick intuition seemed to move too.

"She must have written to you in America," returned the claimant. "We shall have to cut deeper. But I beg your pardon: I hope I have committed no blunder? I hope the young lady is not still living in the district at a more mature age, and that I have not touched on any inconvenient subject?"

"Damn you," said Farnleigh suddenly, "I've stood about enough of this. I can't keep my temper much longer. Will you kindly get out of here?"

"No," said the other. "I mean to break down your

bluff. For it is a bluff, my boy, and you know it. Besides, I think it was agreed that we should wait for Kennet Murray."

"Suppose we do wait for Murray?" Farnleigh spoke with toiling lucidity. "Where will it get us? What will it prove, beyond this fiddle-faddle of questions to which we both apparently know the answers? And yet you don't know the answers, because you're the one who is bluffing. I could ask some myself, just as nonsensical as yours. But that's nothing. How did you ever expect to prove a thing like this? How do you still think you can prove it?"

The claimant sat back, richly enjoying his position.

"By the incontrovertible evidence of finger-prints," he said.

CHAPTER IV

IT was as though the man had been keeping this in reserve, waiting for the proper moment to say it and savouring triumph in advance. He seemed a little disappointed that he had to produce the trump so early, and under circumstances less dramatic than he might have wished. But the others were not thinking of it in terms of drama.

Brian Page heard Burrows breathe in with a shaky kind of noise. Burrows got to his feet.

"I was not informed of this," the solicitor said fiercely.

"But you guessed it?" smiled fat Mr Welkyn.

"It is not my business to guess at anything," returned Burrows. "I repeat, sir, I have not been informed of this. I have heard nothing about finger-prints."

"Nor have we, officially. Mr Murray has kept his own counsel. But," inquired Welkyn, with rich suavity, "does the present holder *need* to be told? If he is the real Sir John Farnleigh, surely he remembers that Mr Murray took the finger-prints of the boy as long ago as the year 1910 or 11."

"I repeat, sir—"

"Let *me* repeat, Mr Burrows: did you need to be informed of it? What does the present holder himself have to say?"

Farnleigh's expression seemed to have retreated, to have become locked up. As usual when he was among mental brambles, he did two things. He began to walk round the room with short, quick steps; and he took a key-ring out of his pocket and twirled it round his forefinger.

"Sir John!"

"Eh?"

"Do you remember," asked Burrows, "any such circumstances as Mr Welkyn mentions? Did Mr Murray ever take your finger-prints?"

"Oh, that," said Farnleigh, as though it were of no importance. "Yes, I remember it now. I'd forgotten it. But it occurred to me when I was talking to you and my wife a while ago—you know. I wondered if that could be it, and it made me a whole lot easier in my mind. Yes, old Murray got my finger-prints right enough."

The claimant turned round. He wore an expression not only of mild astonishment, but of sudden and wondering suspicion as well.

"This will not do, you know," the claimant said. "You don't maintain that you will face the test of finger-prints?"

"Face it? Face it?" repeated Farnleigh, with grim pleasure. "Man, it's the best thing that could have happened. You're the impostor, and you know it. Murray's old finger-print test—by George, now I come to think of it, I can remember every detail of that business!—will settle matters. Then I can throw you out."

And the two rivals looked at each other.

For some time Brian Page had been trying to put weights into a scales which would not remain still. He had been trying, without friendship or prejudice, to see where the imposture lay. The issue was simple. If Patrick Gore (to give him the name by which he had been announced) were the impostor, he was one of the coolest and most smooth-faced crooks who ever walked into another man's house. If the present John Farnleigh

36

were the impostor, he was not only a slippery criminal behind that naïve, straightforward mask: he was a would-be murderer as well.

There was a pause.

"You know, my friend," observed the claimant, as though with refreshed interest, "I admire your cheek. One moment, please. I do not say that as a baiting jeer or to start a row. I state, as a matter of simple fact, that I admire an *aes-triplex* cheek which Casanova himself could not have equalled. Now, I am not surprised that you 'forgot' the finger-prints. They were taken at a time before I began to keep my diary. But to say you forgot them: to SAY you forgot them—"

"Well, what's wrong with that?"

"John Farnleigh wouldn't or couldn't have forgotten a detail of that. I, being John Farnleigh, certainly didn't. That is why Kennet Murray was the only person in the world who had any influence with me. Murray on Footprints. Murray on Disguises. Murray on the Disposal of the Body. Wough! And particularly Murray on Finger-prints, which were then the newest scientific craze. I am aware,"—he interrupted himself, raising his voice and looking round the group—"that finger-prints were discovered by Sir William Herschel in the eighteen-fifties, and rediscovered by Dr Faulds in the late seventies. But they were not admitted as legal evidence in an English court until nineteen-five, and even then the judge was dubious. It took years of argument to establish them. Yet, as a possible 'test' of Murray's, you say you never thought of finger-prints."

"You're doing a hell of a lot of talking," said Farnleigh, who again looked swollen and dangerous.

"Naturally. Though you never once thought of finger-prints before, it all comes back to you now. Tell me this. When the prints were taken, how were they taken?"

"How?"

"In what form?"

Farnleigh pondered. "On a sheet of glass," he said.

"Nonsense. They were taken in a 'Thumbograph', a little book which was quite a popular game or toy at the time. A little grey book. Murray had a lot of other prints, my father's and my mother's and anybody else's he could get."

"Stop a bit. Hold on. I believe there was a book—we sat over in that window—"

"So you profess to remember now."

"Look here," said Farnleigh quietly, "who do you think I am? Do you think I'm that fellow in the music-halls, the one you shoot questions at and he instantly tells you the number of clauses in the Magna Charta or what horse ran second in the Derby in 1882? That's what *you* sound like. There's a lot of rubbish that's better forgotten. People change. They change, I tell you."

"But not their basic characters, as you profess to have changed. That is the point I am making. You cannot turn your whole soul inside out, you know."

During this controversy Mr Welkyn had been sitting back with a massive gravity but with a certain complacence which beamed forth from his protuberant blue eyes. Now he lifted his hand.

"Gentlemen, gentlemen. Surely this wrangling is not —er—seemly, if you will allow me to say so? The matter, I am glad to say, can be settled within a very short time—"

"I still insist," snapped Nathaniel Burrows, "that, not having been instructed about this matter of the finger-prints, I may, in the interests of Sir John Farnleigh—"

"Mr Burrows," said the claimant calmly, "you must have guessed it, even if we did not choose to tell you. I suspect you guessed it from the first, and that is why you tolerated this claim. You are trying to save your face on both sides, whether your man should turn out to be a fraud or whether he should not. Well, you had better come over to our side soon."

Farnleigh stopped pacing. He tossed up the key-ring, caught it with a flat smack against his palm, and closed his long fingers round it.

"Is that true?" he asked Burrows.

"If it were true, Sir John, I should have been compelled to take other steps. At the same time, it is my duty to investigate—"

"That's all right," said Farnleigh. "I only wanted to know where my friends stand. I'm not saying much.

My memories, pleasant or unpleasant: and some of them have kept me awake at nights: I'll keep to myself. Just bring on your finger-prints, and then we shall see. The point is, where is Murray? Why isn't he here?"

The claimant wore a look of Mephistophelian pleasure, in which he contrived to suggest a sinister frown.

"If events ran according to form," he answered with relish, "Murray would already have been murdered and his body hidden in the pond in the garden. There is still a pond there, is there? (I thought so.) As a matter of sober fact, I believe he is on his way here now. Besides, I do not wish to put ideas into anybody's head."

"Ideas?" said Farnleigh.

"Yes. Like your old one. A quick cosh and an easy life."

The way he spoke seemed to put an unpleasant chill in the air. Farnleigh's voice went high and rasping. He lifted his hand, and then rubbed it down the side of his old tweed coat, as though in a nervous gesture of controlling himself. With uncanny skill his opponent seemed to pick out exactly the sentences that would sting him. Farnleigh had rather a long neck, which was now much in evidence.

"Does anybody believe that?" he got out. "Molly—Page—Burrows—do you believe that?"

"Nobody believes it," answered Molly, with level eyes. "You're being foolish to let him put you off balance, which is exactly what he's trying to do."

The claimant turned an interested look on her.

"You too, madam?"

"Me too, what?" asked Molly, and then grew furiously annoyed with herself. "Sorry to sound like a musical scale, but you know what I mean."

"You believe your husband is John Farnleigh?"

"I know it."

"How?"

"I'm afraid I must answer woman's intuition," said Molly coolly. But I mean something sensible by it: something that in its own way, and within its own limits, is always right. I knew it the moment I saw him again. Of course I am willing to listen to reasons, but they have got to be the right sort of reasons."

"Are you in love with him, may I ask?"

This time Molly flushed under her tan, but she treated the question in her usual way. "Well, let's say that I am rather fond of him, if you like."

"Exactly. Ex-actly. You are 'fond' of him; you will always be 'fond' of him. You get on and you will get on very well together. But you are not in love with him and you did not fall in love with him. You fell in love with me. That is to say, you fell in love with an imaginary projection of me from your childhood, which surrounded the impostor when 'I' returned home——"

"Gentlemen, gentlemen!" said Mr Welkyn, like a master of ceremonies to a rowdy banquet. He seemed rather shocked.

Brian Page entered the conversation, with broad amusement, to steady their host.

"Now we're being psychoanalytic," Page said. "Look here, Burrows, what are we to do with this flower of something-or-other?"

"I only know that we are putting in an awkward half-hour," returned Burrows coldly. "Also, we are straying from the point again."

"Not at all," the claimant assured him. The claimant seemed genuinely anxious to please. "I hope I haven't said anything to offend anybody again? You should live with a circus; your skins would grow tougher. However, I appeal to you, sir." He looked at Page. "Don't I state a reasonable proposition with regard to this lady? You may make an objection. You may say that, in order to fix her affections on me as a child, she must have been somewhat older—the age, say, of Miss Madeline Dane? Was that your objection?"

Molly laughed.

"No," said Page. "I wasn't thinking of either a support or an objection. I was thinking of your mysterious profession."

"My profession?"

"The unspecified profession you mentioned, the one you first made a success of at the circus. I can't decide whether you are (1) a fortune-teller, (2) a psychoanalyst, (3) a memory-expert, (4) a conjurer, or even a combination of them. There are mannerisms of them all about

40

you, and much more besides. You are a little too suggestive of Mephistopheles in Kent. You don't belong here. You disturb things, somehow, and you give me a pain in the neck."

The claimant seemed pleased.

"Do I? You all need to be stirred up a bit," he declared. "Regarding my profession, I am perhaps a little of all those things. But there is one person I certainly am: I am John Farnleigh."

Across the room the door opened, and Knowles entered.

"Mr Kennet Murray to see you, sir," he said.

There was a pause. By a trick of the fading light, a last fiery glow of sunset shifted in through the trees and the high window-panes. It kindled the heavy room; then it subsided to a steady, warm light which was just bright enough to make faces and figures a little more than visible.

Kennet Murray himself had been remembering many things in that midsummer dusk. He was a tall, lean, rather shambling man, who, in spite of a first-rate intelligence, had never been cut out to be a particular success at anything. Though he was hardly fifty, his fair moustache and fair beard, so closely cropped that they looked like stubble, were greyish. He had aged, as Burrows had said; he had grown leaner and more sour out of his former easy good-nature. But there was much of that good-nature remaining, and his look showed it as he ambled into the library. His eyes had the slightly squinted-up look of one who lives under hot suns.

Then he stopped, frowning as though at a book, and drawing himself up. And, to one of the contestants for the estate, old days returned with old memories and fierce bitterness against dead people; yet Murray himself did not look a day older.

Murray stood studying the persons before him. He frowned, then he looked quizzical—the eternal tutor— and then grim. He fixed his eyes at a point midway between the holder and the claimant.

"Well, young Johnny?" he said.

CHAPTER V

For a second or two neither of the contestants moved or spoke. First it seemed that each was waiting to see what the other would do and then each went his separate way. Farnleigh moved his shoulder slightly, as though he would not enter this as a debate, but he consented to nod and gesture and even smile stiffly. There had been authority in Murray's voice. But the claimant, after a slight hesitation, showed no such views. He spoke with quiet affability.

"Good evening, Murray," he said; and Brian Page, who knew the ways of students towards their former schoolmasters, suddenly felt the scale-pins dip towards Farnleigh.

Murray looked round.

"Someone—er—had better present me," he said in a pleasant voice.

It was Farnleigh, stung out of apathy, who did this. By tacit consent Murray was the 'old man' of the group, though he was a good deal younger than Welkyn; there was something of the 'old man's' manner about him: something brisk and assured, yet wandering. He sat down at the head of the table, with the light behind his back. Then he gravely fitted on a pair of owlish shell-rimmed reading glasses, and surveyed them.

"I should never have recognised Miss Sutton or Mr Burrows," he went on. "Mr Welkyn I know slightly. It was through his generosity that I was able to take my first real holiday in a long time."

Welkyn, evidently well satisfied, thought that the time had now come for him to take charge and get down to real business.

"Exactly. Now, Mr Murray, my client—"

"Oh, tut, tut, tut!" said Murray, rather testily. "Let me get my breath and talk a moment, as old Sir Dudley used to say." It was as though he wanted to get his breath literally, for he breathed deeply several times, looked round the room, and then at the two opponents. "However, I must say you seem to have landed yourself in the middle of a very bad mess. The affair has not become public property, has it?"

"No," said Burrows. "And you, of course, have not said anything about it?"

Murray frowned.

"There I must plead guilty. I have mentioned it to one person. But, when you hear the name of the person, I don't think you will object. It was my old friend Dr Gideon Fell, a former schoolmaster like myself, of whose connection with detective work you may have heard. I saw him as I was passing through London. And I—er— mention this to give you a word of warning." Despite Murray's benevolence, his squinted grey eyes became bright and hard and interested. "It is possible that Dr Fell himself may soon be in this part of the world. You know that there is another man staying at the Bull and Butcher besides myself, a man of inquisitive habits?"

"The private detective?" Farnleigh asked sharply, and to the ostensible surprise of the claimant.

"So it took you in?" said Murray. "He is an official detective from Scotland Yard. It was Dr Fell's idea. Dr Fell maintained that the best way to conceal your identity as an official detective is to act like a private detective." Though Murray seemed hugely delighted, his eyes remained watchful. "Scotland Yard, on the advice of the Chief Constable of Kent, seem to be curious about the death of Miss Victoria Daly here last summer."

Sensation.

Nathaniel Burrows, who looked fussed, made a vague gesture.

"Miss Daly was killed by a tramp," Burrows said, "later killed himself in escaping the police."

"I hope so. However, I heard it in passing when I mentioned my own little problem in mixed identities to Dr Fell. He was interested." Again Murray's voice became sharp; and, if the word can be used, opaque. "Now, young Johnny—"

Even the air of the room seemed to be waiting. The

claimant nodded. The host also nodded, but Page thought that there was a faint glitter of sweat on his forehead.

"Can't we get on with this?" Farnleigh demanded. "It's no good playing cat and mouse, Mr—it's no good playing cat and mouse, Murray. It's not decent, and it's not like you. If you've got those finger-prints, trot 'em out and then we shall see."

Murray's eyes opened and then narrowed. He sounded annoyed.

"So you know about that. I was reserving it. And may I ask," his voice grew professionally poised and sarcastic, "which of you thought that the final test would be finger-prints?"

"I think I can establish that honour," answered the claimant, looking round as though inquiringly. "My friend Patrick Gore here claims to have remembered it afterwards. But he seems to have been under the impression that you took finger-prints on a sheet of glass."

"And so I did," said Murray.

"That's a lie," said the claimant.

It was an unexpected change of voice. Brian Page suddenly realised that, under his mild and Mephistophelian airs, the claimant concealed a violent temper.

"Sir," said Murray, looking him up and down, "I am not in the habit—"

Then it was as though old days returned; the claimant seemed involuntarily about to move back and beg Murray's pardon. But he conquered this. His face smoothed itself out, and the usual mocking expression reappeared.

"Let us say, then, that I have an alternative suggestion. You took my finger-prints in a 'Thumbograph'. You had several such Thumbographs; you bought them in Tunbridge Wells. And you took the finger-prints of myself and my brother Dudley on the same day."

"That," agreed Murray, "is quite true. The Thumbograph with the finger-prints I have here." He touched the inside breast-pocket of his sports-coat.

"I smell blood," said the claimant.

It was true that a different atmosphere seemed to surround the group at the table.

"At the same time," Murray went on, as though he had not heard this, "the first experiments I made with

44

finger-prints were on small glass slides." He grew even more inscrutable and sharp. "Now, sir, as the claimant or plaintiff here, you must tell me a few things. If you are Sir John Farnleigh, certain things are known to me which are known to nobody else. In those days you were an omnivorous reader. Sir Dudley, who you will admit was an enlightened man, made out a list of books which you were permitted to read. You never spoke your views on these books to anyone else: Sir Dudley once spoke a word of harmless ridicule to you about your notions, and tortures would not have opened your mouth afterwards. But you expressed yourself to me in no uncertain terms. Do you remember all that?"

"Very well indeed," said the claimant.

"Then kindly tell me which of those books you liked best, and which made the most impression on you."

"With pleasure," answered the claimant, casting up his eyes. "All of Sherlock Holmes. All of Poe. *The Cloister and the Hearth*. *The Count of Monte Cristo*. *Kidnapped*. *A Tale of Two Cities*. All ghost stories. All stories dealing with pirates, murders, ruined castles, or— "

"That will do," said Murray noncommittally. "And the books you intensely disliked?"

"Every deadly line of Jane Austen and George Eliot. All snivelling school-stories about ' the honour of the school ' and so on. All 'useful' books telling you how to make mechanical things or run them. All animal-stories. I may add that these, in general, are still my views."

Brian Page was beginning to like the claimant.

"Let us take the younger children who were here-abouts," Murray continued. "For instance, the present Lady Farnleigh, whom I used to know as little Molly Sutton. If you are John Farnleigh, what was your private nickname for her?"

"' The gipsy,'" answered the claimant instantly.

"Why?"

"Because she was always tanned, and was always playing with the children in the gipsy tribe that used to camp at the other side of the Chart."

He glanced at a furious Molly, smiling a little.

"And Mr Burrows, there—what was your nickname for *him*?"

"Uncas."

"The reason for that?"

"At any I-Spy games, or things like that, he could slide through the shrubbery without making a sound."

"Thank you. And now for you, sir." Murray turned to Farnleigh, and eyed him as though he was about to tell him to straighten his tie. "I do not wish to convey the impression that I am playing cat-and-mouse. So I have only one question for you before I proceed to take the finger-prints. On this question, actually, will depend my private judgment before I see the proof in the prints. The question is this. What is the Red Book of Appin?"

It was almost dark in the library. The heat was still strong, but a small breeze had begun to stir with sundown. It moved through the one or two opened panes of the windows; and the trees stirred with it. A grim—a rather unpleasant—smile moved across Farnleigh's face. He nodded. Taking a notebook and a little gold pencil from his pocket, he tore out a sheet and wrote some words on it. This he folded up and pushed across to Murray.

"It has never caught *me*," Farnleigh said. And then: "Is that the right answer?"

"That is the right answer," agreed Murray. He looked at the claimant. "You, sir: will you answer the same question?"

For the first time the claimant seemed uncertain. His gaze flashed from Farnleigh to Murray with an expression which Page could not read. Without a word he beckoned flatly for the notebook and pencil, which Farnleigh handed over. The claimant wrote only two or three words before he ripped out the sheet and gave it to Murray.

"And now, gentlemen," said Murray, rising. "I think we can take the finger-prints. Here I have the original Thumbograph: much aged, you see. Here is an ink-pad, and here are two white cards. If you will just—may I have some light, please?"

It was Molly who went across and touched the electric switch beside the door. In the library there was a chandelier in tiers of wrought iron which had once supported crowns of candles; now there were small electric

46

bulbs, not all of which worked, so that the light was not over-bright. But it pushed back the summer night; a hundred little reflections of bulbs were thrown back from the window-panes; and the books on the tall shelves looked more grimy still. On the table Murray had spread out his paraphernalia. The Thumbograph, at which they all looked first, was a rickety little book with grey paper covers grown thin from use: the title in red letters, and a large red print of a thumb underneath.

"An old friend," said Murray, patting it. "Now, gentlemen. 'Roll' prints are better than flat ones; but I did not bring a roller because I wished to reproduce the original conditions. I want only your left thumb-print; there is only one print to compare. Here is a handkerchief with an end doused in benzoline: it will take away the perspiration. Use it. Next—"

It was done.

During that time Page's heart was in his mouth; he could not have said why. But they were all in unnatural states of agitation. For some reason Farnleigh insisted on rolling up his sleeve before making the print, as though he were going to have a blood-transfusion. The mouths of both solicitors, Page was glad to observe, were open. Even the claimant used the handkerchief briskly before he leaned against the table. But what impressed Page most was the confidence of both contestants. The wild thought occurred to Page: suppose those two thumb-prints turn out to be exactly alike?

The chances of this happening, he recalled, were just one in sixty-four thousand millions. All the same, nobody faltered or cried off before the test. Nobody—

Murray had a bad fountain-pen. It scratched as he wrote names and markings at the foot of each white (unglazed) card. Then he blotted them carefully, while the contestants wiped their fingers.

"Well?" demanded Farnleigh.

"Well! Now if you will be good enough to give me a quarter of an hour to myself, I can get down to work. Forgive my unsociability; but I realise the importance of this as much as you do."

Burrows blinked. "But can't you—that is, aren't you going to tell us—?"

"My good sir," said Murray, whose own nerves appeared to be feeling the strain, "are you under the impression that a glance at these prints will be enough to compare them? Especially with the print of a boy done in faded ink twenty-five years ago? They will require many points of agreement. It can be done, but a quarter of an hour is an unnaturally modest estimate. Double that: you will be nearer the truth. Now may I settle down?"

From the claimant came a low chuckle.

"I expected that," he said. "But I warn you, it is unwise. I smell blood. You will have to be murdered. No, don't scowl; twenty-five years ago you would have relished the position and revelled in your own importance."

"I see nothing funny in the matter."

"In point of fact, there is nothing funny in it. Here you sit in a lighted room, with a wall of windows giving on a dark garden and a screen of trees and the devil whispering behind every leaf. Be careful."

"Well," returned Murray, with a faint smile creeping round his moustache and into his beard, "in that case I shall take all care. The more nervous of you can keep an eye on me through the window. Now you must excuse me."

They went out into the hall, and he closed the door on them. Then six persons stood and looked at each other. Lights had already been turned on in the long, pleasant hall; Knowles stood at the door of the dining-room, in the 'new' wing which had been built out at the back from the centre of the house, like the body of the letter T with its head as the front. Molly Farnleigh, though flushed and strained, tried to speak coolly.

"Don't you think we had better have something to eat?" she said. "I've ordered a cold buffet prepared. After all, there's no reason why we shouldn't carry on as usual."

"Thank you," said Welkyn, relieved; "I should like a sandwich."

"Thank you," said Burrows; "I'm not hungry."

"Thank you," said the claimant, to swell the chorus. "Whether I accepted or refused, it would sound equally bad. I am going somewhere to smoke a long, strong, black cigar; and then I am going to see that no harm comes to Murray in there."

Farnleigh said nothing. Just behind him in the hall there was a door giving on that part of the garden over-looked by the library windows. He studied his guests with a long, careful scrutiny; then he opened the glass door and went out into the garden.

In the same way Page presently found himself deserted. The only person in sight was Welkyn, who stood in the dimly lighted dining-room and ate fish-paste sandwiches with great steadiness. Page's watch said that it was twenty minutes past nine o'clock. He hesitated, and then followed Farnleigh out into the cool dimness of the garden.

This side of the garden seemed shut off from the world, and formed an oblong some eighty feet long by forty feet broad. On one side it was closed in by the new wing; on the other by a stretch of high yew hedge. Through the beech-trees the library windows spread out a faint and broken wall of light from the narrow side of the oblong. In the new wing, too, the dining-room had glass doors opening out into it, with a balcony overlooking it from the bedroom windows above.

Inspired by King William the Third at Hampton Court, a seventeenth-century Farnleigh had laid out the garden in severe curves and angles of yew hedge, with broad sanded walks between. The hedges were built waist-high; it was, in fact, very much like the foundation of a maze. Though you had no actual difficulty in finding your way about the garden, it would be (Page had always thought) a rare place for hiding-games if you kept down below the line of the hedges. In the centre was a large round open space, buttressed with rose-trees; and this space in turn enclosed an ornamental pool some ten feet in diameter, with a very low coping. In the uncertainty between the lights, with faint gleams from the house meeting a faint afterglow from the west, it was a secret and fragrant place. Yet for some reason Page had never liked the *feel* of that garden.

With this thought came another, a more unpleasant one. There was nothing about a mere garden, a handful of hedges, shrubs, flowers, and soil, which could inspire disquiet. It may have been that the minds and thoughts of everyone here were concentrated so fiercely on the library, moving against that lighted box like moths on the glass. Of course, it was absurd to suppose that anything could happen to Murray. Things are not managed like that; they are not so convenient; it was only the claimant's hypnotic personality which had been able to worm in the suggestion.

"However," Page almost said aloud, "I think I might just stroll past the window and have a look."

He did so, and jerked back with muttered profanity, for someone else had been having a look as well. He did not see who the other person was, because the other person drew away from the screen of beeches against the library windows. But Page saw Kennet Murray inside, sitting at the library table with his back to the windows, and Murray seemed to be just opening a greyish book.

Nonsense.

Page moved away, and walked quickly out into the cool garden. He skirted the round pool, looking up at a single clear star (Madeline Dane had a poetic name for it) which you could see just above a cluster of chimneys in the new wing. Working his way through the low labyrinth, he reached the far end in labyrinthine thought.

Well, was Farnleigh the impostor, or the other fellow? Page did not know; and he had changed his mind so many times in the past two hours that he did not like to guess. Then, too, there had been the persistent, accidental introduction at every turn of the name of Madeline Dane—

At the end of this side of the garden there was a laurel hedge which screened a stone bench from the house. He sat down and lighted a cigarette. Tracing his thoughts back as honestly as he could, he admitted to himself that a part of his grouse at the universe was the persistent recurrence of Madeline Dane's name. Madeline Dane, whose blonde and slender good looks suggested the origin of her surname, was the person who mixed up the 'Lives of the Chief Justices' and everything else in Page's thoughts. He was thinking more about her than was good for him.

For here he was, getting on towards being a crusty bachelor—

Then Brian Page jumped up from the stone bench, thinking neither of Madeline nor of marriage: only of the sounds he had heard from the garden behind. They were not loud sounds, but they came with terrifying clarity out of the dim, low hedges. The choking noise was the worst: then the shuffle and scrape of feet: then the splash and thrashings.

For a moment he did not want to turn round.

He did not really believe that anything had happened. He never believed that. But he dropped his cigarette on the grass, set his heel on it, and walked back towards the house at a pace that was almost a run. He was some distance away from the house; and in the hide-and-seek paths he took two wrong turnings. At first the uncertain place seemed deserted; next he saw Burrows's tall figure pounding towards him, and the beam of a flashlight flickered over the hedges into his face. When he came close enough to see Burrows's face behind the light the coolness and fragrance of the garden were lost.

"Well, it's happened," said Burrows.

What Page felt at that moment was a slight physical nausea.

"I don't know what you mean," he lied, "except that it can't have happened."

"I'm simply telling you, that's all," returned a white-faced Burrows, with patient insistence. "Come along quick and help me haul him out. I can't swear he's dead, but he's lying on his face in that pond and I'm pretty sure he's dead."

Page stared in the direction he indicated. He could not see the pool, which was hidden by the hedges; but he now had a good view of the back of the house. From one window of a lighted room over the library, old Knowles the butler was leaning out; and Molly Farnleigh was on the balcony outside her bedroom windows.

"I tell you," Page insisted, "nobody would dare have a go at Murray! It's impossible. It's nonsensical to—and, anyway, what's Murray doing at the pond? "

"Murray? " said the other, staring at him. "Why

51

Murray? Who said anything about Murray? It's *Farnleigh*, man: John Farnleigh. It was all over before I could get there; and I'm afraid it's too late now."

CHAPTER VI

"BUT who the devil," Page asked, "would want to kill Farnleigh?"

He had to adjust his thoughts. Afterwards he had acknowledged that his original notion of murder had been mere suggestion. Yet even when another suggestion replaced it, he remembered his first thought: *if* this were murder, it had been ingeniously conceived. As though by an effect of sleight-of-hand, every eye and ear had been concentrated on Kennet Murray. No person in the house had a thought in his head for anybody but Murray. No one would know where anybody had been, anybody but Murray. A person who acted in that vacuum could attack unseen, so long as he did not attack Murray.

"Kill Farnleigh?" repeated Burrows in a queer voice. "Here, this won't do. Wake up. Stop. Steady. Come on."

Still talking like a man giving directions for backing a car, he led the way with his lanky stride. The beam from the flashlight was steady. But he switched it off before they reached the pond, either because there was still enough light from the sky or because he did not wish to see things too clearly just then.

Round the pool there was a border of packed sand some five feet wide. Forms, even faces, were still dimly visible. Farnleigh lay prone in the pool, turned a little towards the right as you faced the rear of the garden. The pool was just deep enough so that his body rocked with the water, which still slopped and splashed over the low round edge of the coping, running across packed sand. They also saw a darker dye in the water, curling upwards and spreading round him; but they did not see the full colour of this dye until it touched a patch of white water-lilies close to the body.

The slopping agitation of the water began again when Page started to haul him out; Farnleigh's heel just touched the edge of the low coping. But, after one minute, which Page never wished to remember afterwards, he got up.

"We can't do him any good," Page said. "His throat's been cut."

The shock had not worn off yet, and they both spoke calmly.

"Yes. I was afraid of that. It's— "

"It's murder. Or," said Page abruptly, "suicide."

They looked at each other in the dusk.

"All the same," argued Burrows, trying to be official-mannered and human at the same time, "we've got to get him out of there. That rule about touching nothing and waiting for the police is all very well, but we can't let him lie there. It's not decent. Besides, his position has been disturbed as it is. Shall we—? "

"Yes."

The tweed suit, now black and bulging, seemed to have accumulated a ton of water. With difficulty they rolled Farnleigh over the edge, sending a minor tidal wave across themselves. The peaceful evening scent of the garden, especially the roses, had never seemed more theatrically romantic than in the midst of this reality. Page kept thinking: this is John Farnleigh, and he's dead. This is impossible. And it was impossible, except for one thought which grew clearer every second.

"You mean suicide," said Burrows, wiping his hands. "We've had a hallucination of murder put on us, but I don't like this any better. You see what it means? It means he was the impostor after all. He bluffed it out as long as he could, and hoped against hope that Murray might not have the finger-prints. When the test was over he couldn't face the consequences. So he came out here, stood on the edge of the pool, and— " Burrows put up a hand to his throat.

It all fitted very well.

"I'm afraid so," admitted Page. Afraid? Afraid? Yes: wasn't that the worst charge you could make against a dead friend, pile the whole burden on him now that he couldn't speak? Resentment rose up in a dull ache, for John Farnleigh had been his friend. "But it's the

53

only thing we can think. For God's sake what happened here? Did you see him do it? What did he do it with?"

"No. That is, I didn't exactly see him. I was just coming out of the door from the hall back there. I'd got this torch"—Burrows snapped the button on and off, and then held it up—"out of the drawer of the table in the hall. You know how weak my eyes are when I go out in the dark. Just as I was opening the door, I saw Farnleigh standing out here—very dimly, you know—on the edge of the pool, with his back towards me. Then he seemed to be doing something, or moving about a bit: with my eyesight, it's very difficult to tell. You must have heard the noises. After I heard that splash—and the thrashing round, you know, which was worse. There never was a balder, worse story."

"But there wasn't anybody with him?"

"No," said Burrows, spreading out his fingers against his forehead and pressing the tips of them there. "Or at least—not exactly. These hedges are waist-high, and—"

The meaning of the words 'not exactly', spoken by the meticulously careful Nathaniel Burrows, Page did not have time to inquire. Voices and footsteps were stirring from the direction of the house, and he spoke quickly.

"You're the one with authority. They're all coming. Molly mustn't see this. Can't you use your authority and head 'em off?"

Burrows cleared his throat two or three times, like a nervous orator about to begin, and his shoulders straightened. Switching on the flashlight, he walked towards the house with the light pointing in that direction. Its beams picked out Molly, with Kennet Murray following; but it did not shine on their faces.

"I am sorry," began Burrows, in tones of high and unnatural sharpness. "But there has been an accident to Sir John, and you had better not go out there—"

"Don't be a fool," said Molly in a hard voice. With deliberate strength she pushed past him, and came into the gloom beside the pool. Fortunately she could not see the extent of what had been done. Though she tried to give the impression of calmness, Page heard her heel turn in the path. He put an arm around her shoulder to steady her; she leaned against it, and he felt unsteady breathing. But what she said, flung out in a sob, seemed merely cryptic. Molly said:

" D-damn him for being *right*! "

By something in the tone Page knew that she could not be referring to her husband. But for a moment it so startled him that he could not take it in. Then, hiding her face even from the dark, she started in a hurried walk for the house.

" Let her go," said Murray. " It will be better for her."

But Murray did not appear as capable as you might have thought, faced with a thing of this sort. He hesitated. Taking the flashlight from Burrows's hand, he directed its beam on the body beside the pool. Then he let out a whistle, his teeth showing between cropped moustache and beard.

" Did you prove," asked Page, " that Sir John Farnleigh was not Sir John Farnleigh? "

" Eh? I beg your pardon? "

Page repeated his question.

" I have proved," said Murray with heavy gravity, " absolutely nothing. I mean that I had not completed my comparison of the prints; I had barely begun it."

" It would appear "—Burrows spoke rather weakly— " that you would not need to finish."

And so it would. There could not be, in all truth and reason, much doubt of Farnleigh's suicide. Page saw that Murray was nodding, in his sometimes vague manner: nodding as though he were not thinking of the matter at all: and stroking the cheek of his beard like a man who tries to place an old memory. It was not a physical wriggling, yet it gave that impression.

" But you can't have much doubt, can you? " Page was prompted to ask. " Which one of them did you think was the fake? "

" I have already informed you— " Murray snapped.

" Yes, I know, but look here, I was only asking, which one of them do you *think* was the impostor? You surely must have had some notion after you'd talked to them. After all, it's the only really important thing either about the imposture or about this; and you can't have any doubt about it? If Farnleigh is the impostor, he had good reason to kill himself and we can certainly agree that he did. But if by any inconceivable chance he was not the impostor—"

"You are assuming—?"

"No, no, only asking. If he were the real Sir John Farnleigh, there would be no reason for him to cut his throat. So he must be the impostor. Isn't he?"

"The tendency to leap to conclusions without even examining the data," began Murray, in a tone between asperity and comfortable discussion, "is one to which the unacademic mind is strongly—"

"Right you are; question withdrawn," said Page.

"No, no, you misunderstand." Here Murray waved his hand like a hypnotist; he seemed uncomfortable and flustered that the balance of argument had been disturbed. "You intimate that this might be murder on the grounds that, if the—er—unfortunate gentleman before us were the real John Farnleigh, he would not kill himself. But, whether he is or is not the real Johnny, why should anyone kill him? If he is a fraud why murder him? The law will attend to him. If he is real, why murder him? He has done no harm to anyone. You see, I am only taking both sides of it."

Burrows spoke gloomily. "It's all this talk, suddenly produced, about Scotland Yard and poor Victoria Daly. I've always thought I was a sensible sort of fellow; but it's given me all sorts of ideas that I've got to root out of my head. And then I've never liked the feel of this blasted garden."

"You felt that too?" demanded Page.

Murray was regarding them with a blaze of interest.

"Stop," he said. "About the garden: why don't you like it, Mr Burrows? Have you any memories connected with it?"

"Not exactly memories." The other considered; he seemed uncomfortable. "It was only that, when anyone used to tell a ghost-story, it was twice as effective here as anywhere else. I remember one about—but that doesn't matter. I used to think it would be very easy to raise the devil here; and I don't mean cut up a row, either. However, this is still beside the point. We've got work to do. We can't stand here talking—"

Murray roused himself; he grew almost excited. "Ah, yes. The police," he said. "Yes, there is a great deal to be done, in the—er—practical world. You will, I think, allow me to take charge. Will you come with me, Mr Burrows? Mr Page, will you oblige us by remaining with the—er—body until we return?"

"Why?" asked the practical Page.

"It is customary. Oh, yes. Indeed, it is absolutely necessary. Kindly give Mr Page your flashlight, my friend. And now this way. There was no telephone at the Close when I lived here; but I presume there is one now? Good, good, good. We must also have a doctor."

He bustled off, shepherding Burrows, and Page was left beside the pool with what remained of John Farnleigh.

With the shock wearing off, Page stood in the dark and reflected on the increasing uselessness and complexity of this tragedy. Yet the suicide of an impostor was simple enough. What disturbed him was the realisation that he had got absolutely no change out of Murray. It would also have been simple enough for Murray to have said, "Yes, that is undoubtedly the impostor: I knew it from the beginning"; and, in fact, Murray's whole atmosphere had conveyed that this was what he thought. But he had said nothing. Was it, then, merely his own love of mystery?

"Farnleigh!" Page said aloud. "Farnleigh!"

"Did you call me?" asked a voice almost at his elbow. The effect of that voice in the dark was to make Page jump back so that he almost stumbled over the body. Forms and outlines were now completely lost in night. The stir of a footstep on a sanded path was followed by the rasping of a match. The flame of the match sprang up over its box, cupped in two hands; and showed, in one opening of the yew hedge, the face of the claimant— Patrick Gore, John Farnleigh—looking into the space beside the pool. He came forward at his slightly clumsy walk.

The claimant was carrying a thin black cigar, half-smoked

and gone out. He put it into his mouth, lit it carefully, and then peered up.

"Did you call me?" he repeated.

"I didn't," Page said grimly. "But it's a good thing you answered. Do you know what's happened?"

"Yes."

"Where have you been?"

"Wandering."

The match went out; but Page could hear him breathing faintly. That the man was shaken there could be little doubt. He came closer, his fists on his hips and the cigar glowing in a corner of his mouth.

"Poor crook," said the claimant, looking down. "And something about him a good deal to be respected, too. I'm rather sorry I did this. I've no doubt he reverted to the Puritan faith of his fathers and spent a good many years repenting at the same time he kept fast hold on the estate. After all, he could have continued posing and made a better squire than I ever shall. But the wrong Farnleigh stuff was missing, and so he did this."

"Suicide."

"Without a doubt." The claimant took the cigar out of his mouth and blew out a cloud of smoke, which curled in the darkness with the odd effect of a ghost taking form.

"I suppose Murray has finished comparing the prints. You were present at that little inquisition by Murray. Tell me: did you notice the exact point at which our— late friend slipped and gave away the fact that he was not John Farnleigh?"

"No."

Then Page suddenly realised that the claimant's shaken air was due as much to relief as to any other emotion.

"Murray would not be Murray," he said with a certain dryness, "if he had not included a catch question. That always was his nature. I was expecting it and even dreading it: in case it should not really be a catch question, but something I had forgotten. But it was a fairly obvious catch when it came. You remember. 'What is the Red Book of Appin?'"

"Yes. Both of you wrote down something—"

"Of course there is no such thing. I should be

interested to see what gibberish my late rival wrote down in order to explain it. It was all the more intriguing when Murray, with a face as solemn as an owl, assured him that he had written the correct answer; but you observed that the very assurance almost finished my rival. Oh, curse it all," he broke off, and made a gesture with the lighted end of his cigar which was curiously like a question-mark. "Well, let us see what the poor devil did to himself. May I have that electric torch?"

Page handed it over, and moved away while the other squatted down with the light. There was a long silence, with an occasional muttering. Then the claimant got up. Though he moved slowly, he snapped the button of the electric torch on and off.

"My friend," he said in a different voice, "this won't do."

"What won't do?"

"This. I hate what I am going to say. But I will take my oath this man did not kill himself."

(Score one for suggestion, intuition, or the influence of a certain garden at twilight).

"Why?" said Page.

"Have you looked at him closely? Then come and do it now. Does a man cut his own throat with three separate slashes, all of which sever the jugular vein, and any one of which would have caused death? Can he do it? I don't know, but I doubt it. Remember, I began my self-made career in a circus. I never saw anything like this since Barney Poole, the best animal-trainer west of the Mississippi, was killed by a leopard."

A night breeze moved in the labyrinth and stirred the roses.

"Where, I wonder, is the weapon?" he went on. He played the beam of his torch over the misted water. "Probably in the pool here, but I don't think we had better go after it. The police may be more necessary in this business than we think. This alters matters in a way that—that worries me," said the claimant, as though making a concession. "Why kill an impostor?"

"Or a real heir, for that matter," said Page.

Then Page could sense that the other was eyeing him sharply. "You do not still believe—?"

They were interrupted by footsteps coming rapidly if pontifically from the direction of the house. The claimant turned the beam of light on Welkyn, the solicitor, whom Page last remembered eating fish-paste sandwiches in the dining-room. Welkyn, now evidently a very scared man, gripped the edge of the white slip inside his waistcoat as though he were going to make a speech. Then he changed his mind.

"You'd better get back to the house gentlemen," he said. "Mr Murray would like to see you. I *hope*"— he gave the word a sinister emphasis, and looked hard at the claimant—"I hope neither of you gentlemen has been in the house since this thing happened."

'Patrick Gore' whipped round. "Don't tell me anything else has happened."

"It has," said Welkyn snappishly. "It appears that someone has taken advantage of this confusion. In Mr Murray's absence, someone went into the library and stole the Thumbograph containing our only evidence."

PART II

Thursday, July 30th

THE LIFE OF AN AUTOMATON

Then all was silent, and presently Moxon reappeared and said, with a rather sorry smile:

"Pardon me for leaving you so abruptly. I have a machine in there that lost its temper and cut up rough."

Fixing my eyes steadily upon his left cheek, which was traversed by four parallel excoriations showing blood, I said:

"How would it do to trim its nails?"

AMBROSE BIERCE, *Moxon's Master.*

CHAPTER VII

IN early afternoon of the following day, while grey, warm rain darkened the countryside, Page sat again at the desk in his study; but this time with very different thoughts.

Up and down the room, in a way as monotonous as the sound of the rain itself, paced Detective-Inspector Elliot.

And throned in the largest chair sat Dr Gideon Fell.

The doctor's thunderous chuckles were to-day subdued. He had arrived in Mallingford that morning, and he did not seem to like the situation he found. Sitting back in the big chair, he wheezed gently. His eyes, behind the eyeglasses on the broad black ribbon, were fixed with singular concentration on a corner of the desk; his bandit's moustache bristled as though ready for argument, and his big mop of grey-streaked hair had fallen over one ear. On a chair beside him lay his shovel-hat and his stick with the ivory crutch-handle. Though there was a pint tankard of beer at his elbow, he did not seem interested even in this. And, though his red face was even more red in the July heat, it hardly expressed his customary joviality. Page found him even larger, both in height and circumference, than he had been described; when he first came into the cottage, wearing his box-pleated cape, he seemed to fill the place and crowd out even the furniture.

Nor did anybody like the situation within the district of Mallingford and Soane. The district retreated within itself; it was not even eloquently silent. Everybody now knew that the stranger known as a 'folklore authority' at the Bull and Butcher was an inspector of the Criminal Investigation Department. But not a word was said of it. In the taproom of the Bull and Butcher, those who came in for their morning pint spoke in a little lower tone, and drifted away sooner; that was all. Dr Fell had been unable to get accommodation at the pub—inn by courtesy

—since both guest-rooms were occupied; and Page had been only too glad to offer the hospitality of his cottage.

Page liked Inspector Elliot as well. Andrew Mac-Andrew Elliot looked out of place neither as folklore authority nor as Scotland Yard man. He was youngish, raw-boned, sandy-haired, and serious-minded. He liked argument, and he liked subtleties in a way that would have displeased Superintendent Hadley. His education had been that thorough Scots one which deals with the minutest details of the minutest subject. Now, pacing the floor of Page's study while the grey rain fell, he tried to make his position clear.

"H'mf, yes," grunted Dr. Fell. "But exactly what has been done so far?"

Elliot considered. "Captain Marchbanks, the Chief Constable, telephoned to the Yard this morning and washed his hands of the business," he said. "Ordinarily, of course, they'd have sent a chief inspector. But, since I happened to be on the spot and already investigating something that may be connected with this—"

(The murder of Victoria Daly, thought Page. But how connected?)

"You got your chance," said Dr Fell. "Excellent."

"Yes, sir, I got my chance," agreed Elliot, placing a freckled fist carefully on the table and bracing himself over it. "And I mean to make something of it, if I can. It's opportunity. It's—you know all that." He expelled his breath. "But you know the difficulties I'm going to find. People hereabouts have shut up tighter than windows. You try to see inside, but they won't let you inside. They'll drink a glass of beer and talk just as usual; but they fall away as soon as you say anything about it. With what we'll call the gentry of the whole district "—his tone showed a certain faint contempt for the word—"it's been even more difficult, even before this thing happened."

"About the other affair, you mean?" inquired Dr Fell, opening one eye.

"About the other affair. The only one who's been at all helpful is a Miss Dane, Madeline Dane. There," declared Inspector Elliot, with measured carefulness and emphasis, "is a real woman. It's a pleasure to talk to

63

her. *Not* one of your hard-boiled misses who blow smoke in your eye and ring up their lawyers as soon as you send in a card. No. A real woman; reminds me of a girl I used to know at home."

Dr Fell opened both eyes, while Inspector Elliot (so to speak) fidgeted under his freckles for having said this. But Brian Page understood and approved. He was even conscious of a twinge of nonsensical jealousy.

"However," the inspector resumed, "you'll want to know about Farnleigh Close. I've taken a statement from everybody who was there last night: exclusive of servants, as yet. A brief statement. I had to round some of them up. Mr Burrows stayed at the Close last night, to be ready for us to-day. But the claimant, this Mr Patrick Gore, and his solicitor (name of Welkyn) both went back to Maidstone." He looked round at Page. "I gather, sir, there was a bit of a row—or, well, say that things got pretty strained after this Thumbograph had been stolen?"

Page admitted it with some fervour.

"Especially after the Thumbograph was stolen," he replied. "The odd part of it was that to everybody except Molly Farnleigh it seemed more important that the evidence had been stolen than that Farnleigh had been murdered—if he was murdered."

A gleam of interest stirred in Dr Fell's eye. "By the way, what was the general attitude in the question of suicide *v.* murder?"

"Very cautious. A great lack of attitude, which is surprising. The only one who definitely said he'd been murdered (screamed it, in fact) was Molly—Lady Farnleigh, I mean. Otherwise accusations of crookedness hurtled about in a way I hope won't be remembered to-day. I'm glad to say I don't remember half of it. I suppose it was only natural. Beforehand we had all been so strainedly and unnaturally on our best behaviour that the reaction was a little too much. Even solicitors, it appears, are human. Murray tried to take charge, and was swept under. Our local police-sergeant wasn't much better."

"I am endeavouring," said Dr Fell, making a hideous face of emphasis, "to clear the way to the problem. You say, inspector, you don't have much doubt that it is murder?"

Elliot was firm.

"No, sir, I haven't. There were three gashes across the throat, *and* no weapon I've been able to find so far, either in the pool or anywhere at hand. Mind," he said cautiously, "I haven't had the medical report. I don't say it's impossible for a man to inflict three such wounds on himself. But the absence of a weapon seems to decide it."

For a moment they listened to the rain, and to the doubtful wheezing of Dr Fell's breath.

"You don't think," suggested the doctor, "I only—harrumph—put it forward as a suggestion: you don't think he might have killed himself and, in the convulsion, flung the weapon away from him, so that you haven't found it? That has happened before, I think."

"It's remotely possible. But he can't have thrown it clear out of the garden; and, if it's there anywhere, Sergeant Burton will find it." There was a curious look on Elliot's hard face. "Look here, sir: do *you* think this is suicide?"

"No, no, no," said Dr Fell earnestly, as though this rather shocked him. "But, even believing that this is murder, I still want to know what our problem is."

"Our problem is who killed Sir John Farnleigh."

"Quite. You still don't perceive the double-alley of hell into which that leads us. I am worried about this case, because all rules have been violated. All rules have been violated because the wrong man had been chosen for a victim. If only Murray had been murdered! (I speak academically, you understand.) Hang it all, Murray should have been murdered! In any well-constituted plot he would have been murdered. His presence cries out for it. Here is a man possessing evidence which will decide a vital problem at the outset: here is a man who can probably solve the puzzle of identities even without that evidence: well, he is the certain candidate for the death-blow. Yet he remains untouched, and the problem of identities is merely made more inexplicable by the death of one of the claimants. You follow that?"

"I do," said Inspector Elliot grimly.

"Let's clear away some of the underbrush," insisted Dr Fell. "Is the whole thing, for instance, an error on the part of the murderer? Was Sir John Farnleigh (to give him his present name) not intended to be the victim at all? Did the murderer kill him in mistake for somebody else?"

"It seems doubtful," said Elliot, and looked at Page.

"It's impossible," said Page. "I'd thought of that too. Well, I repeat: it's impossible. The light was too good. Farnleigh didn't look like anybody else, and wasn't dressed like anybody else. Even from some distance away you could never have mistaken him, let alone at the close quarters of someone who cuts his throat. It was that queerish watery light where details are blurred but all outlines are clear."

"Then Farnleigh was the intended victim," said Dr Fell, clearing his throat with a long rumbling noise. "Very well. What other possible undergrowths or verbiage can we rake away? For instance, is it possible that this murder has no connection whatever with the battle over the title and estates? Did some person unaffected by this debate—some person who didn't care whether he was John Farnleigh or Patrick Gore—choose just this moment to slide through the screen and kill him for some outside motive we don't know? It is possible. It is possible if the Powers are being coy. But I, for one am not going to worry about it. These things are cohesive; they depend on each other. For, you notice, the Thumbograph evidence was stolen at the same time Farnleigh was murdered.

"Very well. Farnleigh was deliberately murdered, and murdered for some reason connected with the question of the right heir to the estates. But we still haven't decided what our real problem is. The problem is still double-headed, not to say double-faced. Thus, if the murdered man was an impostor, he might have been killed for any one of two or three reasons. You can imagine them. But, if the murdered man was the real heir, he might have been killed for any one of two or three totally different reasons. You can imagine those too. They entail different sides, different eyes, different motives. Therefore, which of those two is the impostor?

66

We have got to know that before we have the remotest idea in which direction we've got to look. Harrumph."

Inspector Elliot's face hardened.

" You mean that the key is this Mr Murray? "

" I do. I mean my old, enigmatic acquaintance, Kennet Murray."

" You think he knows which is which? "

" I've got no doubt of it," growled Dr Fell.

" Nor I," said the inspector dryly. " Let's see, now." He got out his notebook and opened it. " Everyone seems to be agreed—remarkable what a lot of agreement there is—that Mr Murray was left alone in the study at about twenty minutes past nine o'clock. Correct, Mr Page? "

" Correct."

" The murder (we'll call it that) was committed at about half-past nine. Two persons give a definite time about this: Murray and the solicitor, Harold Welkyn. Now ten minutes may not be a long time. But the comparison of finger-prints, though you've got to be careful about it, isn't the all-night job Murray gave you to understand. You can't tell me he didn't have *some* idea—Do you think he's a wrong 'un, sir? "

" No," said Dr Fell, frowning heavily at the tankard of ale. " I think he's trying to do a spot of sensational detection. And in just a minute I'll tell you what I think this case is. You say you got a statement from each of them as to what each was doing during that ten minutes? "

" Bald few lines from everybody," said Elliot, suddenly angry. " No comment. They asked what comments they could make. Well, I mean to ask again, and comment too. Queerish crowd, if you ask me. I know things sound pretty shorn in a policeman's report, because you've got to stick little bits of facts together without anything between: and thankful to get what you do. But there's black murder and plain hell in the midst of them, and this is what they say. Listen."

He opened his notebook.

' *Statement of Lady Farnleigh:* When we left the library I was upset, so I went upstairs to my bedroom. My husband and I have adjoining bedrooms on the first floor of the new wing, over the dining-room. I washed my face and hands. I told my maid to lay out another frock, because I felt grubby. I lay down on the bed. There was only a very small light from the bedside lamp. The windows were open on the balcony of my room overlooking the garden. I heard noises like a fight and a scuffling and a kind of cry, and then a splash. I ran to the balcony and saw my husband. He seemed to be lying in the pool and fighting. He was alone then. I could see this clearly. I ran downstairs by the main staircase, and out to him. I did not see or hear anything suspicious in the garden.

"Next we have:

'*Statement of Kennet Murray:* I remained in the library between nine-twenty and nine-thirty. No one entered the room, and I saw no one else. My back was to the window. I heard the sounds (similarly described). I did not think anything serious had happened until I heard someone run downstairs in the hall. I heard Lady Farnleigh's voice calling out to the butler that she was afraid something had happened to Sir John. I looked at my watch; it was then just nine-thirty. I joined Lady Farnleigh in the hall, and we went out into the garden, where we found a man with his throat cut. I have no comment to make at this time on the finger-prints or my comparisons of them.

"Fine and helpful, isn't it? Then we have:

'*Statement of Patrick Gore, claimant:* I wandered. I was out on the front lawn first, smoking. Then I wandered round the south side of the house to this garden. I did not hear any sounds except a splash, and I heard that very faintly. I think I heard this when I had just started round the side of the house. I did not think anything was wrong. When I came into the garden I heard loud voices talking. I did not want any company, so I kept to the side path along the high yew hedge bounding the garden. Then I heard what they were talking about. I listened. I did not go to the pool until all of them except a man named Page had gone back to the house.

"Finally, we come to:

'*Statement of Harold Welkyn:* I remained in the dining-room and did not leave it at any time. I ate five small sandwiches and drank a glass of port. I agree that the dining-room has glass doors opening out into the garden, and that one of these doors is not far from the pool in a straight line. But the lights were full on in the dining-room, and I could not see anything in the garden because of the contrasting lights—

"A witness dead on the scene. Ground floor: hedges only waist-high: not more than twenty feet from where Farnleigh must have been standing," said Elliot, flicking his notebook with finger and thumb. "But he's dead and blind in his 'contrasting lights'. He concludes:

'At nine thirty-one by the grandfather clock in the dining-room I heard certain noises resembling a scuffle and a stopped cry. This was followed by a series of loud splashings. I also heard a kind of rustling noise in the hedges or shrubbery, and I thought I saw something looking at me through one of the glass panels of the door, one of the panels down nearest the ground. I was afraid that certain things might have happened which were no affair of mine. I sat down and waited until Mr Burrows came in and told me the fraudulent Sir John Farnleigh had committed suicide. During this time I did not do anything except eat another sandwich.'"

Dr Fell, wheezing into a more upright position, reached out after the tankard of ale and took a deep pull. There was a steady, gleaming excitement behind his eyeglasses, a sort of astonished pleasure.

"Oh, Bacchus!" he said in a hollow voice. "'Shorn' statements, hey? Is that your considered opinion? There is something in our Mr Welkyn's statement which tends to give me a cauld grue. H'mf, ha, stop a bit. Welkyn! Welkyn! Haven't I heard that name somewhere before? I'm certain of it, because it cries aloud for bad puns, and therefore it would stick in my—'What is mind?' 'No matter.' 'What is matter?' 'Never mind.' I beg your pardon, I was scatter-braining again. Have you got anything else?"

"Well, there were two other guests, Mr Page here and Mr Burrows. You've heard Mr Page's statement, and you've had the gist of Mr Burrows's."

"Never mind. Read it again, will you?"

Inspector Elliot frowned.

'*Statement of Nathaniel Burrows:* I could have eaten something, but Welkyn was in the dining-room and I did not think it proper for me to talk to him then. I went to the drawing-room at the other side of the house and waited. Then I thought that my proper place was with Sir John Farnleigh, who had gone out into the south garden. I took an electric torch out of the table in the hall. I did this because my eyesight is not good. As I was starting to open the door to the garden I saw Sir John. He was standing on the edge of the pool. He. seemed to be doing something, or moving about a little. From the door to the nearer edge of the pool is about thirty-five feet. I heard the scuffling sounds, and then the splash and the churnings in water. I ran down there and found him. I am not able to swear whether or not there was anybody with him. I cannot give an exact description of the movements he made. It was as though something had got hold of his feet.

"And there we are, sir. You notice certain things. Except Mr Burrows, nobody ever actually saw the victim before he was attacked and fell or was thrown into the pool. Lady Farnleigh didn't see him until he was in the pool; Mr Gore, Mr Murray, Mr Welkyn, and Mr Page didn't see him until afterwards—or so they say. There are other things," he prodded, "which you'll have noticed?"

"Eh?" said Dr Fell vaguely.

"I asked what you made of it."

"Why, I'll tell you what I was thinking. 'A garden is a lovesome thing, God wot,'" said Dr Fell. "But what about the sequel? After the murder, I gather, the Thumbograph was pinched from the library when Murray came out to see what was up. Did you get a statement from the various persons about what they were doing then, or who might have pinched it?"

"I did," said Elliot. "But I won't read it to you, sir. And why? Because it's one great, serene blank. Analysed and boiled down, it amounts to this: that anybody might have stolen the Thumbograph, and that in the general confusion nobody would have noticed who did."

"Oh, Lord!" Dr Fell groaned, after a pause. "We've got it at last."

"Got what?"

"What I've been half-dreading for a long time—an almost purely psychological puzzle. There are no discrepancies in the various stories, in the various times given, even in the various possibilities. There are no incongruities to explain, except the thundering psychological incongruity of why the wrong man should have been so carefully murdered. Above all, there is an almost complete absence of material clues: no cuff-links,

cigarette-ends, theatre-ticket-stubs, pens, ink, or paper.
H'mf. Unless we get our claws into something more
tangible, we shall merely fumble with the greased pig
called human behaviour. Which person, then, would
be most likely to kill the man who was killed? And
why? And which person fits best, psychologically, into
the pattern of devilry you've drawn round Victoria Daly's
murder? "

Elliot began to whistle through his teeth. He said:
" Any ideas, sir? "

" Let me see," muttered Dr Fell, " if I have mastered
the essential facts in the case of Victoria Daly. Age
thirty-five, spinster, pleasant, not intelligent, lived alone.
H'mf. Ha. Yes. Murdered about eleven-forty-five pm
on July 31st, last. Right, my lad? "

" Right."

" Alarm given by farmer driving home past her cottage.
Screams coming from there. Village policeman, passing
on bicycle, follows farmer. Both see a man—tramp known
in district—climbing out of window, ground floor, rear.
Both follow in quarter-mile chase. Tramp, trying to cut
off pursuit by getting over gates and across tracks ahead
of Southern Railway goods-train, is eliminated quickly
if not neatly. Right? "

" Right."

" Miss Daly found in ground-floor room of cottage: her
bedroom. Strangled with boot-lace. When attacked,
was retiring but had not yet gone to bed. Wore night-
dress, quilted dressing gown, and slippers. Apparently a
clear case—money and valuables found on tramp—except
for one fact. On examination by doctor, body found
smeared with dark sooty compound; same compound also
round under all finger-nails. Eh? This substance, analysed
by Home Office man, proved to be composed of juice
of water parsnip, aconite, cinquefoil, deadly nightshade,
and soot."

Page sat up, mentally stuttering. Until the last part
of Dr Fell's statement, he had heard it all a thousand
times before.

" Here! " he protested. " That's the first time anybody's mentioned a thing like that. You found smeared
on the body a substance containing two deadly poisons? "

71

"Yes," said Elliot, with a broad and sardonic grin. "The local doctor didn't have it analysed, of course. The coroner didn't think it was important and didn't even bring it up at the inquest. He probably thought it was some kind of beauty preparation, which it would be indelicate to mention. But the doctor later passed on a quiet word, and—"

Page was troubled. "Aconite and deadly nightshade! All the same, they weren't swallowed, were they? They wouldn't have killed her if they only touched her externally, would they?"

"Oh, no. All the same, it's a fairly clear case. Don't you think so, sir?"

"An unfortunately clear case," admitted Dr Fell.

Above the noise of the rain Page heard a rapping at the front door of the cottage. Trying to place an elusive memory, he went out through the short passage and opened the door. It was Sergeant Burton of the local police, wearing a rubber hood and coat, under which he was shielding something wrapped in newspapers. What he said brought Page's thoughts back from Victoria Daly to the closer problem of Farnleigh.

"Might I see Inspector Elliot and Dr Fell, sir?" Burton said. "I've got the weapon, right enough. And—"

He gestured with his head. Beyond a muddy front garden pricked up into puddles by the rain, a familiar car stood by the front gate. It was an ancient Morris, and there seemed to be two persons behind the side-curtains. Inspector Elliot came to the door hurriedly.

"You said—?"

"I've got the weapon that killed Sir John, inspector. And something else too." Again Sergeant Burton moved his head in the direction of the car. "It's Miss Madeline Dane and old Mr. Knowles, who works up at the Close. He used to work for Miss Dane's father's best friend. When he wasn't sure what to do he went to Miss Dane, and she sent him to me. He's got something to tell you that'll probably straighten out the whole case."

CHAPTER VIII

THEY put down the newspaper-parcel on Page's writing-table, and unfolded it to reveal the weapon. It was a pocket-knife; a boy's pocket-knife of old-fashioned design; and, under the present circumstances, a heavy and murderous-looking pocket-knife.

In addition to the main blade—which was open now—its wooden handle contained two smaller blades, a cork-screw, and an implement once alleged to be useful for removing stones from horses' hoofs. To Page it brought back the days when to possess such a fine knife was the proud mark of almost-manhood: when you were an adventurer, almost a red Indian. It was an old knife. The main blade, well over four inches long, bore two deep triangular nicks, and the steel was ragged in places; but it was not rusty, and it had been kept razor-sharp. There was about it now no suggestion of playing at Indians. From point to handle the heavy blade was dis-coloured with blood-stains which had recently dried.

A feeling of uneasiness touched them all as they looked at it. Inspector Elliot straightened up.

" Where did you find this? "

" Stuck down deep inside one of those low hedges; about "—said Sergeant Burton, half-closing one eye to estimate—" about ten feet away from the lily-pond."

" Away from the pool in which direction? "

" Towards the left, standing with your back to the house. Towards that high hedge that's the south boundary. A bit nearer in to the house than the lily-pond is. You see, sir," explained the sergeant carefully, " it was luck —me finding it. We might have searched for a month and never found it. No more we mightn't, unless we pulled all the hedges to bits. That yew's as thick as sin. It was the rain that did it. I was running my hand along the top of one hedge; not meaning anything, you understand; just wondering where to look. The hedge was wet, and my hand came away with a bit of reddy-brown colour on it. That was where it'd left a bit of blood on the flat top of the hedge when it went through. You couldn't even see the cut in the top where she'd gone through. I dug her out. The hedge kept the rain off, as you see."

"Somebody'd pushed it straight down through the hedge, you think?"

Sergeant Burton considered.

"Yes, it'd be that, I think. She was stuck in there straight, point downwards. Or else—that's a good heavy knife, sir. Blade's as heavy as the handle. If somebody threw her away, or up into the air, she'd have come down blade first and gone through just like that."

There was a certain look on Sergeant Burton's face which no one there failed to intercept. Dr Fell, who had been sunk in some obscure musing, rolled up his head; Dr Fell's large under-lip came out in a mutinous way.

"H'm," he said. "'Threw her away?' After suicide, you mean?"

Burton's forehead altered slightly; he said nothing.

"It's the knife we want, right enough," Inspector Elliot conceded. "I didn't like the jagged, crooked look of two of the three wounds on that fellow. They looked more like mauling or tearing. But look here—look at the notches in this blade. They'll fit or I'm a Dutchman. What do you say?"

"About Miss Dane and old Mr Knowles, sir— "

"Yes; ask them if they'll come in. That's good work, sergeant; damned good work. You might go and see whether the doctor has any news for me."

Dr Fell and the inspector were beginning to argue as Page picked up an umbrella from the passage and went out to bring Madeline in.

Not rain or mud could alter Madeline's trimness, or ruffle her quiet good temper. She was wearing one of those transparent oilskin waterproofs, with a hood, which made her look as though she were wrapped in cellophane. Her blonde hair was done into something like curls above the ears; she had a pale, healthy face, the nose and mouth a little broad, the eyes a little long; yet the whole of a beauty which grew on you the more you noticed it. For

74

she never gave the impression of wanting to be noticed; she was one of those persons who seem cut out to be good listeners. Her eyes were very dark blue, with a deep glance of sincerity. Though her figure was good—Page always damned himself for noticing her figure—she conveyed an impression of fragility. She put her hand on his arm, and gave him an uncertain smile, as he helped her out of the car under the umbrella.

"I'm terribly glad it's at your house," she said in her soft voice. "It makes things easier, somehow. But I really didn't know what to do, and it seemed the best way—"

She glanced back at stout Knowles, who was getting out of the car. Knowles carried his bowler hat even in the rain, and he was picking his way in a pigeon-toed waddle through the mud.

Page took Madeline into the study, and introduced her proudly. He wanted to show her off to Dr Fell. Certainly the doctor's response was everything that could be wished. He beamed down on her in a way that threatened to split several waistcoat buttons, and seemed to turn on lights behind his eye-glasses; he towered up, chuckling, and it was the doctor himself who took her waterproof when she sat down.

Inspector Elliot was at his most brisk and official. He spoke like a shop-assistant behind a counter.

"Yes, Miss Dane? And what can I do for you?"

Madeline regarded her clasped hands, and looked round with a pleasant frown before her candid gaze met the inspector's.

"You see, it's very difficult to explain," she said. "I know I must do it. Someone must do it, after that terrible affair last night. And yet I don't want Knowles to get into trouble. He mustn't, Mr Elliot—"

"If anything's bothering you, Miss Dane, just tell me," said Elliot briskly; "and nobody will get into trouble."

She gave him a grateful look.

"Then perhaps—You'd better tell them, Knowles. What you told me."

"Heh-heh-heh," said Dr Fell. "Sit down, man!"

"No, sir; thank you; I—"

"Sit down!" thundered Dr Fell.

As an alternative to being pushed down, which from the doctor's gesture seemed imminent, Knowles obeyed. Knowles was an honest man: sometimes a dangerously honest man. He had one of those faces which in moments of mental stress go transparently pink, as though you could see through the face like a shell. He sat on the edge of the chair, turning his bowler hat round in his hands. Dr Fell tried to give him a cigar, but he declined this.

"I wonder, sir, if I may speak frankly?"

"I should advise it," said Elliot dryly. "Well?"

"Of course, sir, I know I should have gone to Lady Farnleigh straight away. But I couldn't tell her. I mean quite sincerely that I couldn't make myself do it. You see, it was through Lady Farnleigh that I came to the Close when Colonel Mardale died. I think I can say honestly that I think more of her than anyone else I know. Honest to God," added Knowles, with a sudden and unexpected descent into the human, and a slight surge up out of his chair. Then he relapsed. "She was Miss Molly, the doctor's daughter, from Sutton Chart. I knew—"

Elliot was patient.

"Yes, we appreciate that. But this information you were going to give us?"

"It's about the late Sir John Farnleigh, sir," said Knowles. "He committed suicide. I saw him do it."

The long silence was broken only by the diminishing noise of the rain. Page heard the rustle of his own sleeve as he looked round to see whether they had hidden the stained clasp-knife; he did not want Madeline to see it. It was now concealed under the newspapers on the table. Inspector Elliot, seeming even more hard-boned, was staring steadily at the butler. From Dr Fell's direction there issued a faint ghost of a noise, like half-humming or half-whistling behind closed teeth; he has a habit of whistling thus at times, to the tune of 'Auprès de ma Blonde', though he looked half asleep.

"You—saw—him—do it?"

"Yes, sir. I could have told you this morning; only you didn't question me; and, frankly, I'm not sure I should have told you even then. It's like this. I was standing at the window of the Green Room last night, the room just over the library, looking out into the garden, when it all happened. I saw everything."

(This, Page remembered, was true. When he had gone with Burrows to look at the body first, he had seen Knowles standing at the window of the room above the library.)

"Anybody will tell you about my eyesight," Knowles said warmly. Even his shoes squeaked with vehemence. "I'm seventy-four years old, and I can read a motor-car number-plate at sixty yards. You just go out in the garden there, and you take a box or a sign or something with small letters—" He corrected himself, and sat back.

"You saw Sir John Farnleigh cut his own throat?"

"Yes, sir. As good as."

"'As good as'? What do you mean by that?"

"I mean this, sir. I didn't actually see him draw the—you know—because his back was towards me. But I saw him put his hands up. And there wasn't a living soul near him. Remember, I was looking straight down on him and into the garden. I could see into that circular open space all round the pool; and there's a good five-foot border of sand between the pool and the nearest hedge all round. Nobody could have come near him without my seeing. And he was all alone in that open space, I'll tell you to my dying day."

Still the sleepy and tuneless whistling wheezes from Dr Fell's direction.

"'Tous les oiseaux du monde,'" muttered the doctor, "'viennent y faire leurs nids—'" Then he spoke out. "Why should Sir John Farnleigh kill himself?"

Knowles braced himself.

"Because he wasn't Sir John Farnleigh, sir. The other gentleman is. I knew it as soon as I clapped eyes on him last night."

Inspector Elliot remained impassive.

"What reason have you for saying that?"

"It's hard to tell you so you'll understand, sir," Knowles complained. (For the first time in his life he showed a lack of tact.) "Now, I'm seventy-four. I wasn't any chicken, if you'll excuse me for saying so, when young Mr Johnny went away from home in nineteen-twelve. You see, to old people like myself the younger

77

ones never change. They always seem just the same, whether they're fifteen or thirty or forty-five. Lord bless you, do you think I wouldn't have recognised the real Mr Johnny whenever I met him? Mind! " said Knowles, again forgetting himself and raising his finger. " I don't say that when the late gentleman came here and pretended to be the new Sir John—I don't say I twigged it. No. Not at all. I thought, well, he's different; he's been to America, and you never know them after that; it's only natural, and I'm getting old. So I never really suspected him of not being the right master, though I'm bound to admit that now and again he did say things that— "

" But— "

" Now, you'll say," continued Knowles, in real and blinding earnest, " I wasn't at the Close in the old days. That's true. I've been here only ten years, since Miss Molly asked the late Sir Dudley to offer me the honour. But, when I served Colonel Mardale, young Mr Johnny used to spend a lot of time in the big orchard between the colonel's and the major's— "

" The major's? "

" Major Dane, sir, Miss Madeline's father; he was the colonel's great friend. Well, young Mr Johnny liked that orchard, with the wood behind it. That orchard is close to the Hanging Chart, you know—leads into it. He pretended he was a wizard, and a mediæval knight, and I don't know what; but some things I didn't like at all. Anyway, I knew last night, even before he started asking me about rabbits and the like, that this new gentleman was the real Mr Johnny. He knew I knew it. That's why he had me called in. But what could I *say*? "

Page remembered that interview only too well. But he remembered other things too, and wondered if Elliot had learned them. He glanced across at Madeline.

Inspector Elliot opened his notebook.

" So he killed himself. Eh? "

" Yes, sir."

" Did you see the weapon he used? "

" No, not properly, I'm afraid."

" I want you to tell me just exactly what you did see. For instance, you say you were in the ' Green Room ' when it happened. When and why did you go there?"

Knowles got his wits together.

"Well, sir, it might have been two or three minutes before it happened——"

"Twenty-seven or twenty-eight minutes past nine. Which?" asked Inspector Elliot, with a hard passion for accuracy.

"I can't say, sir. I didn't take any account of the time. One of them. I was in the hall near the dining-room, in case I should be wanted, though there was nobody in the dining-room except Mr Welkyn. Then Mr Nathaniel Burrows came out of the drawing-room, and asked me where he could find an electric torch. I said I thought there was one in the Green Room upstairs, which the late—gentleman used as a kind of study, and I said I would go and fetch it for him. I have since learned," Knowles was now giving evidence, as his diction showed, "that Mr Burrows found one in the drawer of the table in the hall; but I had not known there was one there."

"Go on."

"I went upstairs and I went into the Green Room——"

"Did you turn on the light?"

"Not then," said Knowles, a little flustered. "Not just at that moment. There is no wall-switch in the room. You must turn on the light from the ceiling-fixture. The table where I thought I had seen the electric torch is between the windows. I went towards that table, and when I went past I glanced out of the window."

"Which window?"

"The right-hand one, facing out on the garden."

"Was the window open?"

"Yes, sir. Now, here's how it was. You must have noticed there are trees all along the back of the library; but they've been pruned down so that they don't cut off the view from the windows of the floor above. The ceilings at the close are eighteen feet high, most of them —except the new wing, which is a little low doll's house of a place—and that gives you a good height of tree without having them stretch up past the windows of the Green Room. That's why it's called the Green Room, because you look out over tree-tops. So you see I was high over the garden, looking down into it."

Here Knowles got up from his chair and craned himself forward. He had seldom executed this movement before, and it evidently gave him a twinge, but his grimness was such that he held the position while he talked.

"Here I was, you see. Then there were the green leaves, lit up from underneath by the library windows." He moved his hand. "Then there was the garden, with every hedge and path distinct, and the pool in the centre. The light wasn't bad, sir. I've seen them play tennis in worse. Then there was Sir John—or the gentleman who called himself that—standing by it with his hands in his pockets."

At this point Knowles had to leave off play-acting and sit down.

"That's all," he said, with a slightly quicker breath.

"That's *all*?" repeated Inspector Elliot.

"Yes, sir."

Elliot, pulled up at this unexpected conclusion, stared at him.

"But what happened, man? That's what I'm trying to get you to tell me!"

"Just that. I thought I heard a movement down in the trees under me, and I glanced down. When I looked up again—"

"Are you going to tell me," said Elliot very calmly and carefully, "that YOU didn't see what happened either?"

"No, sir. I saw him fall forward in the pool."

"Yes; but what else?"

"Well, sir, there certainly wasn't time for someone—you know what I mean, sir—to cut his throat three times and then run away. There couldn't 'a' been. He was alone every bit of the time, before and after. So he must have killed himself."

"What did he use to kill himself?"

"A kind of knife, I think."

"You think. Did you see the knife?"

"Not properly, no."

"Did you see it in his hand?"

"Not properly. It was too far away to see that plain. Sir," replied Knowles, remembering that he had a position in the world and drawing himself up with dignity,

"I am trying to give you a true, so-help-me-God story of what I saw——"

"Well, what did he do with the knife afterwards? Did he drop it? What happened to it?"

"I didn't notice, sir. I honestly didn't. I was paying attention to him; and something seemed to be happening to the front of him."

"Could he have thrown the knife from him?"

"He might. I don't know."

"Would you have seen it if he had thrown it?"

Knowles considered long. "That would depend on the size of the knife. And there are bats in that garden. And sometimes, sir, you can't see a tennis-ball until it's——" He was a very old man. His face grew clouded, and for a moment they were afraid he was going to cry. But he spoke again with dignity. "I am sorry, sir. If you don't believe me, have I your permission to go?"

"Oh, hang it all, it isn't that——!" said Elliot, stung to youthful naturalness, and his ears grew slightly red. Madeline Dane, who had said not a word the whole time, was watching him with a faint smile.

"Just one other point, for the time being," Elliot went on stiffly. "If you had a good view of the whole garden, did you see anybody else in the garden at the time of the—attack?"

"At the time it happened, sir? No. Immediately afterwards, though, I turned on the lights in the Green Room, and by that time there were a number of persons in the garden. But beforehand, at the time of the— *excuse* me, sir; yes, there was! " Again Knowles raised his finger and frowned. "There was somebody there when it happened. I saw him! You remember, I said I heard a noise down in the trees round the library windows?"

"Yes; well?"

"I looked down. That was what took away my attention. There was a gentleman down there, looking into the library windows. I could see plainly; because the branches of the trees, of course, don't quite reach to the windows, and everything was all lighted up between, like a little alley between the trees and the windows. He was standing there looking into the library."

"Who was?"

"The new gentleman, sir. The real Mr Johnny that I used to know. The one who now calls himself Mr Patrick Gore."

There was a silence.

Elliot very carefully put down his pencil, and glanced across at Dr Fell. The doctor had not moved; he would have seemed asleep if one little eye had not gleamed half-open.

"Have I got this clear?" Elliot demanded. "At the same time as the attack, or suicide, or murder, or whatever-we-call-it, Mr Patrick Gore was standing down there in your sight by the library windows?"

"Yes, sir. Over to the left he stood, towards the south. That's how I could see his face."

"Now, you'll swear to that?"

"Yes, sir, of course," said Knowles, opening his eyes.

"This was at the time of the various scuffling sounds, the splash and fall, and so on?"

"Yes, sir."

Elliot nodded in a colourless way and leafed back through his notebook. "I should like to read you a part of Mr Gore's testimony dealing with that same time. Listen. *'I was out on the front lawn first, smoking. Then I wandered round the side of the house to this garden. I did not hear any sounds except a splash, and I heard that very faintly. I think I heard this when I had just started round the side of the house.'* He goes on to say that he kept to the side paths along the south boundary.—Now, you tell us that, when the splash occurred, he was standing down underneath you looking into the library. His statement contradicts it."

"I can't help what he says, sir," answered Knowles helplessly. "I'm sorry, but I can't. That's what he was doing."

"But what did he do after you saw Sir John go into the pool?"

"I can't say that. I was looking towards the pool then."

Elliot hesitated, muttering to himself, and then glanced at Dr Fell. "Any questions you'd like to ask, doctor?"

"Yes," said Dr Fell.

He bestirred himself, beaming on Madeline, who

smiled back. Then he assumed an argumentative air as he beamed on Knowles.

"There are several troublesome queries following your theory, my boy. Among them, if Patrick Gore is the real heir, the question of who stole the Thumbograph, and why. But let's stick first to the vexed business of suicide *v.* murder." He reflected. "Sir John Farnleigh—the dead man, I mean—he was right-handed, was he?"

"Right-handed? Yes, sir."

"It was your impression that he had this knife in his right hand when he killed himself?"

"Oh, yes, sir."

"H'mf, yes. Now I want you to tell me what he did with his hands after this curious seizure by the pool. Never mind the knife! We'll admit you didn't properly see the knife. Just tell me what he did with his hands."

"Well, sir, he put them up to his throat—like this," said Knowles, illustrating. "Then he moved a little, and then he lifted them up over his head and threw them out, like this." Knowles made a large gesture, spreading his arms wide. "That was just before he went forward into the pool and began to writhe there."

"He didn't cross his arms? He simply lifted them and threw them out one to each side? Is that it?"

"That's right, sir."

Dr Fell took his crutch-handled stick from the table and hoisted himself to his feet. Lumbering over to the table, he took up the newspaper packet, unfolded it, and showed Knowles the bloodstained clasp-knife inside.

"The point is this," he argued. "Farnleigh has the knife in his right hand, supposing this to be suicide. He makes no gestures except to fling both arms wide. Even if he were helping support the knife with his left hand, his right would have the grip on it. The knife flies from his right hand as the arm is thrown wide. Excellent well. But will someone explain how in blazes that knife completely altered its flight in the air, passed high over the pool, and dropped into the hedge some ten feet to the *left*? And all this, mind you, after he has just inflicted not one, but three fatal wounds on himself? It won't do, you know."

Apparently oblivious to the fact that he was holding

the newspaper with its grisly exhibit almost against Madeline's cheek, Dr Fell frowned at it. Then he looked at the butler.

"On the other hand, how can we doubt this chap's eyesight? He says Farnleigh was alone by the pool; and there is some confirmation. Nathaniel Burrows is inclined to agree that he was alone. Lady Farnleigh, who ran out on the balcony immediately after the splash, saw nobody by the pool or within reach of it. We shall have to take our choice. On the one hand we have a somewhat preposterous suicide; but on the other hand, unfortunately, we have a more than somewhat impossible murder. Will someone kindly oblige me with an idea?"

CHAPTER IX

As vigorously and even violently as he had spoken, Dr Fell had been talking to himself. He had not expected an answer, nor did he get one. For a time he remained blinking at the book-shelves. He appeared to wake up when Knowles ventured a frightened cough.

"I beg your pardon, sir; is that the—?" He nodded towards the knife.

"We think so. It was found in a hedge to the left of the pool. How do you think it squares with suicide?"

"I don't know, sir."

"Did you ever see this knife before?"

"Not to my knowledge, sir."

"Or you, Miss Dane?"

Though Madeline seemed startled and a little shocked, she shook her head quietly. Then she leaned forward. Page noted again how the breadth of her face, the slight breadth and bluntness of her nose, did not in the least detract from her beauty, but seemed to add to it. His mind was always searching for comparisons or images when he saw her; and he found in her something mediæval, something in length of eye or fullness of lip, some inner spring of quietness, which suggested the rose-garden or the turret window. The sentimentality of the comparison must be excused, for he felt it and believed it.

"I'm afraid, you know," Madeline said almost pleadingly, "that I've no right to be here at all, and that I'm talking about things which do not concern me. And yet—well, I suppose I must." She smiled at Knowles. "I wonder if you will wait for me in my car?"

Knowles bowed and was gone—vague and troubled; and still the grey rain fell.

"Yes," said Dr Fell, sitting down again and folding his hands over the top of his stick. "You were the one I wanted to ask the questions, Miss Dane. What do *you* think of Knowles's views? About the real heir, I mean?"

"Only that it's much more difficult than you think."

"Do you believe what he says?"

"Oh, he's absolutely and completely sincere; you must have seen that. But he's an old man. And, among the children, he was always most fanatically devoted first to Molly (her father, you know, saved Knowles's mother's life once), and next to young John Farnleigh. I remember he once made a conical wizard's hat for John, out of cardboard painted blue, with silver-paper stars and whatnots. When this affair came up, he simply couldn't tell Molly; he couldn't. So he came to me. They all do—come to me, that is. And I try to do them what good I can."

Dr Fell's forehead was wrinkled. "Still, I was wondering . . . h'mf . . . you knew John Farnleigh pretty well in the old days? I understand," here he beamed, "that there was a kind of boy-and-girl romance between you?"

She made a wry face.

"You remind me that I'm past my youth. I'm thirty-five. Or thereabouts; you mustn't ask me to be too precise. No, there never was even a boy-and-girl romance between us, really. Not that I should have minded, but it didn't interest him. He—he kissed me once or twice, in the orchard and in the wood. But he used to say that I didn't have enough of the Old Adam—or do I mean Old Eve?—in me. Not enough of the devil, anyhow."

"But you never married?"

"Oh, that's unfair!" cried Madeline, flushing and then

laughing. "You talk as though I were sitting with my dim spectacled eyes over a piece of knitting in the chimney corner—"

"Miss Dane," said Dr Fell, with thunderous solemnity, "I don't. I mean that I can see suitors standing in droves at your door, stretching away like the Great Wall of China; I can see Nubian slaves bowed down by the weight of great chocolate-boxes; I can—ahem. Let us omit that."

It was a long time since Page had seen a genuine blush; he believed, nowadays, that such mainsprings were dried up and with the dodo; but, all the same, he did not mind seeing Madeline blush. For what she said was:

"If you're thinking that I cherished a romantic passion for John Farnleigh all these years, I'm afraid you're hopelessly wrong." There was a twinkle in her eye. "I was always a little frightened of him, and I'm not even sure I liked him—then."

"Then?"

"Yes. I liked him later, but only liked."

"Miss Dane," said Dr Fell, growling out of his several chins and moving his head curiously, "some inner Little Bird seems to tell me that you're trying to convey something to me. You still haven't answered my question. Do you think Farnleigh was an impostor?"

She made a slight gesture.

"Dr Fell, I am not trying to be mysterious. Really and truly I'm not; and I think I can tell you something. But, before I do, will you—or somebody—tell me just what did happen at the Close last night? I mean before the last horrible business happened? I mean, what those two said and did while each was claiming to be the real one?"

"We might as well have the story again, Mr Page," said Elliot.

Page told it, with as many shadings and impressions as he could remember. Madeline nodded her head several times in the course of it; she was breathing rapidly.

"Tell me, Brian: what struck you most about the whole interview?"

"The absolute assurance of both claimants," said Page.

"Farnleigh faltered once or twice, but over what seemed unimportant points; when any real test was mentioned, he was eager. I only saw him smile and look relieved once. That was when Gore was accusing him of attempted murder with a seaman's mallet aboard the *Titanic*."

"Just one other thing, please," Madeline requested, breathing still more rapidly. "Did either of them say anything about the dummy? "

There was a pause. Dr Fell, Inspector Elliot, and Brian Page looked at each other blankly.

"The dummy? " repeated Elliot, clearing his throat. "What dummy? "

"Or about bringing it to life? Or anything about the 'Book'? " Then a mask seemed to close over her face. "I'm sorry. I shouldn't have mentioned that, only I should have thought it would be the first thing to be brought up. Please forget it."

An expression of refreshed pleasure animated Dr Fell's large face.

"My dear Miss Dane," he rumbled, "you demand a miracle. You demand a miracle greater than any that could have happened in that garden. Consider what you demand. You refer to a certain dummy, to the possibility of its being brought to life, and to something you call the 'Book', all presumably in connection with this mystery. You acknowledge that it is the first thing you would have thought should be brought up. And then you ask us to forget it. Do you think that ordinary human beings of feverish curiosity could— "

Madeline looked stubborn.

"But you ought not to have asked me about it," she protested. "Not that I know anything, really. You ought to have asked them."

"'The Book,'" mused Dr Fell. "You don't mean, I suppose, the 'Red Book of Appin'? "

"Yes, I believe I later heard it called that. I read about it somewhere. It's not a book, really; it's a manuscript, or so John once told me."

"Wait a bit," interposed Page. "Murray asked that question, and both of them wrote down answers for it. Gore later told me that it was a catch question, and there was no such thing as the 'Red Book of Appin'. If there is such a thing, it makes Gore out the impostor, doesn't it?"

Dr Fell seemed about to speak, with some excitement and vehemence; but he drew a long breath through his nose and restrained himself.

"I wish I knew," said Elliot. "I never thought there could be so much doubt and confusion caused by only two persons. Now you're certain it's one of them, again you're just as certain it's the other. And—as Dr Fell says—we can't get much farther until we establish that. I hope, Miss Dane, you're not trying to evade the question. You still haven't answered: do you think the late Farnleigh was an impostor?"

Madeline threw her head back against the back of the chair. It was the greatest sign of animation, the only sign of spasmodic action, Page had ever seen her give. She opened and shut her right hand.

"I can't tell you," she said helplessly. "I *can't*. Not until I've seen Molly, anyhow."

"But what has Lady Farnleigh got to do with us?"

"Only that he—told me things. Things he didn't even confide to her. Oh, please don't look shocked!" (As a matter of fact, Elliot did not; but he looked interested.) "Or believe a lot of gossip you may have heard. But I've got to tell Molly first. You see, she believed in him. Of course, Molly was only seven years old when he left home. All she hazily remembers is a boy who took her to a gipsy camp, where they taught her to ride a pony and throw stones better than any man. Besides, any dispute over the Farnleigh name or estates wouldn't trouble her at all. Dr Sutton wasn't a country G.P.; he died worth nearly half a million, and Molly inherited it all in her own right. Also, sometimes I've thought she never really liked being mistress of that house; she doesn't seem to *care* for responsibilities of that sort. She didn't marry him because of his position or income, and she wouldn't really have cared—and won't now—whether his name is Farnleigh or Gore or whatever you like. So why should he have told her?"

Elliot looked rather dazed, as he had reason to do.

"Just a moment, Miss Dane. What are you trying to tell us: that he was or was not an impostor?"

"But I don't know! I don't know which he was!"

"The startling lack of information with which we are provided," said Dr Fell sadly, "proceeds from all sources and o'erflows its basin. Well, let's leave that for the moment. But on one point I insist on having my curiosity satisfied. What's all this about a dummy?"

Madeline hesitated.

"I don't know whether they've still got it," she answered, staring at the window in a fascinated way. "John's father kept it locked up in an attic room, along with the—books he didn't like. The old-time Farnleighs were an unpleasant lot, as you may know, and Sir Dudley was always afraid John had taken after them. Though there certainly didn't seem to have been anything wrong or unpleasant about this figure.

"I—I only saw it once. John stole the key from his father, and took me up all those stairs to see it, with a candle in a dark-lantern. He said the door hadn't been opened for generations. When it was new, they say the figure was as absolutely lifelike and beautiful as a real woman, sitting on a kind of padded box in Restoration costume. But when I saw it it was only old and black and withered-looking, and it frightened me horribly. I suppose it hadn't been touched for well over a hundred years. But I don't know what the story was that made people afraid of it."

There was something about her tone which made Page vaguely uneasy, because he could not place the inflection: he had never heard Madeline speak quite like that before. And he had never, certainly, heard of this 'figure' or 'dummy', whatever it was.

"It may have been very ingenious," Madeline explained, "yet I can't understand why there should have been anything bad about it. Did you ever hear of Kempelen's and Maelzel's mechanical chess-player, or Maskelyne's 'Zoe' or 'Psycho', the whist-playing figure?"

Elliot shook his head, though he looked interested; and Dr Fell was so interested that the eye-glasses tumbled off his nose.

"You don't mean—?" he said. "Archons of Athens, this is better than anything I had hoped for! They were among the best of a series of nearly life-size automatons which puzzled Europe for two hundred years. Didn't you ever read of the harpsichord, exhibited before Louis XIV, which played by itself? Or the dummy invented by Kempelen, shown by Maelzel, which was owned by Napoleon and later lost in the museum fire at Philadelphia? For all practical purposes, Maelzel's automaton was alive. It played chess with you; and usually won. There have been several explanations of how it worked—Poe wrote one—but to my simple mind it still isn't satisfactorily explained. You can see ' Psycho ' in the London Museum to-day. You don't mean there's one at Farnleigh Close? "

"Yes. That's why I should have thought this Mr Murray would have *asked* about it," said Madeline. "As I say, I don't know the story. This automaton was exhibited in England during the reign of Charles II, and bought by a Farnleigh then. I don't know whether it played cards or chess, but it moved and spoke. When I saw it, as I say, it was old and black and withered-looking."

"But this—harrumph—this business of bringing it alive? "

"Oh, that was only the nonsense John used to talk when he was a silly child. I wasn't trying to talk seriously about that, don't you see? I was only trying to go back and test what could be remembered of him in the old days. The room where they used to keep the figure was full of books with—well, with downright evil in them," again she flushed, "and that was what attracted John. The secret of how to make the figure work had been forgotten; I daresay that was what he meant."

On Page's desk the telephone-bell rang. He had been so engrossed in watching Madeline, the slight turns of her head, the intentness of her dark-blue eyes, that he groped after the 'phone before finding it. But at the sound of Burrows's voice on the wire he became very much alert.

"For God's sake," said Burrows, "come up to the Close straight away, and bring the inspector and Dr Fell."

"Steady! " said Page, feeling a certain unpleasant warmth creep round his chest. "What's up? "

"For one thing, we've found the Thumbograph—"

"What! Where? "

They were all looking at him now.

"One of the maids: Betty: do you know her—? "
Burrows hesitated.

"Yes; go on."

"Betty disappeared, and nobody knew what has become of her. They looked all over the place for her:
that is, they looked in the only places she was likely to
be found. No Betty. Everything was a bit disorganised,
because for some reason Knowles wasn't here either.
Finally Molly's maid found her in the Green Room, where
it wasn't Betty's business to go. Betty was lying on the
floor with the Thumbograph in her hand. But that isn't
all. Her face was such a queer colour, and she was
breathing so queerly, that we sent for the doctor. Old
King is worried. Betty's still unconscious, and she won't
be in any condition to tell us anything for a long time.
She's not physically hurt, but King says there's not much
doubt about what caused it."

"Well? "

Again Burrows hesitated.

"Fright," he said.

CHAPTER X

IN the library at Farnleigh Close, Patrick Gore sat back
in the embrasure of the windows and smoked a black
cigar. Ranged near him were Burrows, Welkyn, and a
sleepy-looking Kennet Murray. Inspector Elliot, Dr Fell,
and Brian Page sat by the table.

At the Close they had found a frightened and disorganised household, the more frightened because of a
completely pointless upset in the middle of an ordinary
afternoon, and the more disorganised because of the
absence of the butler.

Facts? What did you mean, facts? The group of
domestics whom Elliot questioned did not know what
he meant. It was only this maid, Betty Harbottle; a nice
girl; ordinary. She had not been seen since mid-day

dinner. When it came time for her to wash the windows of two of the upstairs bedrooms with Agnes, another maid, Agnes had gone to look for her. She was not found until four o'clock. At this time Teresa—Lady Farnleigh's maid—had gone into the Green Room, the late Sir John's study, and found her lying on the floor by a window overlooking the garden. She was lying on her side, with the paper-covered book in her hand. Dr King had been summoned from Mallingford; and neither the expression of his face nor Betty's did anything to reassure the household. Dr King was with the patient still.

This thing was wrong. Terrors should not be domestic terrors. It was like being told that in your own home you may completely disappear for four hours. It was like being told that in your own home you may open a familiar door, and enter not your own room, but a room you have never seen before, where something is waiting. From the housekeeper, the cook, and the other maids he learned little except domestic details; about Betty he learned little except that she liked apples and wrote letters to Gary Cooper.

Knowles's arrival soothed the staff; and Madeline's arrival, Page hoped, would have a good effect on Molly Farnleigh. Madeline had accompanied her to her sitting-room while the men glared at one another in the library. Page had wondered what would happen at a meeting between Madeline and Patrick Gore; yet there was little on which even the imagination could fasten. They were not introduced. Madeline moved past, softly, with her arm round Molly; she and the claimant looked at each other; and Page thought that an amused look of recognition opened Gore's eyes; but neither spoke.

And it was Gore who put the case to the inspector when the others were gathered in the library, just before Dr Fell flung a hand-grenade of remarkable explosive power.

"It's no good, inspector," said Gore, re-lighting a black cigar which would not remain lit. "You asked the same kind of questions this morning, and this time I assure you it's no good. This time it is, where were you when the girl was—well, whatever happened to her—and the Thumbograph was put in her hand? I have replied quite simply that I am damned if I know. So have all the others.

We were here. You ordered us to be here. But you may be sure we were not courting each other's society, and we have not the remotest idea when the girl collapsed."

"Look here, you know," said Dr Fell abruptly, "a part of this had better be settled."

"I only hope you can settle it, my friend," answered Gore, who seemed to have taken a sincere liking to him. "But, inspector, you have already had our statements with the servants. We have been over that again and— "

Inspector Elliot was cheerful.

"That's right, sir," he said. "And, if it's necessary, we shall have to go over them again. And again."

"Really— " interposed Welkyn.

The claimant sat on him again. "But, if you're so interested in the wanderings of that Thumbograph, why not pay some slight attention to what is *in* the Thumbograph?" He glanced at the tattered grey book, which now lay on the table between Elliot and Dr Fell. "Why in the name of sense and sanity don't you settle the matter now? Why don't you decide, between a dead man and myself, which is the real heir?"

"Oh, I can tell you that," said Dr Fell affably.

There was an abrupt silence, broken only by the scrape of the claimant's foot on the stone floor. Kennet Murray took away the hand with which he had been shading his eyes. The expression of cynicism remained on his ageing face; but his eyes were bright and hard and indulgent, and he used one finger to stroke his beard, as though he was listening to a recitation.

"Yes, doctor?" he prompted, in that tone used exclusively among schoolmasters.

"Furthermore," continued Dr Fell, tapping the book on the table, "it's no good getting down to business with *this* Thumbograph. It's a fake. No, no, I don't mean that you haven't got the evidence. I merely say that THIS Thumbograph, the one that was stolen, is a fake. Mr Gore pointed out last night, they tell me, that you had several Thumbographs in the old days." He beamed on Mr Murray. "My boy, you retain your melodramatic soul of old, for which I am glad. You believed that there

93

might be some attempt to pinch the Thumbograph. So you came to the house last night equipped with two of them— "

" Is this true? " demanded Gore.

Murray seemed at once pleased and annoyed; but he nodded, as though he were following the matter carefully.

" —and," continued Dr Fell, " the one you showed to these people in the library was bogus. That was why you were so long in getting down to business. Hey? After you had shoved everybody out of the library, you had to get the real Thumbograph (a clumsy kind of book, apt to tear) out of your pocket, and put the valueless one in. But they had said they were going to keep a close watch on you. And, with a wall of windows stretching across the room, you were afraid somebody might see you and cry trickery if you were seen fooling about with the evidence. So you had to make sure there was nobody watching— "

" I was finally obliged," said Murray gravely, " to get into that cupboard and do it." His nod indicated an old book closet built into the wall on the same side as the windows. " It is somewhat late in life to feel as though I were cheating at an examination."

Inspector Elliot did not say anything. After glancing sharply from one to the other of them, he began to write in his notebook.

" H'mf, yes. You were delayed," said Dr Fell. " Mr Page here, passing the windows only a few minutes before the murder, on his way out to the back of the garden, saw that you were just ' opening ' the Thumbograph. So you hardly had time to get down to real work— "

" Three or four minutes," corrected Murray.

" Very well. You hardly had time to get down to real work before there were alarums of bloodshed." Dr Fell looked pained. " My dear young Murray, you are not simple-minded. Such an alarm might be a trick, especially a trick *you* would suspect. You would never on earth have gone thundering out, leaving the Thumbograph open and inviting on that table. I couldn't believe that when I heard it. No, no, no. Back went the real one into your pocket, and out came the dummy one for a honeyed lure. Hey? "

" Confound you," said Murray without heat.

" You therefore decided to lie doggo and exultantly apply your detective faculties when the dummy was stolen. You have probably been sitting up all night writing out a statement about the prints, with the real Thumbograph in front of you, together with your affidavit that the real heir— "

" The real heir is who? " asked Patrick Gore coolly.

" Is *you*, of course," growled Dr Fell.

Then he looked at Murray.

" Hang it all," he added plaintively, " you must have known that! He was your pupil. You must have known it. I knew it as soon as I heard him open his mouth— "

The claimant, who had got to his feet, now sat down rather awkwardly. The claimant's face expressed an almost simian pleasure; his bright grey eye and even his bald spot seemed to twinkle.

" Dr Fell, I thank you," Gore said, with his hand on his heart. " But I must point out that you have asked me not a single question."

" Look here, you fellows," said Dr Fell. " You had the opportunity to listen to him all last evening. Look at him now. Listen to him. Does he remind you of anybody? I don't mean in appearance; I mean in turn of phrase, in shaping of ideas, in way of expressing himself. Well, of whom does he remind you? Hey? "

And at last the troublesome sense of familiarity fitted into place in Page's mind, while the doctor blinked round at them.

" Of Murray," replied Page, in the midst of a silence.

" Of Murray. Got it in one. Misted by time, of course; pulled round a bit by character; but there and unmistakable. Of Murray, who had him in sole charge during the formative years of his life, and was the only one with influence over him. Study his bearing. Listen to the smooth turn of those sentences, rolling like the *Odyssey*. It's only superficial, I cheerfully acknowledge; they are no more alike in their natures than I am like Elliot or Hadley. But the echo lingers on. I tell you, the only important question Murray asked last night was what books the real John Farnleigh had enjoyed as a boy, and what books he hated. Look at this fellow!" He pointed to Gore. "Didn't I hear how his dead eye glowed when he talked about *The Count of Monte Cristo* and *The Cloister and the Hearth*? And of what books he hated and still hates? No impostor would have dared to talk like that before the person to whom he'd poured out his soul years ago. In a case like this, facts are piffle. Anybody can learn facts. You want the inner boy. I say, Murray: honestly, you'd better come off it and give us the truth. It's all very well to be the Great Detective and play 'possum, but this has gone far enough."

A red bar showed across Murray's forehead. He looked snappish and a trifle shamefaced. But his far-away mind caught at something out of this.

"Facts are not piffle," Murray said.

"I tell you," roared Dr Fell, "that facts are——" He caught himself up. "Harrumph, well. No. Perhaps not. Altogether. But am I correct?"

"He did not recognise the 'Red Book of Appin'. He wrote down that there was no such thing."

"Which he knew only as a manuscript. Oh, I am not his champion. I'm only trying to establish something. And I repeat: am I correct?"

"Confound you, Fell, you do spoil a fellow's pleasure," complained Murray, in a slightly different tone. He glanced across at Gore. "Yes, he's the real Johnny Farnleigh. Hullo, Johnny."

"Hullo," said Gore. And, for the first time since Page had met him, his face did not look hard.

The quiet in that room was of a dwindling and shrinking sort, as though values were being restored and a blurred image had come into focus. Both Gore and Murray looked at the floor, but they looked vaguely, uncomfortably amused. It was Welkyn's rich voice which now arose with authority.

"You are prepared to prove all this, sir?" he asked briskly.

"There goes my holiday," said Murray. He reached into his stuffed inside pocket, and became austere again. "Yes. Here you are. Original Thumbograph, and print —*with* signature of John Newnham Farnleigh as a boy and date. In case there should be any doubt this is the original one I brought with me, I had photographs of it taken and deposited with the Commissioner of Police at Hamilton. Two letters from John Farnleigh, written to me in 1911: compare signatures with the signature on the thumb-print. Present thumb-print, taken last night, and my analysis of their points of agreement— "

"Good. Good, very good," said Welkyn.

Page looked at Burrows, and he noticed that Burrows's face was white. Nor had Page realised that the breaking of the long tension would have such an effect on their nerves.

But he realised it when he looked round, and saw that Molly Farnleigh was in the room.

She had come in unobserved, with Madeline Dane just behind her; she must have heard all of it. They all got up, with an awkward scraping of chairs.

"They say you're honest," she said to Murray. "Is this true? "

Murray bowed. "Madam, I am sorry."

"He was a cheat? "

"He was a cheat who could have deceived nobody who had really known him."

"And now," interposed Welkyn suavely, "perhaps it would be as well if Mr Burrows and I were to have a talk—without prejudice, of course— "

"One moment," said Burrows with equal suavity. "This is still most irregular; and I may point out that I have seen nothing yet in the nature of proof. May I be allowed to examine those documents? Thank you. Next, Lady Farnleigh, I should like to speak with you alone."

Molly had a glazed, strained, puzzled look in her eyes.

"Yes, that would be best," she agreed. "Madeline has been telling me things."

Madeline put a hand soothingly on her arm, but she threw it off with a shake of her sturdy body. Madeline's self-effacing blonde beauty was in contrast to the anger which blazed round Molly and seemed to darken everything away from her. Then, between Madeline and Burrows, Molly went out of the room. They heard Burrows's shoes squeak.

"God! " said Patrick Gore. "And now what have we got? "

"If you'll take it easy and listen to me, sir," Elliot suggested grimly, "I'll tell you." His tone made both Gore and Welkyn look at him. "We've got an impostor who was somehow killed by that pool. Why or by whom we don't know. We've got someone who stole a valueless Thumbograph "—he held up the little book—" and later returned it. Presumably because the person knew it was valueless. We've got a housemaid, Betty, whom nobody had seen since noon; but who was found at four o'clock in the afternoon, half dead of fright, in the room above this library. Who or what frightened her we don't know, or how the Thumbograph got into her hand. By the way, where is Dr King now? "

"Still with the unfortunate Betty, I believe," said Gore, "But what then? "

"Finally, we have some new evidence," Elliot told him. He paused. "As you say, you have all been patiently repeating the stories you told last night. Now, Mr. Gore. In the account you gave of your movements at the time of the murder, were you telling the truth? Think before you answer. There is someone who contradicts your story."

Page had been waiting for it, wondering how long it would be before Elliot would bring it up.

"Contradicts my story? Who contradicts it? " asked Gore sharply, and took the dead cigar out of his mouth.

"Never mind that, if you please. Where were you when you heard the victim fall into the pool? "

The other contemplated him with amusement. "I suppose you've got a witness. I was watching this ancient " —he indicated Murray—" through the window. It suddenly occurs to me that I have now no reason for keeping back the information any longer. Who saw me? "

"You realise, sir, that if what you say is true this provides you with an alibi? "

"Unfortunately as regards clearing me from suspicion, yes."

"Unfortunately? " Elliot froze up.

"A bad joke, inspector. I beg your pardon."

"May I ask why you didn't tell me this at first? "

" You may. And in doing so you might ask me what I saw through the window."

" I don't follow you."

Elliot was always careful to conceal his intelligence. A shade of exasperation passed over Gore's face. " In words of one syllable, inspector, ever since I came into this house last night I suspected the presence of dirty work. This gentleman walked in." He looked at Murray, and did not seem to know how to treat him. " He knew me. I knew he knew me. But he never spoke out."

" Well? "

" What happened? I came round the side of the house—as you have so shrewdly discovered—possibly a minute or so before the murder." He broke off. " By the way, *have* you determined that it was murder? "

" Just one moment, please. Go on."

" I looked in here, and I saw Murray sitting with his back to me like a stuffed dummy, not even moving. Immediately afterwards I heard all the sounds we have so often heard, beginning with the choking noise and ending with the thrashings in water. I moved away from the window, over towards the left, and looked out to see what was happening in the garden. But I did not go nearer. At this time Burrows ran out from the house towards the pool. So I withdrew again, back towards the library windows. The alarm seemed to have gone up inside the house. And this time what did I see? I saw this distinguished, venerable gentleman," again his curt nod indicated Murray, " carefully juggling *two* Thumbographs, guiltily putting one in his pocket and hastily putting the other on the table. . . . "

Murray had been listening with critical interest.

" So, so? " he observed, with an almost Teutonic inflection. " You thought I was working against you? " He seemed pleased.

" Naturally. Working against me— As usual, you understate the case," returned Gore. His face darkened. " So I did not care to tell where I had been. I reserved the knowledge of what I had seen for a shot in the locker in case dirty work had been attempted."

" Have you anything more to add to that? "

"No, inspector, I think not. The rest of what I said was true. But may I ask who saw me?"

"Knowles was standing at the window of the Green Room," said Elliot, and the other began to whistle through his teeth. Then Elliot's gaze moved from Gore to Murray, to Welkyn. "Has any of you ever seen this before?"

From his pocket he took a smaller section of newspaper, in which the stained clasp-knife had been carefully wrapped. He opened it and exhibited the knife.

The expressions of Gore and Welkyn showed a general blankness. But Murray sucked in his bearded cheeks; he blinked at the exhibit and hitched his chair closer.

"Where did you find this?" Murray asked briskly.

"Near the scene of the crime. Do you recognise it?"

"H'm. You have tested it for finger-prints? No. Ah, a pity," said Murray, growing brisker and brisker. "Will you allow me to touch it if I handle it with the greatest circumspection? Correct me if I am wrong. But didn't you, young Johnny"—he glanced at Gore— "use to have a knife exactly like this? Didn't I present it to you, in fact? Didn't you carry it for years?"

"I certainly did. I always carry a pocket-knife," admitted Gore, reaching into his pocket and producing an old knife only slightly smaller and lighter than the one before them. "But—"

"For once," interposed Welkyn, slapping his hand on the table, "for once and all I must insist on exercising the rights with which you, sir, have seen fit to endow me. Such questions are absurd and improper; and as your legal adviser I must tell you to disregard them. Such knives are as common as blackberries. I once had one myself."

"But what is wrong with the question?" asked Gore, puzzled. "I owned a knife like that. It went with the rest of my clothes and effects in the *Titanic*. But it seems absurd to suppose that the one there could be—"

Before anybody could stop him, Murray had whipped a handkerchief out of his pocket, moistened it at his lips (a handkerchief in the mouth is one of the things which always set Page's teeth on edge), and wiped clean a small section of the blade about halfway down. Into the cleared steel had been roughly cut letters forming the word

Madeline

"It is yours, Johnny," said Murray comfortably. "You put this name there one day when I took you through the stone-cutting works at Ilford."

"Madeline," repeated Gore.

Opening a pane of the window behind him, he threw out his cigar into the sodden trees. But Page saw his face reflected momentarily in the gloomy glass: it was a curious, set, indecipherable face, unlike the one of mockery with which Gore usually pointed out the difference between his moods and the world's. He turned back.

"But what about the knife? Are you suggesting that that poor, tortured, would-be-honest crook kept it about him all these years, and finally cut his throat with it by the pool? You seem to have determined that this is a case of murder; and yet—and yet—"

He beat the flat of his hand slowly on his knee.

"I'll tell you what it is, gentlemen," said Elliot, "it's an absolutely impossible crime."

He detailed to them Knowles's story. The interest exhibited by both Gore and Murray was in contrast to the evident disgust and bewilderment of Welkyn. When Elliot described the finding of the knife there was an uneasy movement through the group.

"Alone, and yet murdered," said Gore reflectively. He looked at Murray. "Magister, this is a matter after your own heart. I don't seem to know you. Perhaps we have grown too far apart; but in the old days you would have hopped round the inspector, full of strange theories and bearded like the pard—"

"I am no longer a fool, Johnny."

"Still, let us hear a theory. Any theory. So far, you are the only one who has been reticent about the whole affair."

"I second that motion," observed Dr Fell.

Murray settled himself more comfortably, and began to wag his finger.

"The exercise of pure logic," he began, "is often comparable to working out immense sums in arithmetic and finding at the end that we have somewhere forgotten to carry one or multiply by two. Every one of a thousand figures and factors may be correct except that one; but the difference in the answer to the sum may be disconcerting. Therefore I do not put this forward as pure logic. I make a suggestion.—You know, inspector, that the coroner's inquest is almost certainly going to call it suicide?"

"Can't say that, sir. Not necessarily," declared Elliot. "A Thumbograph was stolen and then returned; a girl was nearly frightened to death—"

"You know as well as I do," said Murray, opening his eyes, "what verdict a coroner's jury will return. It is remotely possible that the victim might have killed himself and flung the knife away; it is impossible that he should have been murdered. But I assume that it is murder."

"Heh," said Dr Fell, rubbing his hands. "Heh-heh-heh. And the suggestion?"

"Assuming that it is murder," said Murray, "I suggest that the victim was not, in fact, killed with the knife you have there. I suggest that the marks on his throat are more like the marks of fangs or claws."

CHAPTER XI

"CLAWS?" repeated Elliot.

"The term was fanciful," said Murray, now so didactic that Page longed to administer a swift kick. "I do not necessarily mean literal claws. Shall I argue out my suggestion for you?"

Elliot smiled. "Go right ahead. I don't mind. And you may be surprised how much there is to argue."

"Put it like this," said Murray in a startlingly ordinary tone. "Assuming that it was murder, and assuming that this knife was used to do it, one question bothers me badly. It is this. *Why didn't the murderer drop the knife into the pool afterwards?*"

The inspector still looked at him inquiringly.

"Consider the circumstances. The person who killed this man had an almost perfect—er——"

"Set-up?" suggested Gore, as the other groped.

"It is a rotten word, Johnny, but it will do. Well. The murderer had an almost perfect set-up for suicide. Suppose he had cut this man's throat and dropped the knife into the pool? Not one person would afterwards have doubted that it was suicide. This man, an impostor, was about to be unmasked: here would have seemed his way out. Even as things are you have difficulty in believing it was not suicide. With the knife in the pool it would have been a clear case. It would even take care of the matter of finger-prints which the dead man might have been assumed to have left on the knife.

"Now, gentlemen, you can't tell me that the murderer did not *want* this to be thought suicide. You can't tell me any murderer ever wants that. If it can be managed, a fraudulent suicide is the best possible way out. Why wasn't that knife dropped in the pool? The knife incriminates nobody—except the dead man, another indication of suicide and probably the reason why the murderer chose it. Yet instead the murderer takes it away and (if I follow you) thrusts it deep into a hedge ten feet away from the pool."

"Proving?" said Elliot.

"No, no. Proving nothing." Murray lifted his finger. "But suggesting a great deal. Now consider this behaviour in relation to the crime. Do you believe old Knowles's story?"

"You're giving the theories, sir."

"No, that is a fair question," said Murray rather sharply. Page felt that he only just checked himself in adding, "Come, come, sir!" "Otherwise we shall get nowhere."

"We shall get nowhere if I say I believe an impossibility, Mr Murray."

"Then you do believe in suicide?"

"I didn't say that."

"Which do you believe in, then?"

Elliot grinned faintly. "If you get the bit in your teeth, sir, you'll convince me that I ought to answer you. Knowles's story is supported by—um—contributory evi-

103

dence. For the sake of argument let's say I believe he was telling the truth, or thought he was telling the truth. What happens then? "

" Why, it follows that he did not see anything because there was nothing to see. That can hardly be doubted. This man was alone in the middle of a circle of sand. Therefore no murderer went near him. Therefore the murderer did not use that notched and suggestively stained knife you have there; and the knife was, in fact, ' planted ' in the hedge afterwards to make you think it was used for the crime. You follow that? Since the knife could not have flown out of the air, cut his throat three times, and dropped into the hedge, it is evident that the knife could not have been used at all. That argument is plain? "

" Not exactly plain," objected the inspector. " You say it was some other weapon? Then some other weapon hung in the air, cut his throat three times, and disappeared? No, sir. I don't believe that. Definitely not. That's worse than believing in the knife."

" I appeal to Dr Fell," said Murray, evidently stung. " What do you say, doctor? "

Dr Fell sniffed. Mysterious wheezes and noises of internal combustion suggested argument; but he spoke mildly.

" I abide by the knife. Besides, you know, there certainly was something moving in that garden; something of damned bluish cast of countenance, if you'll allow me. I say, inspector. You've taken the statements. But d'you mind if I probe and pry into them a bit? I should very much like to ask a few questions of the most interesting person here."

" The most interesting person here? " repeated Gore, and prepared himself.

" H'mf, yes. I refer, of course," said Dr Fell, lifting his stick and pointing, " to Mr Welkyn."

Superintendent Hadley has often wished that he would not do this. Dr Fell is, possibly, too much concerned with proving that the right thing is always the wrong thing, or at least the unexpected thing; and waving flags with both hands above the ruin of logic. Certainly Page would never have taken Harold Welkyn for the most interesting person there. The fat solicitor, with his long disapproving chin, evidently did not think so either. But, as even Hadley admits, the old beggar is often unfortunately right.

"You spoke to me, sir?" inquired Welkyn.

"I was telling the inspector a while ago," said Dr Fell, "that your name seemed very familiar. I remember now. Is it a general interest in the occult? Or are you a collector of curious clients? I rather imagine you collected our friend here"—he nodded towards Gore—"in the same way you collected that Egyptian some time ago."

"Egyptian?" asked Elliot. "What Egyptian?"

"Think! You'll remember the case. Ledwidge *v.* Ahriman, before Mr Justice Rankin. Libel. Mr Welkyn here was instructed for the defence."

"You mean that ghost-seer or whatever he was?"

"Yes," said Dr Fell, with great pleasure. "Little bit of a chap; hardly more than a dwarf. But he didn't see ghosts: he saw through people, or so he said. He was the fashion of London; all the women flocked to him. Of course, he could have been prosecuted under the old Witchcraft Act, still in force—"

"A most infamous act, sir," declared Welkyn, slapping the table.

"—but it was a question of a libel suit, and Mr Welkyn's ingenious defence, combined with Gordon-Bates as counsel, got him off. Then there was Madame Duquesne, the medium, who was up for manslaughter because one of her clients died of fright in her house. (Fascinating point of law, eh?) Mr Welkyn was also instructed for the defence there. The trial, as I remember it, was rather grisly. Oh, yes! And another one: a girl, good-looking blonde as I remember her. The charges against her never got past the Grand Jury, because Mr Welkyn—"

Patrick Gore was looking at his solicitor with quick interest. "Is this true?" he demanded. "Believe me, gentlemen, I did not know it."

"It is true, isn't it?" inquired Dr Fell. "You're the same chap?"

Welkyn's face was full of cold wonder.

"Of course it is true," he answered. "But what of it? What has it to do with the present case?"

Page could not have said why it seemed so incongruous. Harold Welkyn, examining his pink fingernails, then glancing up sharply from little eyes, was a model of business decorum; and yet why not? The white slip inside his waistcoat, the glossy wings of his collar, had no connection with the clients he sought or the beliefs he held.

"You see, Mr. Welkyn," rumbled Dr Fell, "I had another reason for asking. You were the only one who saw or heard anything queer in the garden last night. Will you read out the part of Mr Welkyn's statement I mean, inspector?"

Elliot nodded, not taking his eyes from Welkyn until he opened the notebook.

"'I heard a kind of rustling noise in the hedges or shrubbery, and I thought I saw something looking at me through one of the glass panels of the door, one of the panels down nearest the ground. I was afraid that certain things might be happening which were no affair of mine.'"

"Exactly," said Dr Fell, and closed his eyes.

Elliot hesitated, debating two courses; but Page had a feeling that the matter was out in the open now, and that both Dr Fell and the inspector thought it was better so. Elliot's hard, sandy-haired head bent forward a little.

"Now, sir," he said. "I didn't want to ask you too much this morning, until we—knew more. What does that statement mean?"

"What it says."

"You were in the dining-room, only fifteen feet or so away from the pool, yet you didn't once open one of those doors and look out? Even when you heard the sounds you describe?"

"No."

"'I was afraid that certain things might be happening that were no affair of mine,'" read Elliot. "Does this refer to the murder? Did you think that a murder was being committed?"

"No, certainly not," said Welkyn, with a slight jump. "And I still have no reason to suspect that one was committed. Inspector, are you mad? Clear evidence of suicide is brought to you; and you all go star-gazing after something else—"

"Did you think that suicide was being committed last night, then? "

"No, I had no reason to suspect it."

"Then what were you referring to? " asked Elliot practically.

Welkyn had the palms of his hands flat on the table. By lifting his fingers slightly he conveyed the effect of a shrug; but his bland dumpling countenance betrayed nothing else.

"I'll try to put it in another way. Mr Welkyn; do you believe in the supernatural? "

"Yes," said Welkyn briefly.

"Do you believe that someone is attempting to produce supernatural phenomena here? "

Welkyn looked at him. "And you from Scotland Yard! *You* say that! "

"Oh, it's not so bad as all that," said Elliot; and he wore a curious, dark expression which his countrymen have understood for centuries. "I said 'attempting', and there are various ways of doing that. Real and unreal. Believe me, sir, there may be queer doings here—implanted here—growing from one ancestor to another—queerer doings than you think. I came down here because Miss Daly had been murdered; and there may be more behind that than a purse of money stolen by a tramp. All the same, I wasn't the one who suggested there might be something supernatural here. You suggested it."

"I did? "

"Yes. 'I thought I saw something looking at me through one of the glass panels of the door, one of the panels down nearest the ground.' You said 'something'. Why didn't you say 'someone'? "

A small bead of sweat appeared on Welkyn's forehead, up near the large vein by the temple. It was his only change of expression, if it can be called that; at least it was the only moving thing on his face.

"I did not recognise who it was. Had I recognised the person, I should have said 'someone'. I was merely attempting to be accurate."

"It was a person, then? A 'someone'? "

The other nodded.

"But, in order to peep at you through one of the lower panels, this person must have been crouched down to the ground or lying on the ground?"

"Not exactly."

"Not exactly? What do you mean by that, sir?"

"It was moving too quickly—and jumpily. I hardly know how to express what I mean."

"Can't you describe it?"

"No. I only received the impression that it was dead."

Something like horror had got into Brian Page's bones; how it had come there, even when it had come, he could not tell. Almost imperceptibly the conversation had moved into a new element, yet he felt that this had always been in the background of the case, waiting for a touch to be wakened. Harold Welkyn then made a very quick movement. He took a handkerchief out of his breast-pocket, wiped the palms of his hands quickly on it, and replaced it. When he spoke again he had recovered something of his old solemn, careful manner.

"One moment, inspector," he put in before Elliot could speak. "I have been trying to tell you truthfully and literally what I saw and felt. You ask me whether I believe in—such things. I do. I tell you frankly I wouldn't go into that garden after dark for a thousand pounds. It seems to surprise you that a man of my profession should have such ideas."

Elliot pondered. "To tell you the truth, it does, somehow. I don't know why it should. After all, I suppose even a lawyer may believe in the supernatural."

The other's tone was dry

"Even a lawyer may," he agreed; "and be none the worse man of business for doing so."

Madeline had come into the room. Only Page noticed her, for the others were too intent on Welkyn; she was walking on tiptoe, and he wondered whether she had heard what had gone before. Though he tried to give her his chair, she sat down on the arm of it. He could not see her face: only the soft line of chin and cheek: but he saw that the breast of her white silk blouse was rising and falling rapidly.

Kennet Murray's eyebrows were pinched together. He was very polite, but he had the air of a customs-officer about to examine luggage.

"I presume, Mr. Welkyn," Murray said, "you are—er —honest about this. It is certainly extraordinary. That garden has a bad reputation. It has had a bad reputation for centuries. In fact, it was remodelled in the late seventeenth century in the hope of exorcising the shadow by fresh prospects. You remember, young Johnny, how your demonological studies tried to raise up things there?"

"Yes," answered Gore. He was about to add something, but he checked himself.

"And on your homecoming," said Murray, "you are greeted by a crawling legless something in the garden, and a housemaid frightened into a fit. Look here, young Johnny: you're not up to your old tricks of frightening people, are you?"

To Page's surprise, Gore's dusky face had gone pale. Murray, it appeared, was the only person who could sting him or rouse him out of his urbanity.

"No," Gore said. "You know where I was. I was keeping an eye on you in the library. And just one thing more. Just who the hell do you think you are, to talk to me as though I were still a fifteen-year-old child? You kow-towed to my father; and, by God, I'll have decent respect from you or I'll take a cane to you as you used to do to me."

The outburst was so unexpected that even Dr Fell grunted. Murray got to his feet.

"Is it going to your head already?" he said. "Just as you like. My usefulness is over. You have your proofs. If I am wanted for anything more, inspector, I shall be at the inn."

"That, John," interposed Madeline softly, "was rather a rotten thing to say, don't you think? Forgive me for interrupting."

For the first time both Murray and Gore looked at her fully, and she at them. The latter smiled.

"You are Madeline," he said.

"I am Madeline."

"My old, cold light-of-love," said Gore. The wrinkles deepened round his eyes. He detained Murray, and there was apology in his voice. "It's no good, magister. We can't pick up the past, and now I am quite certain I don't care to. It seems to me that for twenty-five years I have been moving forward, mentally, while you have been standing still. I used to imagine what would happen when I returned to what are poetically known as the halls of my fathers. I used to imagine myself moved by the sight of a picture on a wall or letters cut with a pen-knife into the back of a bench. What I find is a group of alien sticks and stones; I begin to wish I had not intruded. But that is not the point now. Something seems to have gone out of line. Inspector Elliot! Didn't you say a minute ago that you had come down here because 'Miss Daly had been murdered '?"

"That's right, sir."

Murray had sat down again, evidently curious, while Gore turned to the inspector.

"Victoria Daly. That's not by any chance the little girl who used to live with her aunt—Ernestine Daly, was it?—at Rose-Bower Cottage on the other side of the Hanging Chart?"

"I don't know about her aunt," returned Elliot, "but that's where she lived. She was strangled on the night of July 31st, last year."

The claimant was grim. "Then I can at least produce an alibi there. I was happily in America then. All the same, will somebody take us out of this fen? What has the murder of Victoria Daly got to do with this business here?"

Elliot gave an inquiring glance towards Dr Fell. The doctor nodded sleepily but violently; his great bulk hardly seemed to breathe, and he was watching. Taking up the brief-case from beside his chair, Elliot opened it and drew out a book. It was of quarto size, bound in dark calf-skin at some comparatively recent date (say a hundred years ago), and had on its back the somewhat unexhilarating title of *Admirable History*. The inspector pushed it across to Dr. Fell, who opened it. Then Page saw that it was a much older volume, a translation from the French of Sébastien Michaëlis, published at London in 1613. The paper was brownish and ridged, and across from the title-page there was a very curious book-plate.

"H'mf," said Dr Fell. "Has anybody here ever seen this book before?"

"Yes," said Gore quietly.

"And this book-plate?"

"Yes. That book-plate has not been used in the family since the eighteenth century."

Dr Fell's finger traced out the motto. "*Sanguis eius super nos et super filios nostros*, Thos. Farnleigh, 1675. His blood be upon us and upon our children.—Was this book ever in the library here at the Close?"

Gore's eye quickened and gleamed as he looked at the book; but he remained puzzled. He spoke sardonically.

"No, it certainly was not. That's one of the books of darkness which my father, and his father before him, kept locked in the little room in the attic. I stole his key once, and had some duplicates made, so that I could go up there and read. Lord, the time I spent there— under pretext, if anyone should find me, of getting an apple from the apple-room next door." He looked round. "Do you remember, Madeline? I took you up there once to give you a glimpse of the Golden Hag? I even gave you a key. But I am afraid you never liked it.—Doctor, where did you get that book? How did it get out of captivity?"

Inspector Elliot got up and rang the bell for Knowles.

"Will you find Lady Farnleigh," he said to a scared butler, "and ask her if she will come in here?"

With great leisureliness Dr Fell took out pipe and pouch. He filled the pipe, lit it, and inhaled with deep satisfaction before he spoke. Then he made a flourishing gesture and pointed.

"That book? Because of the innocuous title, nobody at the time even glanced into it or thought twice about it. Actually, it contains one of the most unnerving documents in recorded history: the confession of Madeleine de la Palud, at Aix in 1611, of her participation in ceremonies of witchcraft and the worship of Satan. It was found on the table by Miss Daly's bed. She had been reading it not long before she was murdered."

CHAPTER XII

I N the quiet of the library, Page heard very distinctly the footsteps of Molly Farnleigh and Burrows as they came in.

Murray cleared his throat. "Meaning— ? " he prompted. "Didn't I understand that Miss Daly was killed by a tramp? "

"Quite possibly she was."

"Well, then? "

It was Molly Farnleigh who spoke. "I came in here to tell you," she said, "that I am going to fight this ridiculous claim, *your* claim," her whole vigorous nature went into the glance of cold dislike she gave Gore, "to the end. Nat Burrows says it will probably take years and we shall all lose our. shirts, but I can afford that. In the meantime, the important thing is who killed John. I'll call a truce for the time being, if you will. What did I hear you all talking about when we came in here? "

A certain sense of relief went through the group. But one man was instantly on guard.

"You think you have a case, Lady Farnleigh? " asked Welkyn, all solicitor again. "I am bound to warn you— "

"A better case than you may have any idea of," retorted Molly, with a curious significant look at Madeline. "What did I hear you talking about when we came in? "

Dr Fell, fiery with interest now, spoke in a kind of apologetic thunder.

"We're on rather an important aspect of it just now, ma'am," he said, "and we should very much appreciate your help. Is there still, in the attic of this house, a little room containing a collection of books on witchcraft and kindred subjects? Eh? "

"Yes, of course. But what has that to do with it? "

"Look at this book, ma'am. Can you tell us positively whether it comes from that collection? "

Molly approached the table. They had all risen, but she made a gesture of impatience at the formality.

"I think so. Yes, I'm almost sure of it. All of them had that book-plate, and none of the other books have: it's a kind of badge. Where on earth did you get the book?"

Dr Fell told her.

"But that's impossible!"

"Why?"

"Because there was such a terrible fuss and bother and to-do about those books. My husband caused it; I never knew why. We had only been married a little over a year, you know." Her quiet brown eyes looked at the past. She took the chair Burrows set out for her. "When I came here as a—as a bride, he gave me all the household keys except the key to that room. Of course I handed them straight over to Mrs Apps, the housekeeper; but you know the principle of the thing. It interested me, rather."

"Like Bluebeard?" suggested Gore.

"No controversy, please," said Dr Fell sharply, as she turned to the claimant in a cold fury.

"Very well," said Molly. "Anyhow, I heard about it. My husband wanted to burn it—the collection, I mean. It seems that when they were valuing the property just before he came into it, they had a man down from London to look at the books. He said that little collection in the attic was worth thousands and thousands of pounds and almost danced with delight, the silly ass. He said there were all kinds of rarities in it, including something unique. I do remember what that was. It was a manuscript book which was supposed to have been lost since the beginning of the nineteenth century. Nobody knew where it had gone, and there it was right in our attic. They called it the 'Red Book of Appin'. He said it was supposed to be the big harum-scarum hocus-pocus of magic, and it was so magical that anybody who read it had to wear a hoop of iron round his head. I jolly well do remember that, because you were all arguing about it last night, and this man"—she looked at Gore—"didn't even know what it was."

"As Dr Fell suggests, no controversy," said Gore pleasantly. But he addressed Murray. "Fair play, magister. I never knew the sacred volume under that name, you know. But I can tell you what it is, and I can even identify it if it is still upstairs. I'll give you one of its qualities. Anyone who possessed it was said to know what any inquiry would be before the inquirer opened his lips."

"That must have been very useful to you," Molly said sweetly, "last night."

"As proving that I had read the book, yes. It was also said to confer the power of giving life to inanimate objects, which almost suggests that Lady Farnleigh must have read it herself."

Dr Fell hammered the ferrule of his stick on the floor to call for attention. When the threatened storm had been hammered away, he looked at Molly benevolently.

"Heh," said Dr Fell. "Heh-heh-heh. I gather, ma'am, that you don't believe in the magical properties of the ' Red Book of Appin ' or anything else? "

"Oh, so-and-so! " said Molly, using a short Anglo-Saxon word which made Madeline colour.

"H'mf, yes. Exactly. But you were telling us? "

"Well, anyway, my husband was frightfully upset and concerned about those books. He wanted to burn them. I said not to be absolutely silly: if he had to get rid of them, why not sell them, and in any case what harm were they doing? He said they were full of eroticism and wickedness." Molly hesitated, but she went on in her candid way. "That did interest me a bit, if you must know. I peeped into one or two of them—when he showed me the room—but it certainly wasn't anything like that. You never read such horribly dull stuff in your life. There was nothing low about it. It was a lot of long-winded rubbish about the twin life-lines or something, and all done with those funny ' f's ' for ' s's ' that make it look as though the writer lisped. I couldn't get up *any* interest in it. So, when my husband insisted on keeping the place locked, I never bothered any more about it and I'm sure it hasn't been opened since."

"But this book"—Dr Fell tapped it—"came from there? "

"Ye-es, I'm sure of it."

"And your husband always kept the key to that locked room. Yet somehow it got out of there and into Miss

114

Daly's possession. H'm." Dr Fell was smoking in short puffs; now he took the pipe out of his mouth and sniffed massively. "Consequently, we have a connection—on a thread like this—through Miss Daly's death to your husband's death. Eh?"

"But what connection?"

"For instance, ma'am, could he have given Miss Daly the book himself?"

"But I've already told you what he thought about those books!"

"That, you know, ma'am," said Dr Fell apologetically, "was not the question. Could he? After all, we've heard that when he was a boy—if he was the real John Farnleigh, as you claim—he thought very highly of those books."

Molly faced it out.

"You've got me in a cleft stick. If I say he hated such things out of all reason, you can answer that it's too much of a change and proves he wasn't John Farnleigh. If I say he could have given the book to Victoria—well, I don't know what you'll say."

"All we want is an honest answer, ma'am," said Dr Fell. "Or, rather, an honest impression. Heaven pity the person who tries to tell all the truth. But look here: did you know Victoria Daly well?"

"Pretty well. Poor Victoria was the sort who exulted in Good Works."

"Should you have said"—Dr Fell made a vague gesture with his pipe—"should you have said she was the sort to be deeply interested in the subject of witchcraft?"

Molly clenched her hands.

"But will you tell me, please, how on earth this witchcraft talk comes into it? Granting that's what this book is about—if it comes from the attic it must be—does it prove anything just because she was reading it?"

"There is other evidence, believe me," said Dr Fell gently. "Your own native intelligence, ma'am, will show you that the important thing is the connection of Miss Daly+a locked library+that book. For instance: did your husband know her well?"

"H'm. I don't know. Not very well, I should have thought."

Dr Fell's forehead was wrinkled. "And yet consider his behaviour last night, as it has been described to me. Confirm this. A claimant to his estate appears. The possession of this estate, rightfully or wrongfully, is the most important driving force in his life. And now the citadel is attacked. Mr Gore, Mr Welkyn, with their convincing stories and their deadly proof of finger-prints, are closing in on him. It is true that he paces the floor; yet, at the very moment the attack is launched, he seems more concerned over the fact that there is a detective in the village investigating the death of Victoria Daly. Is that true?"

It was true. Page remembered it only too well. And Molly was forced to admit it.

"So, we perceive, the thread spins out. Let's try to follow that thread wherever it leads. I am more and more interested in that locked attic room. Is there anything else up there besides books?"

Molly reflected.

"Only that mechanical robot thing. I saw it once when I was a little girl, and I rather loved it. I asked my husband why we couldn't have it down and see whether we couldn't find a way to make it work: I love things that work: but it stayed there too."

"Ah, the mechanical robot thing," repeated Dr Fell, hauling himself up with a wheeze and flash of interest. "What can you tell us about that?"

It was Kennet Murray who answered, when Molly shook her head.

"Now there is a matter, doctor," Murray said comfortably, settling himself in the chair, "you would do well to investigate. *I* tried to investigate it years ago, and so did young Johnny."

"Well?"

"Here are all the *facts* I could unearth." Murray spoke with emphasis. "Sir Dudley never allowed me to look at the figure, and I had to work from outside. It was constructed by Monsieur Raisin, the organist of Troyes, who made the self-playing harpsichord for Louis XIV; and it was exhibited with great success at the court of Charles II in 1676-7. It was a nearly life-sized figure, sitting on a kind of small couch, and it was said to represent

116

one of the king's ladies: there is argument about which one. Its actions delighted the people of that time. It played two or three tunes on a cittern (what we nowadays call a zither); it thumbed its nose at the spectators, and went through a variety of gestures, some undoubtedly indecorous."

There was no doubt that he had caught the immediate interest of his audience.

"It was bought by Sir Thomas Farnleigh, whose book-plate you have there," said Murray. "Whether it was the immodesty of the automaton that later caused a blight to fall on it, or some other cause, I have never been able to find out. But something happened—dead silence of all records as to what. That seems no reason for the horror it inspired in the eighteenth century, though such a contraption wouldn't have recommended itself to Sir Dudley or his father or grandfather. Presumably old Thomas learned the secret of how to make it work; but that secret has never been passed on. Eh, young Jo . . . I beg your pardon, Sir John?"

At the thick and exaggerated courtesy of his tone, Gore showed some contempt. But he was interested in other matters.

"No, it was not passed on," Gore admitted. "And it will never be learned. I know, gentlemen. In my younger days I racked my brains over the secret of the Golden Hag. I could easily show you why none of the obvious explanations would work. If we—" He looked startled. "By all the gods, why shouldn't we go.up and have a look at her? I only just thought of it. I'm in-hibited. I was thinking of all sorts of excuses and crooked ways by which I could sneak up there as I used to do. But why not? Why not, in the open light of day?"

He thumped his fist down on the arm of the chair, blinking a little as though he himself had just come into light. Inspector Elliot interposed rather sharply.

"Just one moment, sir," Elliot said. "This is all very interesting; and we can go into it another time; but I don't see that it has any bearing on—"

"Are you sure?" asked Dr Fell.

"Sir?"

"Are you sure?" repeated the doctor with great intensity. "I say, somebody! What does this automaton look like?"

"It's a good deal decayed, of course; at least, it was twenty-five years ago—"

"It was," agreed Madeline Dane, and shuddered. "Don't go up there. Please say you won't!"

"But why on earth not?" cried Molly.

"I don't know. I'm afraid."

Gore regarded her with indulgence.

"Yes, I hazily remember that it had a powerful effect on you. But you were asking what it looked like, doctor. It must have been uncannily life-like when it was new. The framework is of jointed iron, of course; but the 'flesh' is wax, with glass eyes—one missing—and real hair. The decay has not improved it; it is rather fat, and used to look somewhat unpleasant when you imagined things. It wears, or used to wear, a brocaded gown. The hands and fingers are of painted iron. In order to play the zither and make gestures, the fingers are long and jointed and sharp, almost like : . . It used to smile, but the smile had rotted away when I saw it last."

"And Betty Harbottle," said Dr Fell abruptly, "Betty Harbottle, like Eve, has a strong fondness for apples."

"I beg your pardon?"

"She has, you know," urged Dr Fell. "Betty Harbottle, the frightened maid, is fond of apples. That was the first thing which was pointed out to us when we questioned the servants. I suspect our good housekeeper, Mrs Apps, of conveying a hint. By the darkness of Eleusis, that's exactly what it was! And you"—the doctor's red face shone with concentration as he blinked at Gore—"you told me a minute ago that you used to have a pretext when you wanted to visit the den of the books and the Golden Hag. You went to the apple-room, next door to it in the attic. Will somebody offer me odds as to where Betty Harbottle was when she was frightened, and where the Thumbograph was hidden last night?"

Harold Welkyn got up and began to walk round the table; but he was the only one who moved. Afterwards Page was to remember that circle of faces in the gloom of the library, and the brief expression he surprised on one of them.

It was Murray who spoke, smoothing his moustache.

"Ah. Yes. Yes, it is undoubtedly interesting. If I still have my geography straight, the stairs to the attic are at the back of the passage beside the Green Room. You suggest that the girl was carried downstairs and put in the Green Room?"

Dr Fell wagged his head. "I only suggest that we have got to follow our dim intelligences or go home to bed. Every thread leads back to that little den. It's the core of the labyrinth and the heart of every disturbance, like the little bowl of fluid in *The House and the Brain*: which is an apter title than we may think. We had better pay a visit there."

Inspector Elliot spoke slowly.

"I think we had. Now. Do you mind, Lady Farnleigh?"

"No, not at all, except that I don't know where the key is. Oh, bother that! Break the lock. It's a new padlock my husband had put on; and if you think it will help you can tear—you can t-tear—" Molly brushed her hand across her eyes, held tight to her feelings, and regained control again. "Shall I lead the way?"

"Thank you." Elliot was brisk. "How many of the rest of you have ever been in that room? Only Miss Dane and Mr Gore? Will you two come with Dr Fell and me, please. And Mr Page. The others please remain here."

Elliot and the doctor went ahead, talking in low tones. Molly then put herself in front of them, as though discreetly deaf, placing them between herself and the claimant. Page followed with Madeline.

"If you'd rather not go up—" he said to Madeline.

She pressed his arm. "No, please. I *want* to go up. I do, really, to see if I can understand what is going on. You know, I'm afraid something I said has upset Molly terribly, but I had to tell her: there was no other way out. Brian. You don't think I'm a cat, do you?"

He was startled. Though her half-smiling mouth made fun of this suggestion, the long eyes had a look of great intensity.

"Good Lord, no! What put that idea into your head?"

"Oh nothing. But she didn't love him, really. She's

only doing all this because she thinks she ought to. In spite of all appearances, I tell you they weren't suited to each other. He was idealistic and she is practical. Wait: I know he was an impostor, but you don't know all the circumstances or you'd understand—"

"Then give me the practical," Page snapped.

"Brian! "

"I mean it. Idealistic my eye! If he did what they say he did, and what you yourself admit he did, our late dead friend was a hundred-carat swine and you know it. Were you by any chance in love with him yourself? "

"Brian! You have no right to say that! "

"I know I haven't; but were you? "

"I was not," said Madeline quietly, and looked at the floor. "If you had better eyes, or understood things better, you would know enough not to ask that." She hesitated; it was clear that she wanted to change the subject. "What do Dr Fell and the inspector think of— all this? "

He opened his mouth to answer, and realised that he had no idea.

He had no idea. Their group had gone up the broad, shallow oak staircase to the floor above, along the gallery, and round the turning of a passage to the left. On the left was the Green Room, its open door showing heavy study furniture of the last century and walls biliously patterned. On the right were two bedroom doors. The passage ran straight down to a window at the end, over-looking the garden. The stairs up to the attic—Page vaguely remembered—were in the outer thickness of the wall at the end of the passage, the door to them being in the left-hand wall.

But he was not thinking of this. Despite Dr Fell's thunderous geniality, and the easy-talking frankness of Inspector Elliot, he realised that he knew nothing what-ever. Both of them would talk until Doomsday, of course. But what about routine police-work: a fingerprint here, a footprint there, a searching of the garden by Elliot or a clue sealed into an envelope? The finding of the knife, yes; he knew of that because under the circum-stances it could hardly have been avoided. What else, even as regarded theories? Certain statements had been taken from certain persons; what were we to think of those statements?

After all, it was their business. Yet it disquieted him. New discoveries were being turned up out of what he had thought was old ground, like skulls at Blenheim, and you had no warning of the skull until it rolled across the table. No, better change the simile. Up ahead towered Dr Fell's huge back, seeming to fill the passage.

"Which room is she in?" Elliot asked in a low voice.

Molly indicated the farther bedroom door, across the passage from the door to the attic. Elliot knocked very lightly at the door; but from inside came a faint muttered cry.

"Betty," whispered Madeline.

"In there?"

"Yes. They put her in the nearest bedroom. She's not," said Madeline, "she's not in very good shape."

The full implications of this were beginning to creep into Page's mind. Dr King opened the bedroom door, glanced behind him, and eased it softly shut as he slipped out into the passage.

"No," he said. "You can't see her yet. Tonight, maybe; to-morrow or next day more likely. I wish the sedatives would take hold. They won't, properly."

Elliot looked puzzled and worried. "Yes, but, doctor, surely it's not—not—?"

"Serious, were you going to say?" asked King, lowering his grizzled head as though he were about to butt with it. "My God! Excuse me."

He opened the door again.

"Has she said anything?"

"Nothing for your notebook, inspector. Delirium, more than half of it. I wish I could find out what she saw."

He was speaking to a very quiet group. Molly, whose expression had altered, seemed to be trying to hold fiercely to accepted rules. Dr King had been a lifelong friend of her father, and they stood on no ceremony with each other.

"Uncle Ned, I want to know. I'd do anything for Betty, and you know it. But I never realised—that is, it's not really what we can call *serious*, is it? It can't be.

People get frightened, but it's not the same thing as being actually ill? It's not dangerous?"

"Oh," said the other, "it's not dangerous. Fine, lusty wench you are; no nerves; surplus energy; see something and biff it one. Yes, you would. Well, maybe it takes people differently. Maybe it was a mouse or wind in the chimney. Only I hope I don't run across it, whatever it was." His tone softened. "No, it'll be all right. No help, thanks; Mrs Apps and I can manage. But you might have some tea sent up."

The door closed.

"Yes, my good friends," observed Patrick Gore, with his hands deep in his pockets, "I think I am safe in saying that something has happened. Shall we go upstairs?"

He went over and opened the door opposite.

The staircase inside was steep-pitched and had that faint, sour smell which comes from old stone enclosed within walls. It was as though you saw the ribs and bones inside the house, unsmoothed by modern crafts. The servants' quarters, Page knew, were at the other side of the house. There was no window here; and Elliot, who went ahead, had to use an electric torch. Dr Fell followed him, then Molly, then Madeline and Page, with Gore in the rear.

Nor had any of this part of the attic been altered since Inigo Jones sketched out his small windows and backed his brick with stone. On the landing the floor sloped in such humped fashion towards the stairs that an unwary footstep might send you down. There was a mighty strength of oak beams, too huge for the picturesque, conveying only power to uphold or crush. Faint grey light entered; the air was thick, damp, and hot.

They found the door they wanted at the far end. It was a heavy door, black, suggesting a cellar rather than an attic. The hinges were of the eighteenth century; the knob was gone and a more modern lock disused; a tight chain and padlock now secured it. But it was not at the lock that Elliot first directed his light.

Something had been flung down and partly crushed by the closing of the door.

It was a half-eaten apple.

CHAPTER XIII

WITH the edge of a sixpence as a screw-driver, Elliot carefully unscrewed the staple which held the chain of the padlock. It took a long time, but the inspector worked carefully, like a carpenter. When the chain had fallen the door swung open of its own accord.

"The lair of the Golden Hag," said Gore with gusto, and kicked the half-eaten apple out of the way.

"Steady on, sir!" said Elliot sharply.

"What? Do you think the apple is evidence?"

"You never know. When we go in here, please don't touch anything unless I tell you to."

"When we go in" was an optimistic phrase. Page had expected to see a room. What he found was a kind of book-closet hardly six feet square, with a sloping roof in which a small and thick-grimed pane of glass showed opaque. There were many gaps in the shelves, where ragged calfskin mingled with more modern bindings. Over everything was a film of dust; but it was that thin, blackish, gritty dust of attics, in which few decipherable marks are left. An early Victorian armchair was pushed into it— and the hag herself seemed to jump out at them when the light of Elliot's torch fell inside.

Even Elliot jumped back a little. The hag was not a beauty. She might once have been an alluring charmer, but now only one eye looked out of half a face: the other side of the head was ruined, like the remnants of the yellow brocaded gown which might once have been yellow. Her appearance was not improved by the cracks opening out across her face.

Had she been standing up, she would have been something under life-size. She sat on an oblong box, once gilded and painted to resemble a couch, but not much broader or deeper than she was, and set up off the floor on wheels which were evidently of later date than the automaton itself. The hands were partly lifted with

123

burlesque and rather horrible coquetry. The whole squat, ponderous machine must have weighed two or three hundredweight.

Madeline uttered a kind of giggle, as of nerves or relief. Elliot growled, and Dr Fell swore. The doctor said:

"Shades of *Udolpho*! Is this anti-climax?"

"Sir?"

"You know what I mean. Did that girl try to get into Bluebeard's room, see this thing for the first time, and—" He paused, blowing out the ends of his moustache. "No. No, that won't do."

"I'm afraid it won't," agreed Elliot soberly. "*If* something happened to her here, that is. How did she get in? And who carried her downstairs? And where did she get the Thumbograph? You can't tell me that the mere sight of this thing would affect her as badly as she seems to have been affected. She might scream, or something of the sort. It might give her a turn. But nothing like this, unless she's a hysterical case. Lady Farnleigh, did the servants know about this dummy?"

"Of course," said Molly. "Nobody has seen it, except Knowles or possibly Mrs Apps, but they all knew about it."

"Then it wouldn't even come as a surprise?"

"No."

"If, as I say, she was frightened by something in this little two-by-four place—of which we haven't any evidence—"

"Look there," said Dr Fell, pointing with his stick.

The beam of the torch played on the floor by the base of the automaton. It found a heap of crumpled linen which, when Elliot picked it up, proved to be a maid's frilled apron. Though it had recently been freshly laundered, it was stained with patches of dust and dirt; and, in one place, there were two short jagged rents in it. Dr Fell took it from the inspector and handed it to Molly.

"Betty's?" he said.

Molly examined a minute tab, with an even more minute name in ink, sewn to the hem of the apron and Molly nodded.

"Stop a bit!" urged Dr Fell, shutting his eyes. He began to lumber back and forth by the door, pressing on his eye-glasses as though to keep them from falling off. When he took his hand away again, his face was lowering and grave. "All right. I'll tell you, my lad. I can't prove it, any more than I could prove the part about the apple and the apple-room. But I can tell you what happened in that book-closet as certainly as though I had seen it. It's no longer mere routine: it's the most vital thing in the case that we should know just when, between lunch-time and four o'clock in the afternoon, that girl was frightened, and what the various people here were doing at that time.

"Because, my lad, the murderer was here—in this book-closet. Betty Harbottle found him here. I don't know what the murderer was doing; but it was vital that nobody should know he had been here at all. Something happened. Afterwards he used the girl's apron to remove possible footprints, finger-prints, marks of any kind in this dust. He carried or dragged her downstairs. He put into her hand the useless Thumbograph he had stolen the night before. And then he went away, as they all do, and left the apron lying neatly in the middle of the floor. Eh?"

Elliot raised his hand.

"Steady on, sir. Not so fast." He thought it over. "There are two bad objections to that, I'm afraid."

"Which are?"

"One. If it was so vital to conceal the fact that he'd been in this little room, doing whatever he was doing, how was he covering his tracks just by moving the unconscious girl from one place to another? He wasn't preventing disclosure; he was only postponing it. The girl's alive. She will recover. And she'll tell who was here, and what he was doing—if anything."

"Apparently a poser," said Dr Fell. "Apparently a stinger whang in the gold. And yet, do you know," he spoke with some violence, "I should not be surprised if the answer to that seeming contradiction is the answer to our problem. What's the other objection?"

"Betty Harbottle wasn't hurt. Physically, she wasn't touched. She was put into the shape she was in by plain old-fashioned fright at something she saw. Yet all she could have seen was an ordinary human being doing something he shouldn't. It's not reasonable, sir; girls are

125

pretty tough these days.—What could have put her into that state, then? "

Dr Fell looked at him.

" Something that the automaton did," he answered. " Suppose it reached out now and took your hand? "

Such is the power of suggestion that every person in the group shied back. Six pairs of eyes turned to the ruined head and the curious hands of the dummy. They would not be pleasant hands to take or touch. Nothing about that figure, from the mildewed gown to the cracked-open wax of the face, would be good to the touch.

Elliot cleared his throat.

" You mean he made the dummy work? "

" He did not make it work," interposed Gore. " I thought of that years ago. That is, he did not make it work unless some electrical system or other trickery has been shoved into it since my time. Damn it all, gentlemen, nine generations of Farnleighs have tried to discover what made it work. And I'll make you a flat offer. I will pay a thousand pounds to the man who can show me how it does work."

" Man or woman? " said Madeline. Page could see that she was forcing a laugh, but Gore spoke in very desperate earnest.

" Man or woman or child or anybody else. To the man or woman who can make it work without modern hocus-pocus, and under the same conditions as it was exhibited two hundred and fifty years ago."

" The offer's generous enough," said Dr Fell cheerfully. " Well, wheel her out and let's have a look at her."

With some effort Elliot and Page, laying hold of the iron box on which the dummy sat, pulled it out of the book-closet with a bump over the sill. She jerked her head and quivered; Page wondered whether the hair would come off. Yet the wheels moved with surprising ease. With a heavy creaking and faint rattling noise, they pushed her over into the light from the window near the head of the stairs.

" Go on. Demonstrate," said Dr Fell.

Gore made a careful examination. " To begin with, you will find that the body of the thing is full of clockwork.

I am no mechanical expert, and I can't tell you whether all the wheels and whatnots are genuine, or whether they were put there for effect. I suspect that most of them are dummies even if some are genuine. Anyhow, the point is that the body is completely filled. There's a long window at the back. It still opens, put your hand through, and—oh, you scratch, do you? "

Gore's face darkened, and he jerked his own hand back. In his absorption he made a gesture too close to the sharp fingers of the automaton; a crooked scratch drew blood on the back of his hand. He put it to his mouth.

" My good old clock-guts! " he said. " My faithful old clock-guts! I ought to knock the rest of your face off."

" Don't! " cried Madeline.

He was amused. "As you wish, little one. In any case, inspector—will you poke about among the works? What I want to establish is that the body is full of them and that nobody could hide in there."

Elliot was as serious as ever. The glass had long gone from the window at the back; with the aid of his flashlight he examined the mechanism and groped inside. Something seemed to startle him, but he only said:

"Yes, that's right, sir. No room for anything here. You mean it was suggested that somebody was hiding in the thing and working it? "

" The only suggestion anybody could hazard. Now, then. That takes care of the automaton itself. The only other part of it, as you can see for yourself, is the couch on which she sits. Watch."

This time he had more difficulty. At the left of the couch's foot there was a small knob; Page could see that the whole front opened out like a little door on a hinge. With some manipulation he managed to get the door open. The interior of the box, bare iron badly corroded with rust, was well under three feet long and not more than eighteen inches high.

Gore beamed with pleasure.

" You remember," he said, " the explanation that was advanced for the chess-playing automaton of Maelzel? The figure sat on a series of large boxes, each with its own little door. Before the demonstration, the showman opened these doors to show that there was no hoax. It was said, however, that inside lurked a *small child*, who deftly contorted himself from one compartment to another; and these movements were so synchronised with the shrewd manipulation of doors that the spectators believed they had seen all of an empty inside.

"Something like that was said about the hag here. But spectators have written that this could not be the case. I don't need to point out that, first, it would have to be a very small child; and, second, no exhibitor could possibly travel all over Europe with a child and have nobody aware of that fact.

"But in the hag there is only one small space and one door. Spectators were invited to feel inside the space and make sure there was no deception. Most of them did so. The figure stood by itself, raised well off the ground and on a carpet provided by the host. Yet, in spite of there being no means by which she could come alive, at the word of command our lively lady received a cittern—played any tune whose name was called out by the spectators—returned the cittern—conversed with the spectators by dumb-show and performed other antics of a nature suited to the time. Do you wonder that my respected ancestor was delighted? But I have always wondered what made him change his mind when he learned the secret."

Gore dropped his lofty manner.

"Now tell me how it worked," he added.

"You little—ape!" said Molly Farnleigh. She spoke in her sweetest manner, but her hands were clenched at her sides. "Will you always prance, no matter what happens? Aren't you satisfied? Would you like to play trains or toy soldiers? My God, Brian, come here; I can't stick this. And you too—and you, a police-officer—fiddling with a dummy—crawling round it like a lot of children, when—don't you realise a man was killed last night?"

"Very well," said Gore. "Let us change the subject. Then, for a change, tell me how *that* was worked."

"I suppose you will say it was suicide, of course."

"Madam," said Gore, with a gesture of despair, "it makes no difference what I say. Somebody invariably jumps down my throat in any case. If I say it was suicide,

I am assaulted by A, B, and C. If I say it was murder, I am assaulted by D, E, and F. I have not suggested that it was accident, if only to avoid incurring the wrath of G, H, and I."

"That's very clever, no doubt. What do you say, Mr Elliot? "

Elliot spoke out of a personal honesty.

"Lady Farnleigh, I'm only trying to do the best I can in the most difficult business I was ever put into, which isn't helped by the attitude of any of you. You must see that. If you'll think for just a minute, you must see this machine has something very much to do with the case. I only ask you not to talk out of plain temper. For there's something else to do with the machine as well."

He put his hand on its shoulder.

"I don't know whether the clockwork inside this is dummy clockwork or not, as Mr Gore says. I'd like to have a go at it in my workshop and find out. I don't know whether the mechanism might still be expected to work after two hundred years; though, if clocks still go after that time, why shouldn't it? But this much I did find out when I looked into the back. The mechanism in this has been recently oiled."

Molly frowned.

"Well? "

"I was wondering, Dr Fell, whether you—" Elliot turned round. "Here! Where are you, sir? "

Page's conviction that anything might happen was strengthened by the disappearance of so very tangible a bulk as the doctor. He was not yet used to Dr Fell's trick of fading from the scene and reappearing somewhere else, usually engaged in some meaningless occupation. This time Elliot was answered by a flicker of light from the book-closet. Dr Fell had been striking a series of matches and blinking with fierce absorption at the lower shelves.

"Eh? I beg your pardon? "

"Haven't you been listening to this demonstration? "

"Oh, that? Harrumph, yes. I can hardly claim to succeed off-hand where so many generations of the family have failed, but I should rather like to know how the original exhibitor was dressed."

" Dressed? "

" Yes. The traditional magician's costume, I daresay, which has always seemed to me singularly unimpressive but suggestive of possibilities. However, I have been pouncing and poking in that cupboard, with or without results— "

" The books? "

" The books are the usual orthodox collection of the unorthodox, though there are several witch-trials that are new to me. I did find what seems to be an account of how the automaton was exhibited, which I hope I may borrow? Thank you. But particularly there's this."

While Gore watched him with bright, wicked eyes of amusement, he lumbered out of the closet carrying a decrepit wooden box. And at the same time it seemed to Page that the attic was filling with people.

It was only that Kennet Murray and Nathaniel Burrows, evidently having grown restive, had insisted on following them upstairs. Burrows's big spectacles, and Murray's towering calm face, appeared over the attic stairs as though out of a trapdoor. For the moment they did not come nearer. Dr Fell rattled the wooden box. He balanced it as well as he could on the narrow ledge of the couch round the automaton.

" Here, steady the machine! " said the doctor sharply. " This floor's got a bad camber, and we don't want her rolling downstairs on us. Now have a look. An odd collection of the dust of years, don't you think? "

In the box they saw a number of child's glass marbles, a rusty knife with a painted handle, some fishing-flies, a small heavy ball of lead into which four large hooks had been welded like a bouquet, and (incongruously) a woman's garter of many years ago. But they did not look at these things. They looked at what lay on top: a double false face or mask made of parchment on wire, and forming a kind of head with a face back and front like the images of Janus. It was blackish, shrivelled, and without features. Dr Fell did not touch it.

" It's beastly to look at," whispered Madeline. " But what on earth is it? "

" The mask of the god," said Dr Fell.

" The what? "

130

"The mask worn by the master of ceremonies presiding at witch-gatherings. Most of those who read about it, and even some of those who write about it, have no idea what witchcraft really was. I firmly do not mean to lecture. But we have an example here. Satanism was an unholy parody of Christian ritual; but it had its old roots in Paganism. Two of its deities were Janus the double-headed, patron of fertility and of the crossroads; and Diana, patron both of fertility and virginity. The master (or mistress) wore either the goat-mask of Satan or a mask such as we have here. Bah!"

He ticked his forefinger and thumb against the mask.

"You have been hinting at something like that for a long time," said Madeline quietly. "Perhaps I shouldn't ask, but will you please answer a straight question? It seems ridiculous even to ask it. Are you saying that there is a Satanist group somewhere hereabouts?"

"That's the joke," declared Dr Fell, with an expression of heavy enlightenment. "The answer is, NO."

There was a pause. Inspector Elliot turned round. He was so surprised that he forgot they were talking in front of witnesses.

"Steady on, sir! You can't mean that. Our evidence—"

"I do mean it. Our evidence isn't worth *that*."

"But—"

"Oh, Lord, why didn't I think of it before!" said Dr Fell vehemently. "A case after my own heart, and I have only just thought of the solution. Elliot, my boy: there have been no sinister gatherings in the Hanging Chart. There have been no goat-pipes or revels by night. A whole group of solid Kentish people have not been snared into any such mad tomfoolery. It was one of the things that stuck in my gullet when you began collecting your evidence, and I see the grimy truth now. Elliot, there is one crooked soul in this whole affair, and only one. Everything, from mental cruelty to murder, is the work of one person. I give you all the truth gratis."

Murray and Burrows joined the group, their footsteps creaking.

"You seem excited," Murray said dryly.

The doctor looked apologetic.

"Well, I am, a bit. I haven't got it all worked out yet. But I see the beginnings of it, and I shall have something to say presently. It's—er—a matter of motives." He stared far off, and a faint twinkle appeared in his eye. "Besides, it's rather novel. I never heard of the trick before. I tell you frankly, Satanism itself is an honest and straightforward business compared to the intellectual pleasures a certain person has invented. Excuse me, gents—and ladies. There's something I should rather like to look at in the garden. Carry on, inspector."

He had stumped towards the stairs before Elliot woke up. Elliot ignored everything, and became brisk.

"Now, then.—Yes? You wanted something, Mr Murray?"

"I wanted to see the automaton," returned the other with asperity. "I've been rather left out of it, I notice, since I produced my proofs-of-identity and ceased to be of any value. So this is the hag. And this: do you mind if I look at it?"

He picked up the wooden box, rattling it, and moved it closer to the faint dust-grimed light from the window. Elliot studied him.

"Have you ever seen any of those things before, sir?"

Murray shook his head. "I have heard of this parchment mask. But I have never seen it. I was wondering—"

And that was when the automaton moved.

To this day Page swears that nobody pushed it. This may or may not be true. Seven persons were jostling round it on a creaking, crackling floor which ran down in a smooth hump towards the stairs. But the light from the window was very uncertain, and Murray, his back to the hag, was fixing their attention with the exhibit he held in his right hand. If a hand moved, if a foot moved, if a shoulder moved, nobody knew. What they did not see was the rotted dummy jerking forward with the stealthy suddenness of a motor-car slipping its brakes. What they did see was three hundredweight of rattling iron darting out of reach and driving like a gun carriage for the well of the stairs. What they heard was the screech of the wheels, the tap of Dr Fell's stick on the stairs, and Elliot's scream:

"*For God's sake, look out below!* "

Then the crash as it went over.

Page reached it. He had his fingers round the iron box, and he might just as well have tried to stop a runaway gun; but he kept it upright when it might have gone head-over-heels-side-to-side, sweeping the whole staircase in crazy descent and crushing anything in its way. The black weight kept to its wheels. Sprawling down the first steps, Page saw Dr Fell peering upwards— half-way down. He saw the daylight from the open door at the foot of the stairs. He saw Dr Fell, unable to move an inch in that enclosed space, throw up one hand as though to ward off a blow. He saw, out of an inferno of crashings, the black shape plunge past within a hair's clearance.

But he saw more; more which no one could have foreseen. He saw the automaton clear the open door, and land in the passage below. One of its wheels snapped off as it struck, but its momentum was too great. Lurching once, it hurtled against the door directly opposite across the passage; and the door came open.

Page stumbled down the stairs. He did not need to hear the cry from the room across that passage. He remembered who was in that room, and why Betty Harbottle was there, and what had just gone in to visit her now. In the cessation of noise after the automaton had been stopped, small sounds crept out. After a time he heard distinctly the squeak of the hinges as Dr King opened the bedroom door, and the physician had a face like white paper.

"You devil up there, what have you done? "

PART III

Friday, July 31st

THE RISE OF A WITCH

Car, au fond, c'est cela le Satanisme, se disait-il; la question
agitée depuis que le monde existe, des visions extérieures, est
subsidiare, quand on y songe; le Démon n'a pas besoin de
s'exhiber sous des traits humains ou bestiaux afin d'attester sa
présence; il suffit, pour qu'il s'affirme, qu'il élise domicile en
des âmes qu'il exulcère et incite à d'inexplicables crimes.

J.-K. HUYSMANS, *Là-Bas*.

CHAPTER XIV

THE coroner's inquest on Sir John Farnleigh was held the following day, and produced a sensation that blew off every journalistic roof in Great Britain.

Inspector Elliot, like most policemen, is not fond of inquests. This is for practical reasons. Brian Page is not fond of them for artistic reasons: because you never learn anything you did not know before, because there is seldom anything of a sensational nature, and because the verdict, whatever it is, brings you no nearer to a solution than before.

But this inquest—held on the morning of Friday, July 31st—he admitted did not go according to pattern. A suicide verdict, of course, was a foregone conclusion. Yet it was spectacular enough to produce a first-class row before the first witness had said ten words, and it ended in a way that left Inspector Elliot dazed.

Page, drinking very black coffee at breakfast, offered up profane thanks that they had not another inquest on their hands from the business of the previous afternoon. Betty Harbottle was not dead. But she had gone through a narrow graze of it after seeing the hag for the second time, and she was still in no condition to speak. Afterwards Elliot's endless questioning ran in a dismal circle. " Did you push it? " " I swear I didn't; I don't know who did; we were tramping on an uneven floor and maybe nobody did."

Elliot summed it up when he and Dr Fell talked late over pipes and beer. Page, after taking Madeline home, forcing her to have something to eat, quieting threatened hysterics, and trying to think of a thousand things at once, heard the conclusion of the inspector's views.

"We're licked," he said briefly. "Not a single ruddy thing we can prove, and yet look at the string of events we've got! Victoria Daly is murdered: maybe by a tramp, maybe not; but with the indications of other dirty work that we needn't discuss now. That's a year ago.

Sir John Farnleigh dies with his throat cut. Betty Harbottle is in some way 'attacked' and brought down from the attic; and her torn apron is found in the book-closet upstairs. The Thumbograph disappears and returns. Finally, a deliberate attempt is made to kill you by pushing that machinery downstairs, an attempt which you only escaped by one whistle and the grace of God."

"Believe me, I appreciate that," muttered Dr Fell uncomfortably. "It was one of the worst moments of my life when I looked round and saw that juggernaut coming down. It was my own fault. I talked too much. And yet—"

Elliot regarded him with sharp inquiry.

"All the same, sir, it showed you were on the right track. The murderer knew you knew too much. As to just what that track is, if you've got any ideas now is the time to tell me. I shall be recalled to town, you know, unless something is done."

"Oh, I'll tell you fast enough," growled Dr Fell. "I'm not making mysteries. Even when I do tell you, though, and even in the event I happen to be right, it still doesn't prove anything. Besides, I'm not sure about another thing. I am very flattered, of course. But I'm not sure the automaton was pushed downstairs with the purpose of what is poetically known as rubbing me out."

"For what purpose, then? It couldn't be just to frighten that girl again, sir. The murderer couldn't have known it would land smack against that bedroom door."

"I know," said Dr Fell stubbornly, and ruffled his hands through his big mop of grey-streaked hair. "And yet—and yet—proof—"

"That's exactly what I mean. Here are all these points, a connected series of events, and not one blasted one of 'em I can prove! Not one thing I can take to my superintendent and say, 'Here; grab this.' Not one bit of evidence that isn't capable of another interpretation. I can't even show that the events are in any way connected, which is the real snag. Now take this inquest to-morrow. Even the police evidence must plump for a suicide verdict—"

"Can't you get the inquest adjourned?"

"Of course. Ordinarily that's what I should do, and

keep on adjourning it until we either had evidence of murder or had to drop the case altogether. But there's the last and greatest snag. What have I got to hope for by more investigation, as matters stand? My superintendent is just about convinced that Sir John Farnleigh's death is suicide, and so is the A.C. When they learned that there are traces of the dead man's finger-prints on that clasp-knife Sergeant Burton found in the hedge— "

(Here was news to Page, the final nail in a suicide's coffin.)

" —that finished it," Elliot corroborated him. " What else can I look for? "

" Betty Harbottle? " suggested Page.

" All right, suppose she does recover and tell her story? Suppose she says she saw somebody in that book-closet? Doing what? And what of it? What connection has it got with a suicide in the garden? Where's your proof, laddie? Anything about the Thumbograph? Well, it's never been suggested that the Thumbograph was in the possession of the dead man, so where do you get with that line of argument? No. Don't look at it sensibly, sir; look at it legally. It's a hundred to one they'll recall me at the end of to-day, and the case will be shelved. You and I know that there's a murderer here, worming so neatly that he or she can keep right on in the same old way unless somebody stops it. And apparently nobody can stop it."

" What are you going to do? "

Elliot gulped down half a pint of beer before he answered.

" There's just one chance, as I say: a full-dress inquest. Most of our suspects will give evidence. It's remotely possible that somebody, under oath, will make a slip. Not much hope, I admit—but it's happened before (remember the Nurse Waddington case?), and it may happen again. It's the last hope of the police when nothing else works."

" Will the coroner play your game? "

" I wonder," said Elliot thoughtfully. " This chap Burrows is up to something; I know that. But he won't come to me and I can't get any change out of him. He's gone to the coroner about something. I gather that the coroner doesn't particularly like Burrows, didn't particularly like the late alleged 'Farnleigh', and himself thinks it's suicide. But he'll play fair, and they'll all stand together against the outsider—meaning me. The ironical part is that Burrows himself would like to prove murder, because a suicide verdict more or less proves his client was an impostor. The whole thing is going to be just one hilarious field-day about lost heirs, with only one possible verdict: suicide, my recall, and the end of the case."

"Now, now," said Dr Fell soothingly. "By the way, where is the automaton now?"

"Sir?"

Elliot roused himself out of grievances and stared at the other.

"The automaton?" he repeated. "I pushed it into a cupboard. After the whacking it took, it's not good for much now except scrap-iron. I was going to have a look at it, but I doubt if a master-mechanic could make sense of the works now."

"Yes," said Dr Fell, taking up his bedroom candle with a sigh. "That, you see, was why the murderer pushed it downstairs."

Page spent a troubled night. There were many things for the next day besides the inquest. Nat Burrows, he reflected, was not the man his father had been; even matters like funeral arrangements had to be turned over to Page. It appeared that Burrows was busying himself over some other aspect of the difficulty. There was also the question of leaving Molly "alone" in a house of questionable atmosphere, and the disquieting news that the servants were threatening to leave almost in a body.

These things churned through sleep into a day of brilliant sunshine and heat. The riot of motor-cars began by nine o'clock. He had never seen so many cars in Mallingford; the Press and the outside world poured in to an extent that made him realise the immense noise this case was making outside their gates. It angered him. It was, he thought, nobody else's damned business. Why didn't they put up swings and roundabouts, and sell hot dogs? They swamped the Bull and Butcher, in whose "hall"—a sort of long shed built for the jollifications of hop-pickers—the inquest was to be held. Sunlight winked on many camera-lenses in the road. There were women. Old Mr Rowntree's dog chased somebody clear up the road to Major Chambers's, and had a hysteria of barking all morning, and couldn't be quieted.

In this the people of the district moved without comment. They did not take sides. In country life each person depends on the other for something, giving and receiving; in a case like this you had to wait and see what happened, so that matters could be reasonably comfortable whichever way verdicts went. But from the outside world came the tumult of LOST HEIR SLAIN OR LOST HEIR FRAUD?; and at eleven o'clock in the hot morning they opened the inquest.

The long, low, gloomy shed was packed. Page felt the appropriateness of a starched collar. The coroner, a forth-right solicitor who was determined to stand no nonsense from the Farnleighs, sat behind a heap of papers at a broad table, with a witness-chair at his left.

First of all, evidence of identification of the body was given by Lady Farnleigh, the widow. Even this—as a rule the merest of formalities—was questioned. Molly had hardly begun to speak when up rose Mr Harold Welkyn, in frock-coat and gardenia, on behalf of his client. Mr Welkyn said that he must protest against this identification in the matter of a technicality, since the dead man was not, in fact, Sir John Farnleigh; and, since the matter was of the utmost importance in determining whether the deceased took his own life or was murdered, he respectfully begged leave to bring it to the coroner's attention.

There ensued a long argument in which the coroner, aided by a frigid and indignant Burrows, quite properly sat on Mr Welkyn. But Welkyn, relapsing, perspired with satisfaction. He had made the point. He had set the pace. He had outlined the real terms of the battle, and everybody knew it.

It also compelled Molly to discuss the matter in reply to the coroner's questions as to the deceased's state of mind. He treated her well, but he was determined to thrash the matter out and Molly looked badly rattled. Page began to realise the state of affairs when the coroner instead of next calling evidence as to the finding of the body, called Kennet Murray. The whole story came out; and, under Murray's gentle firmness, the imposture of the deceased stood out as clear and black as a finger-print. Burrows fought every step of the way, but only succeeded in angering the coroner.

Evidence of finding the body was given by Burrows and Page. (The latter's own voice sounded wrong to him.) Then the medical testimony was called. Dr Theophilus King testified that on the night of Wednesday, July 29th, he had gone to Farnleigh Close in response to a telephone-call from Detective-Sergeant Burton. He had made a preliminary examination and ascertained that the man was dead. The next day, the body having been removed to the mortuary, he had on the instructions of the coroner performed a post-mortem examination, verifying the cause of death.

The coroner: Now, Dr King, will you describe the wounds on the throat of the deceased?

The doctor: There were three fairly shallow wounds, beginning at the left side of the throat and ending under the angle of the right jaw in a slightly upward direction. Two of the wounds crossed each other.

Q: The weapon was passed across the throat from left to right?

A: That is so.

Q: Would this have been the course taken by a weapon held in the hand of a man taking his own life?

A: If the man were right-handed, yes.

Q: Was the deceased right-handed?

A: To the best of my knowledge, he was.

Q: Should you say it was impossible for the deceased to have inflicted such wounds on himself?

A: Not at all.

Q: From the nature of the wounds, doctor, what sort of weapon should you say had been used to inflict them?

A: I should say a ragged or uneven blade some four or five inches long. There was much laceration of tissue. It is a matter in which it is difficult to speak precisely.

Q: We quite appreciate that, doctor. I shall presently call evidence to show that there was found in a hedge some ten feet to the left of the deceased a knife with a blade such as you describe. Have you seen the knife to which I refer?

A: I have.

Q: In your opinion, could the knife in question have inflicted wounds such as you describe on the throat of the deceased?

A: In my opinion, it could.

Q: Finally, doctor, I come to a point which must be put with some care. Mr Nathaniel Burrows has testified that a moment before the deceased's fall the deceased was standing at the edge of the pool with his back to the house. Mr Burrows is unable to say definitely whether or not the deceased was alone at this time, though I have pressed him to do so. Now, in the event—I say in the event—that the deceased was alone, could he have flung a weapon away from him to a distance of say ten feet?

A: It is well within the physical possibilities.

Q: Let us suppose that he had a weapon in his right hand. Could this weapon instead have been thrown towards the left?

A: I cannot venture on a guess as to the convulsions of a dying man. I can only say that such a thing is physically possible.

After this high-handed carrying of matters, the story of Ernest Wilbertson Knowles left no doubt. Everybody knew Knowles. Everybody knew his likes, his dislikes, his nature. Everybody had seen for decades that there was no guile in him. He told of the view from the window, the man alone in a closed circle of sand, the impossibility of murder.

Q: But are you satisfied in your own mind that what you saw was the deceased taking his own life?

A: I am afraid so, sir.

Q: Then how do you account for the fact that a knife held in the right hand was thrown to the left rather than the right?

A: I am not sure I can properly describe the gestures the late gentleman made, sir. I thought I could at first but I have been thinking it over and I am not sure. It was all so rapid that his gesture might have been anything.

Q: But you did not actually see the knife thrown from him?

A: Yes, sir, I am under the impression that I did.

"WOW!" said a voice among the spectators. It sounded rather like Tony Weller speaking out from the gallery. And it was, in fact, Dr Fell, who throughout the proceedings had remained wheezily asleep with his red face smoking in the heat.

"I will have silence in this room," shouted the coroner.

Cross-examined by Burrows as counsel for the widow, Knowles said that he would not swear to having seen the deceased throw the knife. He had good eyesight, but not such good eyesight as that. And his patent sincerity of manner kept the sympathies of the jury. Knowles admitted that he spoke only from an impression and admitted the (remote) possibility of an error, with which Burrows had to be content.

There followed to an inevitable end the police evidence, the evidence of the deceased's movements, to a rounding-up. In that hot shed, with rows of pencils going like spiders' legs, there was determined for practical purposes the imposture of the dead man. Glances were being cast at Patrick Gore, the real heir. Quick glances. Appraising glances. Hesitant glances. Even friendly glances, under which he remained bland and impassive.

" Members of the jury," said the coroner, " there is one more witness to whom I shall ask you to listen, though I am unacquainted with the nature of the witness's testimony. At the request of Mr Burrows and at her own request, the witness comes here to make a statement of importance, which I trust will be of assistance to you in your painful duty. I therefore call Miss Madeline Dane."

Page sat up.

There was a puzzled stir in the court, the reporters quickening with interest at Madeline's very real beauty. What she was doing here Page himself had no idea, but it disturbed him. Way was made for her to come to the witness-chair, where the coroner handed her the Book and she took the oath in a nervous but clear voice. As though for a kind of distant mourning, she wore dark blue, with a dark blue hat the colour of her eyes. Something of the corrugated iron feeling was removed. The corrugated-iron self-consciousness of the men on the jury relaxed. They did not actually beam on her, but Page felt it was not far off. Even the coroner fussed with consideration. Among the males of the population Madeline was a favourite who had few competitors. A handsome feeling went through the inquest.

" Again I must insist on silence in this room! " said the coroner. " Now will you give your name, please? "

" Madeline Elspeth Dane."

" Your age? "

" Th-thirty-five."

" Your address, Miss Dane? "

" Monplaisir, near Frettenden."

" Now, Miss Dane," said the coroner, brisk but gentle, " I believe you wished to make a statement regarding the deceased? What is the nature of the evidence you wish to give? "

" Yes, I must tell you. Only it's so difficult to know where to begin."

" Perhaps I can help Miss Dane out," said Burrows, on his feet with perspiring dignity. " Miss Dane, was it— "

" Mr Burrows," snapped the coroner, losing all control of his temper, " you have constantly interrupted these proceedings with a lack of respect for your rights and mine which I cannot and will not tolerate. You are entitled to question the witness when I have done questioning her, and not until then. In the meantime you will remain silent or leave this court. Hrrrr! Ahem. Now, Miss Dane? "

" Please don't quarrel."

" We are not quarrelling, madam. I am indicating the respect due to this court, a court gathered to determine how the deceased met his death, and a respect which, whatever may be said of it from some sources "—here his eye sought out the reporters—" I have every intention of upholding. Now, Miss Dane? "

" It's about Sir John Farnleigh," said Madeline earnestly, " and whether he was or was not Sir John Farnleigh. I want to explain why he was so anxious to receive the claimant and the claimant's solicitor; and why he didn't show them out of the house; and why he was so eager to have the finger-print taken; oh, and all the things that may help you decide about his death."

" Miss Dane, if you merely wish to give an opinion as to whether the deceased was Sir John Farnleigh, I am afraid I must inform you— "

" No, no, no. I don't know whether he was. But that's the whole dreadful thing. You see, *he didn't know himself.*"

144

By the stir in the dim shed, it was beginning to be felt that this might be the sensation of the day, even if nobody knew what it meant. The coroner cleared his throat, his head turning like an alert marionette's.

"Miss Dane, this is not a court of law; it is an inquiry; and therefore I can allow you to give what testimony you like, provided only it has some bearing which will help us. Will you be so good as to explain what you mean?"

Madeline drew a deep breath.

"Yes, if you let me explain you'll see how important it is, Mr Whitehouse. What is hard to say in front of all of you is how he came to tell me about it. But he had to confide in somebody, you know. He was too fond of Lady Farnleigh to tell *her*; that was a part of the trouble; and sometimes it worried him so horribly that you may have noticed how ill he looked. And I suppose I'm a safe person to confide in"—she wrinkled her forehead half wryly and half smilingly—"so that's how it was."

"Yes, yes? How what was, Miss Dane?"

"You've let them tell all about the meeting the night before last, to argue over the estate and take the finger-prints," resumed Madeline, with a probably unconscious thrust. "I was not there, but I heard all about it from a friend of mine who was there. He said what impressed him most was the absolute assurance of both claimants, right up to the taking of the finger-prints and afterwards. He said that the only time poor John—I beg your pardon: Sir John—smiled at all or looked relieved was when the claimant was talking about that terrible affair on the *Titanic*, and about being hit with a seaman's mallet."

"Yes; well?"

"Here is what Sir John told me months ago. After the wreck of the *Titanic*, as a boy, he woke up in a hospital in New York. But he didn't know it was New York or about the *Titanic*. He didn't know where he was, or how he had got there, or even who he was. He had had

145

concussion of the brain, after getting some knocks on the head accidentally or deliberately in the wreck of the ship, and he was suffering from what they call amnesia. Do you understand what I mean? "

" Perfectly, Miss Dane. Continue."

" They told him his clothes and papers had identified him as John Farnleigh. There was a man standing over the bed in the hospital, a man who said he was his mother's cousin—oh, that's badly put, but you know what I mean—and told him to go to sleep and get well.

" But you know what boys of that age are. He was very frightened and horribly worried. For he didn't know anything about himself. And worst of all, like boys of that age, he didn't dare tell anybody for fear he might be mad or there might be something wrong with him or they might put him in gaol.

" That's how it seemed to him. He hadn't any reason to think he *wasn't* this John Farnleigh. He hadn't any reason to believe they weren't telling the truth in all they told him about himself. He had a hazy recollection of shouting or confusion, something to do with open air or cold; but that was all he could remember. So he never spoke a word about it to anybody. He pretended to his cousin—a Mr Renwick from Colorado—that he remembered everything. Mr Renwick never suspected.

" He nursed that little secret for years. He kept reading his diary, and trying to bring things back. He told me that sometimes he would sit for hours with his hands pressed to his head, concentrating. Sometimes he would think he remembered a face or an event faintly, like something you see under water. Then again it would seem to him that there was something wrong. The only thing he ever brought out of it, as a phrase rather than an image, had to do with a hinge: a crooked hinge."

Under the iron roof the spectators sat like dummies. No papers rustled. Nobody whispered. Page felt his collar damp and his heart ticking like a watch. Smoky sunlight came through the windows, and Madeline winked the corner of her eye in it.

" A crooked hinge, Miss Dane? "

" Yes. I don't know what he meant. Neither did he."

" Go on, please."

146

"In those early years in Colorado he was afraid they would put him in gaol if there should be anything wrong and they found out about it. Handwriting was no good, because two of his fingers were nearly crushed in the wreck and he could never hold a pen properly. He was afraid to write home; that's why he never did. He was even afraid to go to a doctor and ask if he might be mad, for fear the doctor should tell on him.

"Of course, in time it got fainter. He convinced himself that it was an unfortunate thing which happens to some people, and so on. There was the War and all that. He consulted a mental specialist who told him after a lot of psychological tests that he really was John Farnleigh, and that he had nothing to worry about. But he never lost the horror of those years, and even when he thought he had forgotten it he dreamed about it.

"Then it was all revived when poor Dudley died and he inherited the title and estate. He had to come to England. He was—how can I say this?—academically interested. He thought at long last he *must* remember. And he didn't. You all know how he used to go wandering round like a ghost, a poor old ghost who didn't even know whether he was a ghost. You know how jumpy he was. He loved it here. He loved every acre and yard of it. Mind you, he didn't honestly doubt he was John Farnleigh. But he had to KNOW."

Madeline bit her lip.

Her luminous, now rather hard eyes wandered among the spectators.

"I used to talk to him and try to make him quiet. I would ask him not to think too much; then perhaps he would remember. I used to arrange it so that I reminded him of things, and made him think he had remembered them for himself. Maybe it would be a gramophone playing, 'To thee, beautiful lady,' far away in the evening; and he would remember how we danced to it as children. Maybe it would be a detail of the house. In the library there's a kind of cupboard with shelves of books—built into the wall by the windows, you know—and instead of being just a cupboard, it's got a door that used to open out into the garden. It still will open if you find the right catch. I persuaded him to find the right catch. He said he slept well for nights after that.

"But he still had to know. He said he wouldn't mind so much if he could only know, even if it turned out he was not John Farnleigh. He said he wasn't a wild adolescent boy any longer. He said he could face it quietly; and it would be the greatest thing in the world just to know the truth.

"He went to London and saw two more doctors; I know that. You can see how worried he was when he even went to a person who was supposed to have psychic powers —a horrible little man called Ahriman, in Half-Moon Street—who was all the rage then. He took a crowd of us along under pretext of having our fortunes told, and pretended to laugh at it. But he told this fortune-teller all about himself.

"Still he kept wandering about the place. He used to say, 'Well, I am a good steward'; and you know he was. He used to go into the church a lot, too; he liked the hymns best; and sometimes, when they played, 'Abide with Me'—anyway, when he was near the church, and looking up at the walls, he used to say that if ever he were in a position to— "

Madeline paused.

Her breast rose with a deep breath. Her eyes were fixed on the front rows, and her fingers opened wide on the arms of the chair. All passion and mysticism seemed in her then, as deep as roots and as strong as; yet she was, after all, only a woman making what defence she could in a hot and stuffy shed.

"I'm so sorry," she blurted. "Perhaps it is better not to talk about that; it does not concern us, anyhow. I'm sorry if I'm taking up your time with things that don't matter— "

"I will have silence in here," said the coroner, flinging round his head at the rustle that grew. "I am not sure I think you are taking up our time with things that do not matter. Have you anything else to tell the jury? "

"Yes," said Madeline, turning and looking at them. "One other thing."

"Which is? "

"When I heard about the claimant to the estate and

his lawyer, I knew what John had been thinking. You know now what was in his mind all along. You can follow every step of his thoughts and every word he said. You know now why he smiled, and why the relief was almost too much, when he heard the claimant's story about the seaman's mallet and the blows on the head in the wreck of the *Titanic*. For *he* was the one who suffered from concussion of the brain and a loss of memory that lasted for twenty-five years.

"Please wait! I don't say the claimant's story isn't true. I don't know, or profess to decide. But Sir John— the one you call the deceased as though he had never been alive—must have felt a mighty relief when he heard something that in his eyes couldn't possibly have been true. He saw his dream being fulfilled at last, that his identity should be proved. You know now why he welcomed that finger-print test. You know why he was the most eager of all. You know why he would hardly wait, why he was all wire and nerves, to learn the result."

Madeline grasped the arms of the chair.

"Please. Perhaps I'm putting all this stupidly, but I hope you understand me. To prove things one way or the other was the one end of this life. If he were Sir John Farnleigh, he would be happy to the end of his life. If he were not, it wouldn't matter so much once he really knew. Like winning a football pool, you know. You put your sixpence on it. You think perhaps you've won thousands and thousands of pounds. You're almost sure of it, you could swear it's true. But you can't be sure until the telegram comes. If it doesn't come, you think, 'Well, that's that,' and let it go. Well, that's John Farnleigh. This was his football pool. Acres and acres of things he loved: they were his football pool. Respect and honour and sound sleep at night forever: they were his football pool. The end of torture and the beginning of the future: they were his football pool. He believed now that he had won it. And now people are trying to tell you he killed himself. Don't you think it for a minute. You know better. Can you believe, dare you believe, that he'd have deliberately cut his throat half an hour before he could learn the result?"

She put her hand over her eyes.

There was a genuine uproar, which the coroner put down. Mr Harold Welkyn was on his feet. Page saw that his shiny face was slightly pale, and he spoke as though he had been running.

"Mr Coroner. As a piece of special pleading, all this is no doubt very interesting," he said acidly. "I shall not be impertinent enough to remind you of your duties. I shall not be impertinent enough to point out that no question has been asked in the last ten minutes. But if this lady has completely finished her remarkable statement, which if true tends to show that the deceased was an even greater impostor than we believed, I shall ask leave, as counsel for the real Sir John Farnleigh, to cross-examine."

"Mr Welkyn," said the coroner, flinging round his head again, "you will ask questions when I give you leave and you will remain silent until then. Now, Miss Dane—"

"Please let him ask questions," said Madeline. "I remember seeing him at the house of that horrible little Egyptian, Ahriman, in Half-Moon Street."

Mr Welkyn got out a handkerchief and mopped his forehead.

And the questions were asked. And the coroner summed up. And Inspector Elliot went into another room and privately danced the saraband. And the jury, throwing the case straight to the police to handle, brought in a verdict of murder by a person or persons unknown.

CHAPTER XVI

ANDREW MACANDREW ELLIOT lifted a glass of very passable hock and inspected that.

"Miss Dane," he declared, "you're a born politician. No, I'll say diplomat; it sounds better; I don't know why. That touch about the football pools was sheer genius. It brought things home to the jury as certainly as sixpence and two wrong. How did you come to think of it?"

In the long, warm afterglow of sunset, Elliot, Dr Fell, and Page were having dinner with Madeline at the unfortunately named but comfortable Monplaisir. The table stood by the French windows of the dining-room, and the French windows opened on a deep garden of laurels. At the end of it were two acres of apple-orchard. In one direction a footpath went through the orchard to what used to be Colonel Mardale's. In another it wound across a brook and up through the Hanging Chart, whose slope of trees showed dark against the evening sky to the left of the orchard. If you followed the latter path up through the Chart, over its shoulder, and down again, you came to the back gardens of Farnleigh Close.

Madeline lived alone, having a woman who came in by day to "cook and do." It was a trim little house, bright with military prints that were a heritage from her father, full of brass and bustling clocks. It stood rather isolated, the nearest house being that of the unfortunate Victoria Daly; but Madeline had never minded the isolation.

She sat now at the head of the table beside the open windows, beyond polished wood and silver in a dusk which was not quite dark enough for the lighting of the dinner-table candles. She wore white. The great, low oak beams of the dining-room, the pewter and the busy clocks, all were a background for her. Dinner over, Dr Fell had lit a Gargantuan cigar; Page had lit a cigarette for Madeline; and, at Elliot's question, Madeline laughed in the light of the match.

"About the football pools?" she repeated. She flushed a little as well. "As a matter of fact, I didn't think of it. It was Nat Burrows. He wrote it out and made me get it word-perfect like a recitation. Oh, every word I said was true. I felt it terribly. It was the most awful cheek of me to carry on like that before all those people; and every second I was afraid poor Mr Whitehouse was going to stop me; but Nat said it was absolutely the only way. Afterwards I went upstairs at the Bull and Butcher and had hysterics and cried and felt better. Was it very awful of me?"

They were certainly staring at her.

"No," said Dr Fell quite seriously, "it was a remarkable performance. But, oh, Lord! Burrows coached you? Wow!"

"Yes, he was here half of last night doing it."

"Burrows? But when was he here?" asked Page, surprised. "I brought you home."

"He came here after you left. He was full of what I had just told Molly, and terribly excited."

"You know, gents," rumbled Dr Fell, taking a meditative pull at the large cigar, "we mustn't underestimate our friend Burrows. Page here told us long ago that he was an unco' intelligent chap. Welkyn seemed to run rings round him at the beginning of this circus; but all the time, psychologically—confound that word—he had the inquest exactly where he wanted it. He'll be fighting, naturally. It will naturally make a big difference to the firm of Burrows & Burrows whether they keep the management of the Farnleigh estate. And he's a fighter. When, as, and if the case of Farnleigh *v.* Gore ever comes to trial, it ought to be a sizzler."

Elliot faced something else.

"Look here, Miss Dale," he said stubbornly. "I'm not denying you did us a good turn. It's a victory, if only an outward and newspaper victory. Now the case won't be closed officially, even if the A.C. tears his hair and swears the jury were a pack of thick-witted yokels under the spell of a good-looking—er—female. But what I want to know is why you didn't come to *me* with all this information in the first place. I'm not a twister. I'm not—er—a half bad fellow, if you can put it like that. Why didn't you tell me?"

The odd and almost comic part of it was, Page thought, that he sounded personally hurt.

"I wanted to," said Madeline. "Honestly I did. But I had to tell Molly first. Then Nat Burrows made me swear all kinds of horrid oaths I wouldn't breathe a word of it to the police until after the inquest. He says he doesn't trust the police. Also he's working on a theory to prove—" She checked herself, biting her lip, and made an apologetic gesture with her cigarette. "You know how some people are."

"Still, where do we stand?" asked Page. "After this morning, have we gone round in the old circle to wondering which of them is the real heir? If Murray swears Gore is, and if they don't upset that finger-print evidence, that seems to end it. Or so I thought. This morning, once or twice, I wasn't quite so sure. Certain hints and innuendoes—you made them yourself—seemed to centre round good old Welkyn."

"Really, Brian! I only said what Nat told me to say. What do you mean?"

"Well, possibly that the whole claim to the estate might have been engineered by Welkyn himself. Welkyn, the spooks' solicitor and spiritualists' advocate. Welkyn, who collects some rather rummy friends, and may have collected Gore as he collected Ahriman and Madame Duquesne and the rest of them. (I said when we met Gore he was some kind of showman.) Welkyn, who said he saw a ghost in the garden at the time of the murder. Welkyn, who at the time of the murder was only fifteen feet away from the victim and with only a sheet of glass between. Welkyn—"

"But surely, Brian, you don't suspect Mr Welkyn of the murder?"

"Why not? Dr Fell said—"

"I said," interposed the doctor, frowning at his cigar, "that he was the most interesting person in the group."

"It usually amounts to the same thing," said Page gloomily. "What's your real opinion, Madeline, about the real heir? You told me yesterday you thought the late Farnleigh was an impostor. Do you?"

"Yes, I do. But I don't see how anybody could keep from feeling sorry for him. He didn't want to be an impostor, don't you see? He only wanted to know who he was. As for Mr Welkyn, he couldn't possibly be the murderer. He was the only one of us who wasn't in the attic when—well, it seems horrible to talk about after dinner and on a nice evening, but who wasn't in the attic when that machine fell."

"Sinister," said the doctor. "Very sinister."

"You must be terribly brave," said Madeline with the utmost seriousness, "to laugh about that iron idol tumbling down—"

"My dear young lady, I am not brave. The wind was blowing violently and I felt ill. Afterwards I began, like St Peter, to curse and swear. Then I made jokes. Harrumph. Fortunately I began thinking about that girl

153

in the other room, who hasn't my padding to sustain her. And I swore a mighty oath myself—" His fist hovered over the table, huge in the twilight. They had the impression of a dangerous force behind jokes and absence of mind, a force that could fall and bind. But he did not bring the fist down. He looked out into the darkening garden, and continued to smoke mildly.

"Then where do we stand, sir?" asked Page. "Have you found you can trust us by now?".

It was Elliot who answered him. Elliot took a cigarette out of the box on the table. He lit it with careful movings of the match. In the light of the match his expression was again brisk, impassive, but as though conveying a hint Page could not interpret.

"We must be moving along soon," the inspector said. "Burton is driving us to Paddock Wood, and Dr. Fell and I are catching the ten-o'clock train for town. We have a conference with Mr Bellchester at the Yard. Dr Fell has an idea."

"About—what to do here?" Madeline asked eagerly.

"Yes," said Dr Fell. For a time he continued to smoke with a sleepy air. "I was wondering. Perhaps it would be as well if I gave a few hollow subterranean whispers. For example, that inquest to-day served a double-barrelled purpose. We hoped for a murder verdict and we hoped that one of the witnesses would make a slip. We got the murder verdict; and somebody blundered."

"Was that where you said 'wow' out loud?"

"I said wow many times," answered the doctor gravely. "To myself. At a price, the inspector and I will tell you what caused both of us to say wow, or at least a hint of it. I say: at a price. After all, you ought to do for us what you did for Mr Burrows, and under the same pledge of secrecy. A minute ago you said he was working on a theory to prove something. What theory? And what does he want to prove?"

Madeline stirred, and crushed out her cigarette. In the semi-darkness she looked cool and clean in white, her short throat swelling above the low-necked dress. Page always remembered her at that moment: the blonde hair done into something like curls above the ears, the broad face even more softened and etherealised by twilight, the slow closing of her eyes. Outside a faint wind stirred in the laurels. Towards the west over the garden the low sky was thin yellow-orange, like brittle glass; but over the mass of the Hanging Chart there was a star. The room seemed to have retreated, as though it were waiting. Madeline put her hands on the table and seemed to push herself back.

"I don't know," she said. "People come and tell me these things. They think I can keep a secret; I look the sort of person who can keep a secret; and I can. Now it seems as though all the secrets were being dragged out of me, and I feel as though I had done something indecent by all that talking to-day."

"And?" prompted Dr Fell.

"All the same, you ought to know this. You really and truly ought to know it. Nat Burrows suspects someone of murder, and hopes he can prove it."

"And he suspects—?"

"He suspects Kennet Murray," said Madeline.

The glowing end of Elliot's cigarette stopped in the air. Then Elliot struck the table with the flat of his hand. "Murray! Murray?"

"Why, Mr Elliot?" asked Madeline, opening her eyes. "Does it surprise you?"

The inspector's voice remained impersonal. "Murray is the last person who should be suspected, both in the real sense and in what the doctor here calls the detective-story sense. He was the person everyone was watching. Even if it might have been only a joke, he was the person they were all thinking of as the victim. Burrows is a damned sight too clever by half!—I beg your pardon, Miss Dane: 'ware language. No. And again no. Has Burrows got any reason to think this, except the idea of being clever? Why, the man's got an alibi as big as a house!"

"I don't understand part of it," Madeline said, wrinkling her forehead, "because he didn't tell me. But that's the point. Has he got an alibi, really? I'm only telling you what Nat told me. Nat says that if you go by the evidence there wasn't anybody actually watching him except this Mr Gore, standing down by the library windows."

The inspector and Dr Fell exchanged a glance. They did not comment.

"Go on, please."

"You remember my mentioning at the inquest to-day the little cupboard or book-closet built into the wall of the library—like the one in the attic? The one that's got a door opening into the garden if you find the spring?"

"I do," said Dr Fell rather grimly. "Humph. Murray mentioned that place to us himself, when he said he went in there during his vigil to change the bogus Thumbograph for the real one so that he shouldn't be seen from the windows. I begin to understand."

"Yes. I told that to Nat, and he was terribly interested. He said to be sure to mention it so that it could go into the records. If I understand him at all, he says you're concentrating your attention on the wrong man. He says all this is a trumped-up conspiracy against poor John. He says that because this 'Patrick Gore' has a clever tongue and an interesting way with him, you've mistaken him for the leader of the group. But Nat maintains that Mr Murray is the real—what's that horrid word they use in thrillers—"

"Master-mind?"

"That's it. Of the gang. Of a gang composed of Gore and Welkyn and Murray; Gore and Welkyn being puppets who wouldn't have the courage for any real crime."

"Go on," said Dr Fell in a curious voice.

"Nat was wildly excited when he explained it. He points to the rather odd behaviour of Mr Murray all through this. Well, of course I—I wouldn't know about that. I haven't seen enough of him. He does seem a bit different from the old days, but then I know we all must be.

"Poor Nat has even got a theory of how the scheme might have been worked. Mr Murray was in touch with a shady lawyer (Mr Welkyn). Mr Welkyn was in a position to tell him, through one of the fortune-tellers of his clientèle, that Sir John Farnleigh was suffering from loss of memory and mental trouble over you know what. So Murray, the old tutor, thought of presenting an impostor with forged credentials. Through Welkyn he found a suitable impostor (Gore) among Welkyn's clients. Murray drilled him for six months in every particular. Nat says that's why Gore's way of speaking and conducting himself is so much like Murray's: the thing Nat says you noticed, Dr Fell."

The doctor stared across the table at her.

He put his elbows on the table and his head in his hands, so that Page could not tell what he was thinking. The air stirring through the open windows was very warm and full of fragrance; yet it is a fact that Dr Fell shivered.

"Go on," Elliot prompted again.

"Nat's idea of what happened is—is horrible," replied Madeline, closing her eyes again. "I could see it, even if I didn't want to see it. Poor John, who had never done anybody any harm, had to be killed so that there would be nobody to fight their claim, and so that it should be believed he had killed himself. Just as most people do believe, you know."

"Yes," said Elliot. "Just as most people do believe."

"Welkyn and Gore, the sawdust-men without the courage, had their parts to play. They had the two sides of the house guarded, you see. Welkyn was in the dining-room. Gore was to watch the library windows for two reasons: first, to swear to Mr Murray's alibi; and, second, to keep any other person away from looking in the window while Mr Murray was out of the library.

"They stalked poor John like a—oh, you know. He never had a chance. When they knew he was in the garden, Mr Murray came out ever so softly. He's a big man. He caught John and killed him. He didn't do it until the last moment. That is, they hoped that John might break down and confess he had lost his memory and might *not* be the real heir. Then they mightn't have had to kill him. But he didn't. And so they did. But Mr Murray had to explain why he had been so unneces- sarily long in 'comparing finger-prints'. So he invented the story of juggling with Thumbographs, and stole one and later returned it. And Nat says," she concluded rather breathlessly, looking at Dr Fell, "—he says you tumbled straight into their trap, as Mr Murray planned you should."

Inspector Elliot carefully put out his cigarette.

"That's it, eh? Does this Mr Burrows explain how Murray committed a murder unseen under the eyes of Knowles and practically under the eyes of Burrows himself?"

She shook her head.

"He wouldn't tell me that. Either he didn't want to, or he hasn't got it worked out yet."

"He hasn't got it worked out yet," said Dr Fell in a hollow voice. "A slight slowness of cerebral activity. A little late with the homework. Oh, my ancient hat. This is awful."

Once again that day Madeline had talked herself into a state of quickened breathing. It was as though she herself, at the end of a great nervous strain, had been touched by that wind from the garden or the sense of expectancy and waiting from the house.

"What do you think of it?" she asked.

Dr Fell reflected.

"There are flaws in it. Bad flaws."

"That doesn't matter," said Madeline, looking straight at him. "I don't think I believe it myself. But I've told you what you wanted to know. What were the hints you were going to give us, about what really happened?"

He regarded her in a curious way, as though he wondered.

"Have you told us everything, ma'am?"

"Everything I—I can or dare to. Don't ask me any more. Please."

"Still," argued Dr Fell, "at risk of seeming to make more mysteries, I'm going to ask you another question. You knew the late Farnleigh very well. Now, the point is nebulous and psychological again; but find the answer to the following question and you come near the truth. Why did Farnleigh worry for twenty-five years? Why was he weighed down and oppressed in the blindness of his memory? Most men would have been troubled for a while; yet it should not have left such a terrifying scar in his mind. Was he, for instance, tormented by a memory of crime or evil?"

She nodded. "Yes, I believe he was. I've always thought of him as being like those old Puritans in books, brought up to date."

"But he couldn't remember what it concerned?"

"No—except this image of the crooked hinge."

Page found the words themselves disturbing and bothersome. It seemed as though they ought to convey something or suggest something. What was a crooked hinge? Or, for that matter, a straight hinge?

"Sort of polite version of a screw loose?" he asked.

"N-no, I don't think so. I mean, it wasn't a figure of speech. Sometimes he seemed to see a hinge; a hinge on a door; a *white* hinge. It would become crooked as he looked, and droop or crack somehow. He said it stuck in his mind in the way you notice the pattern of a wall-paper when you are ill."

"A white hinge," said Dr Fell. He looked at Elliot. "That rather tears it, my lad. Eh?"

"Yes, sir."

A long sniff rumbled in the doctor's nose.

"Very well. Now let's see if there are any suggestions of the truth in all this. I will give you a few.

"First. There has been much talk from the beginning about who was or wasn't battered on the head with what has been described as a 'seaman's wooden mallet' There has been a great amount of curiosity about the fact, but very little about the mallet. Where did anybody get such an implement? How was it obtainable at all? Such an article wouldn't be of much use to sailors aboard modern mechanised ships. I can think of only one thing answering the description.

"You have probably seen such mallets if you have crossed the Atlantic. One of them hangs by each of the steel doors which are set at intervals along the passages below decks in a modern liner. These steel doors are, or are supposed to be, water-tight. In the event of disaster they can be closed, to form a series of bulkheads or compartments against water flooding in. And the mallet by each door—a sombre reminder—is for use as a weapon by the steward in case of panic and a stampede on the part of passengers. The *Titanic,* you remember, was famous for its water-tight compartments."

"Well?" prompted Page, as the doctor paused. "What of it?"

"It doesn't suggest anything to you?"

"No."

"Second point," said Dr Fell. "That interesting automaton, the Golden Hag. Find out what made the automaton work in the seventeenth century, and you will have the essential secret of this case."

"But it doesn't make *any* sense!" cried Madeline. "At least, I mean, it doesn't have any connection with what I was thinking. I thought you were thinking just the same things as I was, and now— "

Inspector Elliot looked at his watch. "We shall have to be moving, sir," he said in a flat voice, "if we want to catch that train and still step in at the Close on our way."

"Don't go," said Madeline abruptly. "Don't go. Please. You won't, will you, Brian? "

"I thought we should come to it, ma'am," Dr Fell told her in a very quiet voice. "Just what is wrong? "

"I'm afraid," said Madeline. "I suppose that's why I've been talking so much, really."

The realisation of something different about her, and the reason for it, came to Brian Page with a kind of shock.

Dr. Fell laid his cigar in the saucer of his coffee-cup. Striking a match with great care, he leaned across and lit the candles on the table. Four golden flames curled and then drew up steadily in the warm, still air; they seemed to hover as though disembodied above the candles. The twilight was pushed back into the garden. In the snug little nook on the edge of it, Madeline's eyes reflected the candlelight; they were steady but dilated. It was as though in the fear there showed a measure of expectancy.

The doctor seemed uneasy. "I'm afraid we can't stay, Miss Dane. We shall be back to-morrow, but there are some ends of the case we've got to gather up in town. All the same, if Page could—? "

"You won't leave me, will you, Brian? I'm sorry to be such a fool and to bother you— "

"Good Lord, of course I won't leave you! " roared Page, feeling such a fierce protectiveness as he had never known before. "I'll cause a scandal. I won't let you beyond arm's length until morning. Not that there's anything to be afraid of."

"Aren't you forgetting the date? "

" The date? "

" The anniversary. July 31st. Victoria Daly died a year ago to-night."

" It is also," supplied Dr Fell, looking curiously at both of them, " —it is also Lammas Eve. A good Scot like Elliot will tell you what that is. It's the night of one of the Great Sabbaths and the powers from down under are exalted. H'mf. Hah. Well. I'm a cheerful blighter, eh? "

Page found himself puzzled and nervy and angry.

" You are," he said. " What's the good of putting non-sense into people's heads? Madeline is upset enough as it is. She's played other people's games and done things for other people until she's worn out. What the devil do you mean by trying to make it worse? There's no danger here. If I see anything hanging about I'll wring its ruddy neck and ask permission from the police after-wards."

" Sorry," said Dr Fell. For a moment he stood looking down from his great height with tired, kindly, vaguely troubled eyes. Then he took his cloak, his shovel-hat, and his crutch-handled stick from a chair.

" Good night, sir," said Elliot. " If I've got the geo-graphy of the neighbourhood right, we can go up that path to the left from the garden here, and through the wood, and down to Farnleigh Close on the other side. Is that right? "

" Yes."

" Well—er—good night, then. Thank you again for everything, Miss Dane, for a very pleasant and instructive evening. And just—keep your eye out, you know, Mr Page."

" Yes. And watch out for bogles in the wood," Page shouted after them.

He stood in the French window and watched them go down the garden among the laurels. It was a very warm night, and the scents of the garden were thick and ener-vating. In the east stars were brightening against a slope of sky, but they winked dimly as though distorted by heat-waves. Page's irrational anger grew.

" Bunch of old women," he said. " Trying to— "

He turned round and saw the fleeting of Madeline's smile. She was calm again; but she looked flushed.

" I'm sorry to make such an exhibition of myself, Brian," she said gently. " I know there's no danger of any kind." She got up. "Will you excuse me for a moment? I want to go upstairs and powder my nose. Shan't be a second."

" Bunch of old women. Trying to— "

Alone, he lit a cigarette with care. After a very brief time he was able to laugh at his own annoyance, and he felt better. On the contrary, an evening alone with Madeline was one of the pleasantest things he could imagine. A brown moth flashed through the window and dived in a long sweep towards one flame; he brushed it away, and shifted as it passed his face.

This little core of candlelight was very soothing and pleasant, but they might as well have more light. He went to the electric switch. Subdued wall-lamps brought out the grace of the room and the pattern of chintzes. It was odd, he thought, how clear and sharply defined the ticking of a clock could be. There were two of them in the room; they did not vie with each other, but each filled up the beats the other lacked, and produced a kind of quick rustling. The tiny pendulum of one switched backwards and forwards in a way that drew the eye.

He went back to the table, where he poured himself some almost cold coffee. The noise of his own footsteps on the floor, the rattle of the cup in the saucer, the clink of the china coffee-pot on the edge of the cup: all these made sounds as clearly defined as those of the clocks. For the first time he became aware of mere emptiness as a positive quality. His thoughts ran progressively: this room is absolutely empty: I am alone: what of it?

The emptiness of the place was emphasised by the clearness of the lights. To one subject he kept his mind closed, though he had guessed a certain secret that afternoon and confirmed it from a book in his library. Something cheerful was indicated—for Madeline, of course. This house, neat as it might be, was too isolated. Round it was a wall of darkness stretching for half a mile.

Madeline was taking rather a long time to powder her nose. Another moth zigzagged through the open window and flapped on the table. Curtains and candle-flames stirred a little. Better close the windows. He went across the bright, hard room, stood in one French window looking out into the garden, and then stood very still.

In the garden, in the darkness just beyond the thin edge of light from the windows, sat the automaton from Farnleigh Close.

CHAPTER XVII

FOR the space of perhaps eight seconds he stood looking at it, as motionless as the automaton itself.

The light from the windows was faint yellow. It stretched out ten or a dozen feet across the grass, just touching the once-painted base of the figure. Even wider cracks gaped across her wax face; she leaned a little sideways from her fall downstairs, and half of her clockwork insides were gone. Some effort had been made to mend this by pulling the decayed gown across the wounds. Old and smashed and half-blind, she looked at him malignantly from the shadow of the laurels.

He had to force himself to do what he did. He walked out slowly towards her, feeling that his steps took him farther than need be from the lighted windows. She was alone, or seemed alone. Her wheels had been mended, he noticed. But the ground was so baked from long July drought that the wheels left hardly a trace in the grass. Not far to the left was a gravel drive which would leave no traces.

Then he hurried back to the house, for he heard Madeline coming downstairs.

Carefully he closed all the French windows. Then he picked up the heavy oak table and carried it to the middle of the room. Two of the candlesticks rocked. Madeline, appearing in the doorway, found him steadying one of them as he set down the table.

"Moths getting in," he explained.

"But won't it be awfully stuffy? Hadn't you better leave one— "

163

"I'll do it." He set the middle window open about a foot.

"Brian! There's nothing wrong, is there?"

Again he became aware, with intense clarity, of the ticking of the clocks; but most of all of the sympathetic presence of Madeline, exuding the wish to be protected. Uneasiness takes people in strange ways. She did not now seem so remote or self-effacing. The aura of her—there is no other word for it—filled the room.

He said:

"Good Lord, no; of course there's nothing wrong. It's just that moths are a nuisance, that's all. That's why I closed the windows."

"Shall we go into the other room?"

Better not be out of touch with it. Better not have it free to go where it liked.

"Oh, let's stay here and smoke another cigarette."

"Of course. What about some more coffee?"

"Don't trouble."

"It's no trouble. It's all prepared on the stove."

She smiled, the bright smile of one strung up by nerves, and went across to the kitchen. While she was gone he did not look out of the window. She seemed to be in the kitchen a long time, and he went in search of her. He met her in the doorway, carrying a fresh pot of coffee. She spoke quietly.

"Brian, there *is* something wrong. The back door is open. I know I left it shut, and Maria always closes it when she goes home."

"Maria forgot it."

"Yes. If you say so. Oh, I'm being silly. I know I am. Let's have something cheerful."

She seemed to wake up, with an apologetic and yet defiant laugh, and a brighter complexion. In one corner of the room, unobtrusive like Madeline herself, there was a radio. She switched it on. It took a few seconds to grow warm; then the resulting volume of noise startled them both.

She toned it down, but the flooding jingles of a dance-orchestra filled the rooms like surf on a beach. The tunes seemed as usual; the words rather worse than usual. Madeline listened to it for a moment. Then she returned to the table, sat down, and poured out their coffee. They were sitting at right angles to each other, so close he could have touched her hand. Her back was to the windows. All the while he was conscious of something outside, waiting. He wondered what his feelings would be if a cracked face were poked against the glass.

Yet, at the same time his nerves were touched, his brain stirred as well. It seemed to him that he woke up. It seemed to him that he was rationally reasoning for the first time; that bonds fell apart and the brain emerged from iron bands.

Now what were the facts about that dummy? It was dead iron and wheels and wax. It was no more dangerous of itself than a kitchen boiler. They had examined it, and they knew. Its only purpose was to *terrify*, a human purpose managed by a solid hand.

It had not pushed itself across the path from Farnleigh Close, like a malignant old woman in a wheel-chair. It had been brought here to terrify, again the solid purpose managed by the solid hand. And it seemed to him that this automaton was fitting itself into a pattern which the case had taken since the beginning, and which from the beginning he should have seen. . . .

"Yes," said Madeline, into his thoughts. "Let's talk about it. That would be better, really."

"It?"

"The whole thing," said Madeline, clenching her hands. "I—I may know rather more about it than you think."

She swam into his vision again. Again she had put the palms of her hands flat on the table, as though she were going to push herself back. The faint, frightened smile still lingered about her eyes and mouth. But she was quiet, almost coquettish; and she had never been more persuasive.

"I wonder if you know," he said, "what I've guessed?"

"*I* wonder."

He kept his eyes fixed on the partly open window. It seemed to him that he was talking less to Madeline than to something out there, something waiting, whose presence surrounded the house.

"It'll probably be best to get this out of my system," he

went on with his eye still on the window. "Let me ask you something. Had *you* ever heard of a—a witch-cult hereabouts?"

Hesitation.

"Yes. I've heard rumours. Why?"

"It's about Victoria Daly. I had the essential facts yesterday from Dr Fell and Inspector Elliot; I even had the information to interpret them; but I hadn't the wits to put the whole thing together. It's come to daylight now. Did you know that after Victoria's murder her body was found smeared with a substance composed of the juice of water parsnip, aconite, cinquefoil, deadly night-shade, and soot?"

"But whatever for? What have all those beastly things got to do with it?"

"A great deal. That is one of the formulas for the famous ointment—you've heard of it right enough—with which Satanists bedaubed themselves before going off to the Sabbath.[1] It lacks one of the original ingredients: the flesh of a child: but I suppose there are limits even to a murderer's efforts at realism."

"Brian!"

For it seemed to him that the picture which was emerging from these sly and tangled events was less that of a Satanist than that of a murderer.

"Oh, yes, it's true. I know something about that sub-ject, and I can't imagine why I didn't remember it from the first. Now, I want you to think of the obvious deduc-tions we can draw from that fact, the deductions Dr Fell and the inspector made long ago. I don't mean about Victoria's indulgence, or pretended indulgence, in Satanist practices. That's clear enough without any deduction."

"Why?"

"Follow it out. She uses this ointment on Lammas Eve, the night of one of the great Satanist meetings. She is murdered at eleven forty-five, and the Sabbath begins at Midnight. It's clear that she had applied this ointment

[1] For a medical analysis of these ointments, see Margaret Alice Murray, *The Witch-Cult in Western Europe* (Oxford University Press, 1921), Appendix V, 279-80; and J. W. Wickwar, *Witchcraft and the Black Art* (Herbert Jenkins, 1925), 36-40. See also Montague Summers, *History of Witchcraft and Demonology* (Kegan Paul, 1926).

166

some minutes before the murderer caught her. She is murdered in her ground-floor bedroom, the window of which is set wide open: traditionally the way in which Satanists left, or thought they left, for their gatherings."

Though he was not looking directly at her, he thought that a slight frown had gathered on Madeline's forehead.

"I think I see what you're getting at, Brian. You say ' thought they left ' because— "

"I'm coming to that. But, first, what deductions can we make about her murderer? Most important, this: Whether or not the tramp killed Victoria Daly, *there was a third person in that house at the time of the murder or just afterwards.*"

Madeline sprang to her feet. He was not looking at her, yet he felt that her large blue eyes were fixed on his face.

"How so, Brian? I still don't follow that."

"Because of the nature of the ointment. Do you realise what a substance like that would do? "

"Yes, I think I see that. But tell me."

"For six hundred years," he went on, "there's been a vast mass of testimony from those who claim to have gone to Witches' Sabbaths and seen the presence of Satan. What impresses you as you read it is the absolute sincerity, the careful detail, with which people have described things that couldn't possibly be true. We can't deny, as a matter of history, that the Satanist cult really existed and was a powerful force from the Middle Ages to the seventeenth century. It had an organisation as carefully arranged and managed as the Church itself. But what about these miraculous journeys in the air, these wonders and ghosts, these demons and familiars, these incubi and succubi? They can't be accepted as facts (not by my practical mind, anyhow); and yet they are firmly presented as facts by a great number of people who weren't demented and weren't hysterical and weren't tortured.—Well, what would make a person believe them to be facts? "

Madeline said quietly: "Aconite and belladonna, or deadly nightshade."

They looked at each other.

"I believe that's the explanation," he told her, still

with his attention on the window. "It's been argued, and I think reasonably, that in a great number of cases the 'witch' never left her own house or even her own room. She thought she had attended the Sabbath in the grove. She thought she had been conveyed by magic to the defiled altar and found a demon lover there. She thought so because the two chief ingredients of the ointment were aconite and belladonna. Do you know anything about the effects of poisons like that, rubbed into the skin externally?"

"My father had a *Medical Jurisprudence* here," said Madeline. "I was wondering—"

"Belladonna, absorbed through the pores of the skin— and under the quicks of the nails—would rapidly produce excitement, then violent hallucinations and delirium, and finally unconsciousness. Add to this the symptoms produced by aconite: mental confusion, dizziness, impaired movement, irregular heart-action, and an end in unconsciousness. A mind steeped in descriptions of Satanist revels (there was a book dealing with them on the table by Victoria Daly's bed) would do the rest. Yes, that's it. I think we know now how she 'attended the Sabbath' on Lammas Eve."

Madeline walked her fingers along the edge of the table. She studied them. Then she nodded.

"Ye-es. But even suppose that were true, Brian? How does it prove there was anybody else in the house the night she died? Anybody, I mean, aside from Victoria and the vagabond who killed her?"

"Do you remember how she was dressed when the body was found?"

"Of course. Night-gown, dressing-gown, and slippers."

"Yes—when the body was found. That's the point. A careful new night-gown, to say nothing of the extra flourishing of a dressing-gown, over that sticky, oily soot-coloured ointment? Acute discomfort and unusual marks afterwards? A dressing-gown for the Sabbath? The costume for the Sabbath consisted of the merest rags, which would not impede movement or get in the way of the ointment, when it consisted of any costume at all.

"Don't you see what happened? The woman was

falling from delirium into unconsciousness in a dark house. A poor devil of a derelict, seeing a dark house and an open window, thought he had found an easy crib to crack. What he met was a woman roused and screaming in delirium: and it must have been rather an unnerving apparition which rose up at him from the bed on the floor. He lost his head and killed her.

"Anyone suffering delirium from that ointment couldn't have and wouldn't have put on the night-dress, dressing-gown, and slippers. The murderer wouldn't have put them on her. He was interrupted and chased before he had finished his work.

"But there was somebody else in the dark house. Victoria Daly was lying there dead with the ointment on her body and in a queer kind of costume which would cause a furious scandal when her body was found. Some wiseacre might even guess what had happened. To avert discovery, this third person crept into the bedroom before the body had been seen by anybody. (Remember? The two men who heard the screams saw the murderer escaping from the window, and gave chase; they didn't return until some time afterwards.) This third person then removed whatever 'witch's' clothes Victoria wore, and decorously dressed the body in night-gown, dressing-gown, and slippers. That's it. That's got it. That's what really happened."

His heart was thumping. The mental images, hidden for so long, were of such clarity that he knew he was right. He nodded towards Madeline.

"You know that's true, don't you?"

"Brian! How could I know it?"

"No, no, you don't understand. I mean you're as certain as I am, aren't you? That's the assumption on which Elliot has been working all this time."

She took a long time before she replied.

"Yes," she admitted, "I'd thought that. At least, I'd thought so until to-night, when those hints Dr Fell gave didn't seem in the least to square with my ideas—and I told him so. Besides, it doesn't even seem to fit in with what they think either. You remember, he said yesterday there was no witch cult hereabouts?"

"And so there isn't."

" But you've just explained— "

" I've explained what one person did. One person, and only one. Remember, Dr Fell told us that yesterday. ' Everything from mental cruelty to murder, is the work of one person.' And, ' I tell you frankly, Satanism itself is an honest and straightforward business compared to the intellectual pleasures a certain person has invented.' Put all these words together; put them into a pattern. Mental cruelty, plus intellectual pleasures, plus the death of Victoria Daly, plus a vague and undefined rumour of witchcraft among—what did Elliot tell me?—the gentry of the neighbourhood.

" I wonder what prompted this person to take it up? Pure boredom? Boredom with life, utter and simple, coming from an inability to take an interest in ordinary things? Or a tendency inherited from childhood, under the surface, but always growing up and feeding on secret things? "

" To take what up? " cried Madeline. " That's what I'm trying to get at. To take what up? "

Behind her a hand rapped on the glass of the window, with a malevolent tearing sound like a scratch.

Madeline screamed. That knock or blow had almost closed the partly open window, which rattled with a small noise against the frame. Page hesitated. The jingle of the dance-orchestra still filled the room. Then he went to the window and pushed it open.

CHAPTER XVIII

D R FELL and Inspector Elliot did not catch the train. They did not catch it because, when they arrived at Farnleigh Close, they were told that Betty Harbottle was awake and could speak to them.

They did not talk much on their way through the orchard and up through the wood. What they said, too, might have seemed cryptic to a listener. But it had a very deadly bearing on events which were to take place only an hour or two later, when one of the most cunning murderers in Dr Fell's experience was (perhaps prematurely) snared into the open.

It was close and dark in the wood. Leaves made a heavy pattern against the starlight; Elliot's flashlight threw a beam ahead on a path of bare earth, making the green spectral. From the gloom behind it sounded two voices, the harsh tenor of the inspector and the wheezing bass of Dr Fell.

" Still, sir, are we any nearer to proving it? "

" I think so. I hope so. If I've read one person's character correctly, he'll give us all the proof we need."

" And if your explanation works."

" H'mf, yes. If it works. Of sticks and stones and rags and bones I made it; but it ought to serve."

" Do you think there's any danger," Elliot seemed to jerk his head over his shoulder in the direction of Madeline's house, " back there? "

There was a pause before Dr Fell answered, while their footsteps swished among ferns.

" Dammit, I wish I knew! Hardly think so, though. Consider the character of the murderer. A sly, cracked head—like the dummy's; under that pleasant exterior— just as the dummy used to have. But emphatically not a fabled monster, intent on strewing the place with corpses. Not a monster at all. A moderate murderer, my lad. When I think of the number of persons who, by all the laws of progressive homicide, SHOULD have been murdered in this case, I have a tendency towards gooseflesh.

" We've known cases in which the murderer, after taking careful pains about his original crime, then goes berserk and begins to eliminate people all over the place. It seems to be like getting olives out of a bottle: you have infinite trouble with the first one, and the rest roll out all over the table. Without, indeed, anybody seeming to pay much attention to them. This murderer is human, my lad. I'm not, you understand, praising the murderer for this sporting restraint and good manners in refraining from killing people. But my God, Elliot, the people who have gone in danger from the first! Betty Harbottle might have been killed. A certain lady we know of might have been killed. For a certain man's safety I've had apprehensions from the start. And not one of 'em has been touched. Is it vanity? Or what?"

In silence they came out of the wood and down the hill. Only a few lights burned at Farnleigh Close. They went through the part of the garden on the opposite side from the place where the murder had been committed, and round to the front door. A subdued Knowles admitted them.

"Lady Farnleigh has retired, sir," he said. "But Dr King asks me to say that he wishes you gentlemen would join him upstairs, if you will."

"Is Betty Harbottle—?" Elliot stopped.

"Yes, sir. I think so."

Elliot whistled through his teeth as they went upstairs and into the dimly lighted passage between the Green Room and the bedroom where the girl lay. Dr King held them off a moment before they entered.

"Now, look here," King said in his abrupt fashion. "Five minutes, ten minutes maybe: no more. I want to warn you. You'll find her as quiet and easy-spoken as though she were talking about a bus-ride. But don't let that deceive you. It's a part of the reaction, and she's got a dose of morphia in her. You'll also find her quick with her eyes and tolerably intelligent—curiosity was always Betty's chief feature—so don't start her going with too many suggestions and general fol-de-rol. Is that understood? Right, then. In you go."

Mrs Apps, the housekeeper, slipped out as they entered. It was a large room in which every globe was illuminated in the old-fashioned chandelier. Not an impressive room: large old-fashioned photographs of Farnleighs were framed on the walls, and the dressing-table held a menagerie of china animals. The bed was black, square, and uncompromising. From it Betty regarded them with vague interest.

She had one of those faces called 'bright', with very straight bobbed hair. Her pallor, and the slightly sunken look of the eyes, were the only signs of illness. She seemed pleased to see them rather than otherwise; and the only thing or person that seemed to make her uncomfortable was Dr King. Her hands slowly smoothed the counterpane.

Dr Fell beamed on her. His vast presence made the whole room comfortable.

" Hullo," he said.

" Hullo, sir," said Betty with an effort at brightness.

" Do you know who we are, my dear? And why we're here? "

" Oh, yes. You want me to tell you what happened to me."

" And can you? "

" I don't mind," she conceded.

She fixed her eyes on the foot of the bed. Dr King took out his watch and put it on the dressing-table.

" Well—I don't know how to tell you, hardly. I went upstairs there to get an apple— " Betty abruptly seemed to change her mind. She shifted in bed. " No, I didn't! " she added.

" You didn't? "

" I didn't go up to get an apple. When I get well my sister's taking me away from here (I'm going to have a holiday at Hastings, too), so that's why I'll tell you. I *didn't* go up there to get an apple. I went up often to see if I could get a peep at what's in the cupboard there, the locked cupboard."

Her tone was not in the least defiant: she was too listless to be defiant: she was merely speaking out truth as though she were under the influence less of morphia than of scopolamine.

Dr Fell looked heavily puzzled. " But why should you be interested in the locked cupboard? "

" Oh, everybody knows about it, sir. Somebody'd been using it."

" Using it? "

" Sitting up there with a light. There's a little window in the roof, like a skylight. At night, if you're a little way off from the house, and there's a light inside, you can see it against the roof. Everybody knows about it, though we're not supposed to. Even Miss Dane knows about it. I was over at Miss Dane's house one evening, taking her a parcel from Sir John, and I was going back through the Chart. Miss Dane asked me whether I wasn't afraid to go through the Chart after dark. I said, Oh, no; perhaps I should see the light in the roof, and that would be worth it. I only said it as a joke, because the light was always on the south side, and the path through the Chart takes you to the north side. Miss Dane laughed and put her arm round my shoulder and asked whether I was the only one who had seen it. I said, Oh, no, everybody had; because we had. Besides, we were all interested about that machine like a gramophone, that dummy— "

The look in her eyes altered slightly.

There was a pause.

" But who was 'using' the room? "

"Well, mostly they said it was Sir John. Agnes saw him come down from the attic one afternoon, with his face all perspiring and something like a dog-whip in his hand. I said, So would you be perspiring, too, if you sat in a little bit of a place like that with the door shut. But Agnes said he didn't look quite like that."

"Anyway, my dear, will you tell us what happened yesterday? Hey? "

Dr King interposed sharply. "Two minutes, my lads."

Betty looked surprised.

"I don't mind," she responded. "I went up there to get an apple. But this time, when I went past the door of the little room, I saw the padlock wasn't fastened. The padlock was open, hanging on the staple. The door was closed, but with something stuck in between the door and the frame to hold it shut."

"What did you do? "

"I went and got an apple. After that I came back and looked at the door and started to eat the apple. Then I went to the apple-room again, and finally I came back and thought I would see what was inside after all. But I didn't want to, as much as usually."

"Why not? "

"Because there was a noise in there, or I thought so. A rattly kind of noise, like winding a grandfather clock; but not very loud."

"Do you remember what time this was, Betty? "

"No, sir. Not properly. It was past one o'clock, maybe a quarter past or more than that."

"What did you do then? "

"I went over ever so quickly, before I should decide

not to do it, and opened the door. The thing that was keeping it shut was a glove. Stuck into the door, you know, sir."

"A man's glove or a woman's glove?"

"A man's, I think. It had oil on it; or it smelt like oil. It dropped on the floor. I went inside. I could see the old machine-thing there, a bit sideways to me, like. I didn't want one more look at it: not that you could see very well in there. But I no sooner stepped inside than the door closed ever so softly; and somebody put up the chain across the door and I heard the padlock close together outside; so I was locked in, you see."

"Steady!" said the physician sharply. He took up his watch from the dressing-table.

Betty was twisting the fringe of the counterpane. Dr Fell and the inspector looked at each other; Dr Fell's red face was heavy and grave.

"But—are you still all right, Betty?—who was in there? Who was in the little room?"

"Nobody. Nobody except the old machine-thing. Nobody at all."

"You're sure of that?"

"Oh, yes."

"What did you do?"

"I didn't do anything. I was afraid to call out and ask to be let out. I was afraid I should get the sack. It wasn't quite dark. I stood there and didn't do anything for, oh, maybe it was a quarter of an hour. And nobody else did anything either: I mean the machine-thing didn't. Presently I started to move away from it, and got back as far as I could, because it started to put its arms around me."

If, at that moment, so much as the ash of a cigar had fallen into an ash-tray, Dr Fell swears it would have been heard. Elliot heard the breath drawn through his own nostrils. Elliot said:

"It moved, Betty? The machine moved?"

"Yes, sir. It moved its arms. They didn't move fast, and neither did the body, the way it sort of ducked forward towards me; and it made a noise when it moved. But that wasn't what I minded so much. I didn't seem to feel anything, because I had been standing in there with it for a quarter of an hour already. What I minded was the eyes it had. It didn't have eyes in the proper place. It had eyes in the skirt, right by the knees of the old dummy thing; and they looked up at me. I could see them move round. I don't mind even them so much. I expect I shall get used to them. At that time I don't remember anything more about it; I must have fainted or something; but it's outside the door now," continued Betty, with absolutely no change of expression or tone while she nodded at the door.

"I should like to go to sleep," she added in a plaintive tone.

Dr King swore under his breath.

"That's done it," he said. "Out you go, now. No, she'll be all right; but—out you go."

"Yes," agreed Elliot, looking at Betty's closed eyes, "I think we had better."

They went out with guilty quietness, and King made a pantomime of slamming the door after them. "I hope," he muttered, "hearing common delirium helps you." Still without speaking, Dr Fell and the inspector went across to the dark Green Room. It was furnished as a study in heavy antique style; and the windows were rectangles of starlight. They went across and stood by one window.

"That settles it, sir? Even aside from the—er—answer to the inquiries—?"

"Yes. That settles it."

"Then we'd better get on to town, and—"

"No," said Dr Fell after a long pause, "I don't think it'll be necessary. I think we'd better try the experiment now, while the metal is hot. Look there!"

The garden below showed in clear etching-lines against the dark. They saw the maze of hedges veined with whitish paths, the clear space round the pool, and the white smears of the water-lilies. But they were not looking at this. Someone, carrying an object recognisable even in that light, slipped past under the library windows and round the south corner of the house.

Dr Fell expelled his breath. Lumbering across the room to the central light fixture, he turned on the lamp and swung round with a vast billow of his cape.

"Psychologically, as we've come to say," he told Elliot with sardonic dryness, "to-night is the night. Now's the time, man. Now, or we may lose the whole advantage. Get 'em together, I tell you! I should like to do a little explaining as to how a man can be murdered when alone in a circle of sand; and then we can pray Old Nick will come and get his own. Hey?"

A small cough interrupted them as Knowles came into the room.

"I beg your pardon, sir," he said to Dr Fell. "Mr Murray is here, and asking to see you gentlemen. He says he's been looking for you for some time."

"Has he, now?" inquired Dr Fell, with ferocious affability. The doctor beamed and shook his cape. "Did he say what he wanted?"

Knowles hesitated. "No, sir. That is—" Knowles hesitated again. "He says he's disturbed about something, sir. He also wishes to see Mr Burrows. And, as regards that—"

"Speak up, man! What's on your mind?"

"Well, sir, may I ask whether Miss Dane received the automaton?"

Inspector Elliot whirled round from the window.

"Whether Miss Dane received the automaton? What automaton? What about it?"

"You know the one, sir," returned Knowles, with a guilty expression which (less smoothly done) might have been a leer. "Miss Dane rang up this afternoon, and asked whether she might have the automaton sent over to her home this evening. We—er—we thought it was an odd request; but Miss Dane said a gentleman was coming there, an expert on such things, and she wished him to have a good look at it."

"So," observed Dr Fell without inflection. "She wished him to have a good look at it."

"Yes, sir. Macneile (that's the gardener) mended the wheel, and I had it sent over in a cart. Macneile and Parsons said there was nobody at home at Miss Dane's at the time, so they put it into the coal-house. Then—er—Mr Burrows arrived here, and expressed annoyance that it had gone. He also knows of a gentleman who is an expert on such things."

"How popular the hag is becoming in her old age," rumbled Dr Fell, with a wheeze of what might or might not have been pleasure. "How excellent to eke out her days among throngs of admirers. By thunder, how excellent! A perfect woman, nobly planned, to warn, to comfort, and command. Cold eyelids that hide like a jewel hard eyes that grow soft for an hour—waugh!" He stopped. "And is Mr Murray also interested in the automaton?"

"No, sir. Not that I know of."

"A pity. Well, shoot him into the library. He is remarkably at home there. One of us will be down in a moment. And what," he added to Elliot, when Knowles had gone, "do you make of this little move?"

Elliot rubbed his chin. "I don't know. But it doesn't seem to fit in with what we saw. In any case, it mightn't be a bad idea for me to get back to Monplaisir as fast as I can."

"I agree. Profoundly."

"Burton ought to be here with the car. If he is, I can make it by the road in three minutes. If he isn't—"

He wasn't. What adjustment had gone wrong with the scales or the night Elliot did not know. Nor could he get a car from the garage at the Close, whose doors were (revealingly) locked. Elliot set off for Monplaisir by the path through the wood. The last thing he saw before he left the house was Dr Fell descending the main staircase, lowering himself step by step on his crutch-handled stick; and on Dr Fell's face was an expression that is very seldom seen there.

Inspector Elliot told himself that he had no reason to hurry. But, as he mounted the hill through the Hanging Chart, he found himself walking fast. Nor did he particularly like his surroundings. He knew that they were the victims, no longer gullible, of a series of ingenious hoaxes no more to be feared than the black Janus-face in the attic. The hoax at best was unpleasant and at worst was murderous; but it was no more than a hoax.

And yet, even as he increased his step, he kept the beam of his electric torch playing from side to side. Something stirred in him that was rooted in his blood and race. Out of his boyhood he sought a word to describe

the present doings, and found it. The word was
'heathenish'.

He did not expect anything to happen. He knew that
he would not be needed.

It was not until he was almost out of the wood that he
heard a shot fired.

CHAPTER XIX

BRIAN PAGE stood in the open French window and
looked out into the garden. After that knock he had
been prepared, in the usual fashion, for anything except
nothing. And there was nothing—or so it seemed.

The automaton had gone. The quiet light, almost
draining the grass of its colour, barely showed the wheel-
marks where iron had rested. But the presence or
absence of that dead metal meant nothing; someone or
something had rapped on the window. He took one step
across the sill.

"Brian," said Madeline quietly, "where are you
going?"

"Just to see who called on us, or started to call on us."

"Brian, don't go out there. Please." She came
closer, and her voice was full of urgency. "I've never
asked you to do anything for me before, have I? Well,
I ask you to do something now. Don't go out there. If
you do I'll—well, I don't know what I will do, exactly,
except that it will be something you won't like. Please!
Come in and close the window, won't you? You see, I
know."

"Know?"

She nodded towards the garden. "What was sitting
out there a moment ago, and isn't there now. I saw it
from the back door when I was in the kitchen. I didn't
want to worry you in case you hadn't seen it, though I—I
was pretty sure you had." She slid her hands up the
lapels of his coat. "Don't go out there. Don't go after
it. That's what it wants you to do."

He looked down at her, at the pleading eyes and the

179

curve of the short throat upturned. In spite of what he was thinking and feeling just then, he spoke with a kind of impassionate detachment.

He said:

" Of all the extraordinary places to say what I am going to say, this is the most extraordinary. Of all the inappropriate times to say what I am going to say, this is the most inappropriate. I maintain this because I have got to use superlatives somehow in getting my feelings off my chest, and what I mean is that I love you."

" Then there's some good in Lammas Eve," said Madeline, and lifted her mouth.

It is a problem how far, in accounts of violence, there may be expressed the things he thought and said then. Yet, without a violence that moved round the edges of a lighted window, it is possible that he would never have learned or heard the things he learned and heard then. He was not concerned with this. He was concerned with other matters: the paradox of how remote and mysterious a loved face looks by very reason of being closer: the strange chemistry of kissing Madeline, which altered his life and in whose actuality he could not even yet believe. He wanted to utter a mighty shout of pure joy; and, after many minutes at that window, he did.

" Oh, God, Brian, why didn't you ever tell me so before? " said Madeline, who was half laughing and half crying. " I mustn't swear! My moral character is falling deplorably. But why didn't you ever tell me so before? "

" Because I didn't see how you could possibly be interested in me. I didn't want you to laugh."

" Did you think I would laugh? "

" Frankly—yes."

She held to his shoulders and studied him with her face upturned. Her eyes were shining curiously.

" Brian, you do love me, don't you? "

" For some minutes I have been trying to make that clear. But I haven't got the slightest objection to beginning all over again. If— "

" A spinster like me— "

" Madeline," he said, " whatever else you do, don't use that word ' spinster '. It is one of the ugliest-sounding words in the language. It suggests something between 'spindle' and 'vinegar'. To describe you properly, it is necessary to—"

Again he noticed the curious shining in her eyes.

"Brian, if you really do love me (you do?) then I may show you something, mayn't I?"

Out in the garden there was a noise of a footstep in the grass. Her tone had been odd, so odd as to make him wonder; but there was no time to reflect on this. At that swishing of the footstep they stood apart quickly. Among the laurels a figure was taking shape and coming closer. It was a lean, narrow-shouldered figure, with a walk between a brisk stride and a shamble; after which Page saw, with relief, that it was only Nathaniel Burrows.

Burrows did not seem to know whether to keep his halibut-faced expression or to smile. Between the two he appeared to struggle: producing something of an amiable contortion. His large shell-rimmed spectacles were grave. His long face, which had a very genuine charm when he chose to exercise it, now showed only a part of that charm. His very correct bowler hat was set at a somewhat rakish angle.

"Tsk! Tsk!" was his only comment, with a smile. "I've come," he added pleasantly, "for the automaton."

"The—?" Madeline blinked at him. "The automaton?"

"You should not stand in windows," said Burrows severely. "It upsets your mental equilibrium when you have visitors afterwards. You shouldn't stand in windows either," he added, looking at Page. "The dummy, Madeline. The dummy you borrowed from Farnleigh Close this afternoon."

Page turned to look at her. She was staring at Burrows, her colour heightening.

"Nat, what on earth are you talking about? The dummy *I* borrowed? I never did any such thing."

"My dear Madeline," returned Burrows, putting his gloved hands wide apart and bringing them together again, "I've not yet properly thanked you for all the good work you have done for me—at the inquest. But hang it!"—here he looked at her sideways past his spectacles—" you rang up and asked for that dummy this afternoon. Macneile and Parsons brought it over. It's in the coal-house now."

"You must be absolutely mad," said Madeline, in a high and wondering voice.

Burrows, as usual, was reasonable. "Well, it's there. That's the supreme answer. I couldn't make anyone hear at the front of the house. I came round here, and I—er —still couldn't make anyone hear. My car's out in the main road. I drove over to get the automaton. Why you should want it I can't imagine; but would you mind very much if I took it along? I can't quite see, as yet, how it fits into the picture. However, after my expert has a look at it, it may give me an idea."

The coal-house was built into the wall a little to the left of the kitchen. Page went over and opened the door. The automaton was there. He could make out its outlines faintly.

"You see?" said Burrows.

"Brian," said Madeline rather frantically, "will you believe I never did anything of the kind? I never asked for the thing to be sent here, or thought of it, or anything of the sort. Why on earth should I?"

"Of course I know you didn't," Page told her. "Somebody seems to have gone completely mad."

"Why not go inside?" suggested Burrows. "I should like to have a little talk with both of you about this. Just wait a moment until I put on the side-lights of my car."

The other two went inside, where they looked at each other. The music from the radio had stopped; somebody was talking instead, about a subject Page does not remember, and Madeline shut off the set. Madeline seemed to be in the grip of a reaction.

"This isn't real," she said. "It's all illusion. We're dreaming it. At least—all but a part of it, I hope." And she smiled at him. "Have you any idea what's happening?"

As for what happened in the few seconds after that, Page is still confused in his mind. He remembers that he had taken her hand, and opened his mouth to assure her that he did not particularly give a curse what had happened, provided those minutes by the window were not illusion. They both heard the detonation from the direction of the garden or the orchard behind. It had a flat and bursting noise. It was loud enough to make them jump. Yet it seemed to have no connection with them, to be remote from them, in spite of the fact that a wiry sound sang close to their ears—and one of the clocks stopped.

One of the clocks stopped. Page's ears took note of that at the same time his eyes noted the small round hole, starred with a faint web of cracks, in the glass of the window. It then became clear that the clock had stopped because there was a bullet buried in it.

The other clock ticked on.

"Get back from the window," Page said. "This can't be: I don't believe it: but there's somebody firing at us from the garden. Where the devil has Nat got to?"

He went over and switched out the lights. The candles remained; and he blew them out just as a sweating Burrows, his hat crushed down on his head, ducked low through the window as though for safety.

"There's somebody— " Burrows began in a strange voice.

"Yes. We had noticed that."

Page moved Madeline across the room. He was calculating, by the position of the bullet in the clock, that two inches to the left would have sent it through Madeline's head, just above the small curls there.

No other shot was fired. He heard Madeline's frightened breathing, and the slow, sharp breathing of Burrows from across the room. Burrows stood inside the last of the windows: only his polished shoe was visible as he braced himself there.

"Do you know what I think happened?" Burrows asked.

"Well?"

"Do you want me to show you what I think happened?"

"Go on."

"Wait," whispered Madeline. "Whoever it is— listen!"

Burrows, startled, poked his head out like a turtle's past the line of the window. Page heard the hail from the garden and answered it. It was Elliot's voice. He hurried out and met the inspector, whose run through the grass from the orchard was easy to follow. Elliot's face was inscrutable in the gloom as he listened to Page's story; also, his manner was at its most heavily official.

"Yes, sir," he said. "But I think you can put on those lights now. I don't think you will be troubled again."

"Inspector, are *you* going to do nothing?" demanded Burrows in a wiry voice of remonstrance. "Or are you accustomed to this sort of thing in London? I assure you we're not." He mopped his forehead with the back of a gloved hand. "Aren't you going to search the garden? Or the orchard? Or wherever the shot was fired from?"

"I said, sir," repeated Elliot woodenly, "that I don't think you will be troubled again."

"But who did it? What was the point of it?"

"The point is, sir," said Elliot, "that this nonsense is going to stop. For good. We've had a bit of a change in plans. I think, if you don't mind, I'd like to have you all come back to the Close with me—just in case, you understand. I'm afraid I've got to make the request something like an order."

"Oh, nobody's got any objection," said Page cheerfully; "though it would almost seem that we'd had enough excitement for one evening."

The inspector smiled in a way that was not reassuring.

"I think you're wrong," he said. "You haven't seen anything like excitement to-night. But you will, Mr Page. I promise you you will. Has anybody got a car?"

That uneasy suggestion remained with them while Burrows drove them all to Farnleigh Close. All efforts to question the inspector were useless. To Burrows's insistence that the automaton should be removed with them, Elliot only answered that there was not time and that it was not necessary.

A worried-looking Knowles admitted them to the Close. The centre of tension was in the library. There, as two nights ago, the gaping crown of electric-bulbs from the ceiling was reflected in a wall of windows. In the chair formerly occupied by Murray sat Dr Fell, with Murray across from him. Dr Fell's hand was supported on his stick, and his lower lip outthrust above the chins. The echo of emotion came to them as soon as the library door was opened. For Dr Fell had just finished talking, and Murray shaded his eyes with an unsteady hand.

"Ah," said the doctor with dubious affability. "Good evening, good evening, good evening! Miss Dane. Mr Burrows. Mr Page. Good. I'm afraid we have commandeered the house in a reprehensible way; but something has made it necessary. It is very necessary to have a gathering for a little conference. Couriers have been despatched for Mr Welkyn and Mr Gore. Knowles: will you ask Lady Farnleigh to join us? No: don't go yourself; send a maid; I should prefer that you remain here. In the meantime, certain matters can be discussed."

The tone of his voice was such that Nathaniel Burrows hesitated before sitting down. Burrows raised a hand sharply. He did not look at Murray.

"We cannot go as fast as that," Burrows returned. "Stop! Is there anything in this discussion that is likely to be of a—er—a controversial nature? "

"There is."

Again Burrows hesitated. He had not glanced in Murray's direction; but Page, studying them, felt a twinge of pity for Murray without knowing why. The tutor looked worn and old.

"Oh. And what are we going to discuss, doctor? "

"The character of a certain person," said Dr Fell. "You will guess who it is."

"Yes," agreed Page, hardly conscious that he had spoken aloud. "The person who initiated Victoria Daly into the pleasantries of witchcraft."

It was remarkable, he thought, the effect that name had. You had only to introduce the words 'Victoria Daly', like a talisman, and everybody shied away from it; the prospect seemed to open into new vistas which were not liked. Dr Fell, vaguely surprised but interested, turned round and blinked at him.

"Ah! " said the doctor, wheezing with approval. "So you guessed that."

"I tried to work it out. Is that person the murderer? "

"That person is the murderer." Dr Fell pointed his stick. "It will help us, you know, if the view is also shared by you. Let's hear what you think. And speak out, my lad. There will be worse things said in this room before any of us leaves it."

With some care, and a vividness of image which he hardly sought to use, Page repeated the story he had already told to Madeline. Dr Fell's sharp little eyes never left his face, nor did Inspector Elliot miss a word. The body smeared with ointment, the dark house with the open window, the panic-mad vagabond, the third person waiting: these images seemed to be enacted in the library like pictures on a screen.

At the end of it Madeline spoke. "Is this true? Is it what you and the inspector think?"

Dr Fell merely nodded.

"Then I ask you what I was trying to ask Brian. If there is no witch-cult—as he says—if the whole affair was a dream, what was this 'third person' doing or trying to do? What about the *evidences* of witchcraft?"

"Ah, the evidences," said Dr Fell.

After a pause he went on:

"I will try to explain. You have among you somebody whose mind and heart have been steeped for years in a secret love of these things and what they stand for. Not a belief in them! That I hasten to point out. That I emphasise. Nobody could be more cynical as regards the powers of darkness and the lords of the four-went-ways. But a surpassing love of them, made all the more powerful and urgent by an (altogether prudish) necessity for never letting it show. This person, you understand, figures before you in a very different character. This person will never admit before you to even an interest in such matters, an interest such as you and I might have. So that secret interest—the desire to share it—the desire, above all, to experiment on other people—grew so strong that it had to burst its bonds somehow.

"Now what was this person's position? What could this person do? Found a new witch-cult in Kent, such as existed here in previous centuries? It must have been a fascinating idea; but this person knew that it was as wild as wind. This person is, essentially, very practical.

"The smallest group in the organisation for the worship of Satan was (may I say?) the coven. The coven consisted of thirteen persons, twelve members and a masked leader. To be the Janus-masked leader of such a cotillion must have appealed to our person as a fine dream; but no more than a dream. It was not only that the practical difficulties were too great to be overcome. It was also that for the thing to be interesting—to be shared with a few others—the number of persons concerned must be very small. As the interest was secret, so it must be narrow and personal and individual.

"This, I emphasise, was no measured affiliation with the powers of evil, supposing any such powers to exist. It had no such high ambition; or, to put it more properly, no such high-falutin. It was not carefully planned. It was not managed by a person of any great intelligence. It was not a cult as we know cults seriously developed. It was simply an idle and greedy liking for such things, a kind of hobby. Lord love you, I don't suppose any great harm would have been done—if the person had kept away from poisonous drugs to produce hallucinations. If people choose merely to act the fool, if they don't violate any laws or even any conventions, then it's no concern of the police. But, when a woman just outside Tunbridge Wells dies from the application of belladonna to the skin (which is exactly what happened, eighteen months ago, though we've never been able to prove it), then, by thunder, it *is* a concern of the police! Why do you think Elliot was sent here to begin with? Why do you think he's been so much concerned with the story of Victoria Daly? Hey?

"Do you begin to see what somebody has been doing?

"This person chose a few suitable and sympathetic friends to confide in. There were not many: two or three or four, perhaps. We shall probably never know who they are. This person had many talks with them. Many books were given or loaned. Then, when the friend's mind was sufficiently stuffed and excited with wild lore, it was time. It was time to inform the friend that there really was a Satanist cult hereabouts, to which the candidate could now be admitted."

There was a sharp noise as Dr Fell struck the ferrule of his stick on the floor. He was impatient and he was annoyed.

"Of course there never was any such thing. Of course the neophyte never left the house or stirred from one room on the night of the gatherings. Of course it was all a matter of an ointment whose two chief ingredients were aconite and belladonna.

"And of course, as a rule, the person who instigated this never went near the friend, much less joined any gathering, on the night of an alleged 'meeting'. That might have been too dangerous, if the poisonous effects of the ointment were too great. The pleasure lay in spreading this gospel: in sharing accounts of (mythical) adventures: in watching the decay of minds under the effects of the drug and under the effects of what they thought they had seen at the Sabbaths: in short, of combining a degree of rather heavy-witted mental cruelty with the pleasure of letting loose this interest in a safe and narrow circle."

Dr Fell paused. And in the silence that followed Kennet Murray spoke thoughtfully.

"It reminds me," he said, "of the mentality which writes poison-pen letters."

"You've got it," said Dr Fell, nodding. "'It is almost exactly the same, turned to different and more harmful outlets."

"But if you can't prove the other woman died of poison—the one near Tunbridge Wells, whom I hadn't heard of—where are you? Has the 'person' done anything which is concretely illegal? Victoria Daly didn't die of poison."

"That depends, sir," observed Inspector Elliot suavely. "You seem to think that poisons aren't poisons unless they are taken internally. I can tell you different. But that's not the point now. Dr Fell was only telling you the secret."

"The secret?"

"This person's secret," said Dr Fell. "In order to preserve that secret, a man was murdered beside the pool in the garden two nights ago."

There was another silence, this time of an eerie quality as though everyone had drawn back a little.

Nathaniel Burrows put one finger inside his collar.

"This is interesting," he said. "Very interesting. But at the same time I feel I've been brought here under false pretences. I'm a solicitor, not a student of heathen religions. I don't see that the heathen religions have anything to do with the only thing that matters to me. In the story you outline, there is no connection whatever with the proper succession to the Farnleigh estates—"

"Oh, yes, there is," said Dr Fell.

He went on:

"It is, in fact, at the root of the whole matter, as I hope to make you understand in about two seconds.

"But you—" he looked argumentatively at Page—"you, my friend, asked a little while ago what caused this person to take up such practices. Was it sheer boredom? Was it a kink inherited from childhood, never lost, and increasing from year to year? I'm inclined to suspect that it was a little of both. In this case all things grow up together, like the poison *Atropa belladonna* plant in the hedgerow. They are entwined and inseparable.

"Who might be a person with these instincts, always obliged to repress them? Who is there in whom we can trace the kink, with all the evidence before us? Who can be shown to be the one person, and the only one, with direct access to the toys of both witchcraft and murder? Who did undoubtedly suffer from the boredom of a loveless and miserable marriage, and at the same time suffered from the super-abundant vitality which—"

Burrows sprang to his feet with a ringing oath of enlightenment.

And at the same time, in the open door of the library, there was a whispered conference between Knowles and someone outside.

Knowles's face was white when he spoke.

"Excuse me, sir, but they—they tell me her ladyship is not in her room. They say she packed a bag some time ago, and took a car from the garage, and—"

Dr Fell nodded.

"Exactly," he said. "That's why we don't have to hurry to London. Her flight has blown the gaff. And we shall have no difficulty now in obtaining a warrant for the arrest of Lady Farnleigh on a charge of murder."

CHAPTER XX

"OH, come!" said Dr Fell, rapping his stick on the floor and peering round the group with an air of benevolent expostulation. He was both amused and exasperated. "Don't tell me it surprises you. Don't tell me it shocks you. You, Miss Dane! Didn't you know about her all along? Didn't you know how she hated you?"

Madeline passed the back of her hand across her forehead. Then she reached out and took Page's arm.

"I didn't know about her," Madeline said. "I guessed. But I could hardly tell you that outright, could I? I'm afraid you've thought me enough of a cat as it is."

For Page some readjustment of thought was necessary. So, it appeared, was it necessary for the others. Yet a new notion caught and held in Page's brain even as he tried to assimilate the first. The thought was:

This case is not finished.

Whether it was a slight expression flickering in Dr Fell's eyes, a turn of his hand on the stick, a slight quiver even in that mountain, he could not tell. But the impression was there, and Dr Fell still held the room as though he had not ended with revelation. Somewhere there was an ambush. Somewhere there were guns to be fired on the brain.

"Go on," said Murray quietly. "I don't doubt you; but go on."

"Yes," said Burrows in a vacant way—and sat down.

The doctor's big voice sounded sleepily in the quiet library.

"From the physical evidences," he continued, "there could hardly have been much doubt about it from the first. The centre of all disturbances, psychic and otherwise, was always *here*. The centre of all disturbances was that locked book-closet in the attic. Somebody had been haunting it. Somebody had been juggling with its contents, removing and replacing its books, playing with its trinkets. Somebody, always distinguished for exuberance of action, had made it into a kind of lair.

"Now, the notion that some outsider had done this—

that some neighbour had crept into the nest—was so fantastic as not to be worth serious consideration. Such a course of action would have been impossible, both psychologically and practically. You do not make a sort of one-man club in the attic of someone else's house, particularly under the eyes of a staff of curious servants. You do not come and go through that house at night, unseen by servants or anybody else. You do not so casually treat a new padlock watched by the master of the house. For it will be observed that though Miss Dane, for instance— " here there was a broad and cherubic beam on Dr Fell's face—" though Miss Dane had once possessed a key to that little room, it was the key to a lock no longer in use.

"Next question: what ailed Sir John Farnleigh?

"Just reflect on that, ladies and gentlemen.

"Why did that restless Puritan, already be-dazed with troubles of his own, never find any solace at home? What else was on his mind? Why does he, on the very night his great inheritance is to be challenged, do nothing but pace the floor and talk of Victoria Daly? Why is he so uneasily concerned with detectives asking 'folklore' questions in the vicinity? What is the meaning of his cryptic hints to Miss Dane? In moments of emotion he used to 'look up at the church, and say that if he were in a position to—'

"To do what? Speak out against the defamers of the church? Why does he once visit that attic with a dog-whip in his hand; but come down white and sweating, unable to use the whip on the person he finds there?

"The points in this case are mental ones, as revealing as the physical clues with which I shall deal in a moment; and I can't do better than to trace them."

Dr Fell paused. He stared heavily and rather sadly at the table. Then he got out his pipe.

"Let's take the history of this girl, Molly Sutton: a resolute woman and a fine actress. Patrick Gore said one true thing about her two nights ago. He appears to have shocked most of you by saying that she had never fallen in love with the Farnleigh you knew. He said that she had seized upon and married a 'projected image' of the boy she had known all those years before. And so she had. Whereupon she discovered, with what fury we may never know, that it was not the same boy or even the same person.

"What was the origin of that obsession or kink, even in the brain of a child of seven?

"It's not difficult. That's the age at which our essential tastes begin to be stamped on us by outside impressions. They are never eradicated, even when we think we have forgotten them. To my dying day I shall like pictures of fat old Dutchmen playing chess and smoking churchwarden pipes, because I remember one hanging on the wall of my father's study when I was a small child. You may like ducks or ghost-stories or motor-mechanisms for the same reason.

"Well, who was the only person who had idolised the boy John Farnleigh? Who was the only one to defend him? Who did John Farnleigh take to gipsy-camps (I call the gipsy-camps to your attention as significant), and take with him into the wood? What manner of Satanist lessons did she hear him recite, before she understood them or even before she understood the lessons she learned at Sunday School?

"And the intervening years? We don't know how the taste grew and developed in her brain. Except this: that she spent much time among the Farnleighs, for she had enough influence with old and young Sir Dudley to get Knowles his position as butler here.—Didn't she, Knowles?"

He peered round.

From the moment he had made that announcement Knowles had not moved. He was seventy-four. The transparent colour of his face, which seemed to show every emotion there, now showed nothing at all. He opened and shut his mouth and nodded in pantomime of reply; but he did not say anything. About him there was only a look of horror.

"It is probable," continued Dr Fell, "that she was borrowing books from that sealed library a long time ago. When she first instituted her private Satanist-cult Elliot has not been able to trace; but it was several years before her marriage. The number of men in the district who have been her lovers is large enough to surprise you. But they cannot or will not say anything about the Satanist business. And that, after all, is the only thing with which we are concerned. It is the thing with which *she* was most concerned, and it brought about the tragedy. For what happened?

"After a long and romantic absence, the supposed ' John Farnleigh ' returned to the supposed home of his fathers. For a short time Molly Sutton was transfigured. Here was her ideal. Here was her preceptor. Him she was determined to marry in spite of hell and himself. And something over a year ago—to be exact, a year and three months —they were married.

"Oh, Lord, was there ever a worse match?

"I ask that quite solemnly. You know who and what she thought she was marrying. You know instead the sort of person she did marry. You can guess the silent, cold contempt he had for her; and the frigid politeness he had for her when he learned. You can imagine what she felt for him, and the mask of concerned wifeliness she had to adopt, knowing always that he knew. And between them lay always the polite fiction that neither was aware of the other's knowledge. For, just as he knew about her, so she as certainly knew after a very short time that he was not the real John Farnleigh. So there together they shared each other's secret, in unadmitted hate.

"Why didn't he ever give her away? It wasn't merely that she was what he in his Puritan soul condemned first to the pit. It wasn't merely that he would have taken a whip to her if he had dared. But she was a criminal (make no mistake about that, gentlemen) as well. She was a supplier of more dangerous drugs than heroin or cocaine; and he knew it. She was accessory after the fact in Victoria Daly's murder; and he knew it. You have heard of his outbursts. You know his thoughts. Why, then, didn't he ever give her away as he longed to do?

"Because he was not in a position to do so. Because they held each other's secret. He didn't *know* he was not Sir John Farnleigh; but he feared it. He didn't *know* she could prove he was not, and might do so if he provoked her; but he feared it. He didn't *know* whether she might suspect; but he feared it. He had not quite the character of sweetness and light which Miss Dane gave him. No, he was not a conscious impostor. His memory was blind and he groped there. Very often he was sure he must be the real Farnleigh. But he would not, in the depths of a natural human soul, challenge fate too far, unless it pinned him in a corner and he had to face it out. For he might be a criminal as well."

Nathaniel Burrows jumped to his feet.

" I cannot put up with this," he said in a shrill voice. " I refuse to put up with this. Inspector, I call on you to stop this man! He has no right to prejudice an issue not yet decided. As a representative of the law, you have no right to say that my client— "

" Better sit down, sir," said Elliot quietly.

" But— "

" I said sit down, sir."

Madeline was speaking to Dr Fell.

" You said something like that earlier to-night," she reminded him. " Something about his ' labouring under a sense of crime ', even though he did not know what it was. His ' sense of crime ', that made him a worse Puritan, seems to run all through this; and yet, really and truly, I can't see what that has to do with it. What's the explanation? "

Dr Fell put the empty pipe in his mouth and drew at it.

" The explanation," he answered, " is a crooked hinge, and the white door the hinge supported. It's the secret in this case. We shall come to it presently.

" So these two, each having a secret like a dagger in the sleeve, mopped and mowed and pretended in front of the world: even in front of themselves. Victoria Daly died, a victim of the secret witch-cult, only three months after they had been married. We know what Farnleigh must have felt by that time. *If I were ever in a position to—* had become with him a fetish and a refrain. So long as he was never in a position to speak out, she was safe. For over a year she was safe.

" But then occurred the thunderclap that a claimant to the estate had appeared. Whereupon certain eventualities presented themselves to her as flat and clear and inevitable as A, B, C. Thus:

" He was not the real heir, as she knew.

" It seemed probable that the claimant would prove to be the real heir.

" If the claimant were proved to be the real heir, her husband would be dispossessed.

"If he were dispossessed, he would no longer have a reason for not speaking out about her, and he would speak out.

"Therefore he had to die.

"As simple and certain as that, ladies and gentlemen." Kennet Murray shifted in his chair, taking away the hand with which he had been shading his eyes.

"One moment, doctor. This was a long-planned crime, then?"

"No!" said Dr Fell with great earnestness. "No, no, no! That's what I want to stress. It was brilliantly planned and executed in desperation on the spur of the moment two nights ago. It was as quickly flung out as the automaton was pushed downstairs.

"Let me explain. As she believed from the time she had first heard of the claimant (farther back, I suspect, than she would admit), she had nothing to fear *just yet*. Her husband would fight the claim; she must make him fight, and, ironically, fight for him. Far from wishing to see the hated one ousted, she must clasp him even more tightly than before. It was quite possible that he would win his claim, the law being what it is and the courts being very wary of claimants to an established estate. At all events the law's delays would give her breathing-space to think.

"What she did not know, what had been carefully concealed by the other side until two nights ago, was the existence of the finger-prints. Here was solid proof. Here was certainty. With that deadly finger-print, the whole question could be settled in half an hour. Knowing her husband's mind, she knew he was coldly honest enough to admit the imposture as soon as it had been proved to him: as soon as he knew in his own soul that he was not John Farnleigh.

"When this hand-grenade exploded, she saw imminent peril. You recall Farnleigh's mood that night? If you have described it correctly to me, through every word he said and every move he made runs one strong and reckless flavour: "Well, here's the test. If I survive it, well and good. If I don't, there is one compensation which almost reconciles me to everything else: I can speak out about the woman to whom I am married."—Harrumph, yes. Have I interpreted the mood correctly?"

"Yes," admitted Page.

"So she took desperate measures. She must act at once. At once, at once! She must act before the finger-print comparison had been completed. She took these measures —just as yesterday, in the attic, she struck back at me before the words were out of my mouth—she acted magnificently; and she killed her husband."

Burrows, white-faced and sweating, had been vainly hammering on the table to call for order. Now there was a gleam of hope in his manner.

"There seems to be no way of stopping you," Burrows said. "If the police won't do it, I can't do more than protest. But now, I think, you are at a place where these glib theories won't do. I say nothing of the fact that you have no evidence. But until you can show how Sir John was murdered—alone, mind you, with nobody near him— until you can show that—" His words choked him; he only stuttered, and made a broad gesture. "And that, doctor, that you cannot show."

"Oh, yes, I can," said Dr Fell.

"Our first real lead came at the inquest yesterday," he went on reflectively. "It's good that the testimony is in the records. After that we had only to pick up certain pieces of evidence which had been lying under our noses from the first. Behold a miracle dropped into our laps. We are given hanging evidence by word of mouth. We apply it. We arrange the bits in order. We hand them to the prosecuting counsel. And "—he made a gesture—" we draw the bolt of the gallows-trap."

"You got your evidence at the inquest?" repeated Murray, staring at him. "Evidence from whom?"

"From Knowles," said Dr Fell.

A whimpering kind of cry came from the butler. He took a step forward, and put his hand up to his face. But he did not speak.

Dr Fell contemplated him.

"Oh, I know," the doctor growled. "It's sour medicine. But there you are. It's an ironical turn of the screw. But there you are. Knowles, my lad, you love that woman. She's your petted child. And by your testimony at the inquest, in all innocence, in all desire to tell the truth, you have hanged her as surely as though you drew the bolt yourself."

Still he kept his eyes fixed on the butler.

"Now, I daresay," he continued comfortably, "that some people thought you lied. I knew you didn't lie. You said that Sir John Farnleigh had committed suicide. You clinched your story by saying—something you had remembered in your subconscious mind—that you saw him fling away the knife. You said you saw the knife in the air.

"I knew you weren't lying, because you had had exactly the same trouble with that point when you talked to Elliot and me the day before. You had hesitated. You had groped after an uncertain memory. When Elliot pressed you about it, you puzzled and shook. 'It would depend on the size of the knife,' you said. 'And there are bats in that garden. And sometimes you can't see a tennis-ball until it's—' The choice of words is significant. In other words: *at about the time of the crime you had seen something flying in the air.* What puzzled your subconscious mind was that you saw it just before the murder rather than just afterwards."

He spread out his hands.

"A very remarkable bat," said Burrows, with shrill sarcasm. "A still more remarkable tennis-ball."

"Something very like a tennis-ball," agreed Dr Fell seriously, "though much smaller, of course. Very much smaller.

"We will return to that. Let's go on and consider the nature of the wounds. Already we have heard much astonished and feeling comment about those wounds. Mr Murray here maintained that they were like the marks of fangs or claws; he maintained that the blood-stained clasp-knife found in the hedge could not have produced them. Even Patrick Gore, if you have correctly quoted him to me, made a very similar comment. And what did he say? 'I never saw anything like this since Barney Poole, the best animal-trainer west of the Mississippi, was killed by a leopard.'

"The claw-mark motif runs all through the case. We find it coming out with curious guardedness and in a strikingly suggestive way in Dr King's medical evidence at the inquest. I have some notes here of his testimony. Harrumph! Hah! Let me see:

"'There were three fairly shallow wounds,' says the

physician." Here Dr Fell looked very hard at his audience. "'Three fairly shallow wounds, beginning at the left side of the throat and ending under the angle of the right jaw in a slightly upward direction. Two of the wounds crossed each other.' And presently this still more damning statement: 'There was much laceration of the tissue.'

"Laceration of tissue, eh? Surely that is odd, gents, if the weapon were that exceedingly sharp (if notched) knife which Inspector Elliot is showing you now. Laceration of the throat suggests—

"Well, let's see. Let's return to the claw-mark motif and examine it. What are the characteristics of wounds made by claws, and how are they fulfilled in the death of Sir John Farnleigh? The characteristics of marks left by claws are these:

"1. They are shallow.

"2. They are made by sharp points which tear and scratch and lacerate rather than cut.

"3. They are not separate cuts, but are all made at the same time.

"Every one of these qualifications, we find, is fulfilled by the description of the wounds in Farnleigh's throat. I call your attention to the somewhat odd testimony given by Dr King at the inquest. He does not tell a direct lie; but he is obviously working like blazes and talking wildly in order to make Farnleigh's death a suicide! Why? Observe—he too, like Knowles, has a petted child in Molly Farnleigh, the daughter of his oldest friend, who calls him 'Uncle Ned' and whose traits of character are probably known to him. But, unlike Knowles, he screens her; he does not send her out to have her neck cracked in two at the end of a rope."

Knowles put out his hands as though in supplication. His forehead was smeary with perspiration; but he still did not speak.

Dr Fell went on.

"Mr Murray suggested the basis of our case to us some time ago, when he spoke of something flying in the air and pertinently asked why the knife had not been dropped in the pool if it were really the weapon. But what have we got now? We've got something that flew at Farnleigh in the dusk, something smaller than a tennis-ball. We've got something equipped with claws or points which would make marks like claws— "

Nathaniel Burrows uttered a ghost of a chuckle.

" The episode of the flying claws," he jeered. " Really, doctor! And can you tell us what the flying claws were? "

" I'll do better than that," said Dr Fell. " I'll show them to you. You saw them yesterday."

From his capacious side-pocket he took out something wrapped in a large red bandana handkerchief. Unfolding it so that the needle-sharp points should not catch in' the handkerchief, he disclosed an object which Page recognised with a shock, even though it was a puzzled shock. It was one of the objects which Dr Fell had unearthed from the wooden box put away in the book-closet. It was (to be precise) a small but heavy leaden ball into which at intervals had been set four very large hooks of the sort used to catch fighting deep-sea fish.

" Did you wonder at the purpose of this singular instrument? " asked the doctor amiably. " Did you wonder what earthly use it could be to anybody? But among the Middle-European gipsies—among the gipsies, I repeat —it has a very effective and dangerous use. Let me have Gross: will you, inspector? "

Elliot opened his brief-case and took out a large flat book in a grey jacket.

" Here," pursued Dr Fell, juggling the book, " we have the most complete text-book on crime ever compiled.[1] I sent to town for it last night to verify a reference. You'll find a full description of this leaden ball on pages 249-50.

" It is used by the gipsies as a throwing weapon, and accounts for some of their mysterious and almost super-natural thefts. Into the other end of this ball is fastened a long length of very light but very strong fishing-line. The ball is thrown; and, at whatever it is thrown, the hooks lightly catch no matter in what direction they fall—like a ship's anchor. The leaden ball lends the necessary weight

---

[1] *Criminal Investigation:* A Practical Textbook for Magistrates, Police Officers, and Lawyers, Adapted from the System der Kriminalistik of Dr Hans Gross, Professor of Criminology in the University of Prague, by John Adam, M.A., Barrister-at-Law, and J. Collyer Adam, Barrister-at-Law; edited by Norman Kendal, Assistant Commissioner, Criminal Investigation Dept., Metropolitan Police. (London, Sweet & Maxwell, 1934.)

for throwing, and the fishing-line draws it back with the booty. Hear Gross on the use of it:

"As regards the throwing, gipsies, especially the children, are remarkable skilful. Among all races children amuse themselves by throwing stones, but their particular object in doing so is to throw them as far as possible. Not so the young gipsy; he gathers together a heap of stones about the size of a nut and then chooses a target, such as a fairly large stone, a small plank, or an old cloth, at a distance of about ten to twenty paces; he then launches his stock of projectiles . . . . He keeps going for hours and soon acquires such skill at this exercise that he never misses anything larger than one's hand. When he reaches this stage he is given a throwing hook. . . .

"The young gipsy comes out of his apprenticeship when he is able to strike and carry off a piece of rag thrown upon the branches of a tree among which he has to cast his hook.

"Into a tree, mind you! This is how, with amazing skill, he is able to carry off linen, clothes, and so on, through barred windows or in enclosed yards. But as a throwing weapon you can imagine its horrible effectiveness. It will tear the throat from a man, and back it goes—"

Murray uttered a kind of groan. Burrows did not speak.

"H'mf, yes. Now, we've heard of Molly Farnleigh's uncanny and amazing ability at throwing, a trick she learned among the gipsies. Miss Dane told us of it. We know of her deadly snap-judgments, and the suddenness with which she could strike.

"Where, then, was Molly Farnleigh at the time of the murder? I hardly need to tell you: she was on the balcony of her bedroom overlooking the pool. My eye, *directly* above the pool; and her bedroom, as we know, is built over the dining-room. Like Welkyn in the room below, she was much less than twenty feet away from the pool, and raised above it. Very high up? Not at all. As Knowles here— invaluable at giving us hints on how to hang her—as Knowles told us, that new wing of the house is 'a little low doll's house of a place', the balcony hardly eight or nine feet above the garden.

"So there she is in the dusk, facing her husband below, and raised up high enough to give purchase to her arm. The room behind her is dark—as she admitted. Her maid was in the next room. What brought her to that deadly

200

snap-decision? Did she whisper something to make her husband look up? Or was it because he was already looking at a star, with his long throat upturned? "

With an expression of growing horror in her eyes, Madeline repeated:

" Looking at a star? "

" Your star, Miss Dane," said Dr Fell sombrely. " I've talked a great deal with the various persons in this case; and I think it was your star."

Again memory returned to Page. He himself had thought of 'Madeline's star' when he walked through the garden beside the pool on the night of the murder: the single eastern star to which she had given a poetic name, and which from the pool you could just see by craning your neck to look over the farther chimney-tops of the new wing. . . .

" Yes, she hated you. Her husband's attentions to you had done that. It may have been the sight of him looking up, staring at your star and facing her blindly, that brought out murder in a flood. With the line in one hand and the leaden ball in the other, she lifted her arm and struck.

" Gents, I call your attention to the curious, the weird behaviour of that poor devil when something caught him. It has vaguely troubled everybody who has tried to describe it. The shufflings, the chokings, the jerkings of the body before he was yanked forward into the pool—what has it reminded you of? Ah! Got it, have you? Shows clearly, does it? Of a hooked fish on a line; and that is what it was. The hooks did not penetrate deeply: she saw to that. There was a good deal of mauling, on which everybody commented. The direction of the wounds, obviously, was from left to right, running upwards, as he was pulled off balance; and he went into the pool (you recall?) with his head slightly towards the new wing. When he was in the pool she jerked back the weapon."

With a heavy grimness of expression Dr Fell held up the leaden ball.

" And this little beauty?

" Obviously, of course, it left no blood-trail or any traces when it was pulled back. It had landed in the pool and had been washed clean. You recall that the water in the pool had been so agitated (naturally, by his strugglings) that it was slopped over the sand for some feet round. But

201

the ball did leave one trace—it rustled in the shrubbery.

"Reflect. Who was the only person who heard that curious rustling? Welkyn, in the dining-room below: the only person who was near enough to hear it. That rustling was an intriguing point. Clearly it had not been made by any *person*. If you will try the experiment of attempting to slip through yew hedges as thick as a wide screen (as Sergeant Burton noticed when he later found the knife 'planted' there, with the dead man's finger-prints conveniently on it), you will realise what I mean.

"I spare you details. But that, in essence, is how she planned and carried out one of the wickedest murders in my experience. It was all flash and hate; and it succeeded. She fished for men as she has always done; and she caught her victim. She won't get away, naturally. She will be nabbed by the first policeman she passes. Then she will hang. And all, happily for the cause of justice, because of Knowle's happy inspiration in telling us about the flight of a tennis-ball at dusk."

Knowles made a slight waggling gesture of his hand as though he were trying to stop a bus. His face was like oiled paper, and Page was afraid he was going to faint. But still he could not speak.

Burrows, with his eyes gleaming, seemed inspired.

"It's ingenious," Burrows said. "It's clever. But it's a lie, and I'll beat you in court with it. It's all false and you know it. For other people have sworn things too. There's Welkyn! You can't explain away what *he* said! Welkyn saw somebody in the garden! He said he did! And what have you got to say to that?"

Page noted with alarm that Dr Fell himself was looking somewhat pale. Very slowly Dr Fell pushed himself to his feet. He stood towering over them, and he made a gesture towards the door.

"There's Mr Welkyn now," he replied. "Standing just behind you. Ask him. Ask him if he's now so sure of what he saw in the garden."

They all looked round. How long Welkyn had been standing in the doorway they could not tell. Immaculate, brushed as ever, the overgrown cherubic countenance was uneasy, and Welkyn pulled at his lower lip.

"Er—" he said, clearing at his throat.

202

"Well, speak up! " thundered Dr Fell. "You've heard my say. Now tell us: ARE you sure you saw something looking at you? ARE you sure there was anything there to see? "

"I have been reflecting," said Welkyn.

"Yes? "

"I—er—gentlemen." He paused. "I wish you would cast your minds back to yesterday. You all went up to the attic, and I am given to understand that you investigated certain curious articles you found there. Unhappily I did not go along with you. I did not see any of those articles until to-day, when Dr Fell called them to my attention. I—er—refer to the black Janus-faced mask which you seem to have found in a wooden box there." Again he cleared his throat.

"This is a plot," said Burrows, looking rapidly right and left like a man hesitating before wild traffic in a road. "You can't get away with this. It's all a deliberate conspiracy, and you're all in it— "

"Kindly allow me to finish, sir," retorted Welkyn with asperity. "I said I saw a face looking at me through the lower panel of the glass door. I know what it was now. It was that Janus mask. I recognised it as soon as I saw it. It occurs to me, as Dr Fell suggests, that the unhappy Lady Farnleigh—in order to prove to me the presence of someone actually in the garden—merely let down that mask on another length of fishing-line; and unfortunately sent it too low against the window, so that . . ."

Then Knowles spoke at last.

He came up to the table and put his hands on it. He was crying; and for a moment the tears would not let him speak coherently. When the words did come out, they shocked his listeners as though a piece of furniture had spoken.

"It's a bloody *lie*," said Knowles.

Old and muddled and pitiful, he began to beat with his hand on the table.

"It's like Mr Burrows said. It's all lies and lies and lies and lies. You're all in it." His voice grew frantic, rising to a quaver, and his hand beat frantically on the table. "You're all against her, that's what you are. You none of you will give her a chance. What if she did carry on a bit? What if she did read them books and maybe carry on with a lad or two? What difference is it, much, from the games they used to play when they were kids? They're all kids. She didn't mean any harm. She never meant any harm. And you shan't hang her. By Christ, you shan't. I'll see nobody harms my little lady, that's what I'll do."

His voice grew to a scream through the tears, and he waggled his finger at them.

"I'll fool you, with all your grand ideas and your grand guesses. She didn't kill that crazy silly beggar that come here pretending to be Master Johnny. Master Johnny my foot! That beggar a Farnleigh? *That* beggar? He got just exactly what he deserved, and I'm sorry he can't be killed all over again. Came out of a pigsty, that's where he came from. But I don't care about him. I tell you you're not going to hurt my little lady. She never killed him; she never did; and I can prove it."

In the vast silence they heard the tap of Dr Fell's stick on the floor, and the wheezing of his breath, as he walked over to Knowles, and put his hand on Knowles's shoulder.

"I know she didn't," he said gently.

Knowles stared at him with blurred frenzy.

"Do you mean," shouted Burrows, "that you've been sitting here telling us a pack of fairy-tales just because——"

"And do you think I like what I'm doing?" asked Dr Fell. "Do you think I like one word I've said or one move I've had to make? Everything I told you about the woman and her private witch-cult and her relations with Farnleigh was true. Everything. She inspired the murderer and directed the murder. The only difference is that she did not kill her husband. She did not make the automaton work and she was not the person in the garden. But"—his hand tightened on Knowles's shoulder—"you know the law. You know how it moves and how it crushes. I've set it in motion. And Lady Farnleigh will hang higher than Haman unless you tell us the truth. Do you know who committed the murder?"

"Of course I know it," snarled Knowles. "Yah!"

"And who was the murderer?"

"That's an easy one," said Knowles. "And that silly beggar got everything that was coming to him. The murderer was——"

PART IV

Saturday, August 8th

There was one thing which Flambeau, with all his dexterity of disguise, could not cover, and that was his singular height. If Valentin's quick eye had caught a tall apple-woman, a tall grenadier, or even a tolerably tall duchess, he might have arrested them on the spot. But all along his train there was nobody who could be a disguised Flambeau, any more than a cat could be a disguised giraffe.

G. K. CHESTERTON, *The Blue Cross.*

CHAPTER XXI

*Being a letter from Patrick Gore (born John Farnleigh) to
Dr Gideon Fell*

Outward bound,
At a certain date.

MY DEAR DOCTOR:

Yes, I am the culprit. I alone killed that impostor, and
produced all the manifestations which seem to have alarmed
you.

I write you this letter for a number of reasons. First:
I retain (however foolishly) a genuine liking and respect for
you. Second: You have never done anything better. The
way in which you forced me step by step through every
room, through every door, and out of the house into flight,
rouses my admiration to such an extent that I should like
to see whether I have correctly followed your deductions.
I pay you the compliment of saying that you are the only
person who has ever outwitted me; but then I have never
been at my best against schoolmasters. Third: I believe
I have found the one really perfect disguise and, now that
it is no longer of use to me, I should rather like to brag
about it.

I shall expect an answer to this letter. By the time you
receive it, I and my adored Molly will be in a country which
has no extradition treaty with Great Britain. It is rather
a hot country, but then both Molly and I are fond of hot
countries. I will drop you a line as to the address when
we are settled in our new home.

One request I should like to make. In the debacle of
horrified talk which will follow our flight, I shall doubtless
be presented by newspapers, judges, and other distorters
of the public eyesight as a Fiend, a Monster, a Werewolf,
and so on. Now, you are quite well aware that I am nothing
of the sort. I have no liking for murder; and if I cannot
feel any repentance over the death of that swine it is, I hope,

because I am not a hypocrite. Certain people are consti-
tuted in certain ways, like Molly and myself. If we prefer
to make the world a more exciting place with our studies
and our day-dreams, I should think it would be an inspiration to Suburbia and a hint towards better things. When,
therefore, you hear someone indulging in maudlin speech
about the Fiend and his Witch-bride, kindly inform the
person that you have had tea with both of us, and perceived
no sign of horns or stigmata.

But now I must tell you my secret, which is also the secret
of the case you have been so earnestly investigating. It is
a very simple secret, and can be expressed in four words:

I have no legs.

I have no legs. Both of them were amputated in
April, 1912, after being crushed by that swine in a little
affair aboard the *Titanic*, which I shall describe in a moment.
The admirable sets of artificial legs I have since worn have
not altogether, I fear, disguised this disability. I saw that
you noticed my walk—which is not exactly a limp, but is
always clumsy and sometimes awkward enough to betray
me if I attempt to move rapidly. I cannot, in fact, move
rapidly; and with this also I shall deal in a moment.

Have you ever thought of the remarkable opportunity
presented by artificial legs for the purposes of disguise?
We have had mummeries of wig and beard and grease-
paint; we have had faces altered with clay and figures with
padding; we have had the subtlest turns to the subtlest
illusion. But, astonishing to state, we have never had the
eyes deceived in the simplest way—by a difference in height.
There has always been the statement, ' This and that a man
can do, but there is one thing he cannot disguise: his height.'
I beg leave to state that I can make my height anything I
please, and that I have been doing so for quite a number
of years.

I am not a tall man. That is, to be strictly accurate,
I believe that I should not be a tall man had I any means
of estimating what my height would have been. Let us
say that, without the interference of my small friend on the
Titanic, I should have been about five feet five inches tall.

The removal of underpinning (observe my delicacy)
leaves my actual body less than three feet high. Should you
doubt this, measure your own height against a wall and ob-

serve the proportion taken up by these mysterious appendages we call legs.

With several sets of limbs made to order—this was first done in the circus—and a good deal of painful practice in the harness, I can make my height what I choose. It is interesting to discover how easily the eye is deceived. Imagine, for example, a small and slender friend of yours appearing before you as a six-footer; your brain would refuse to take it in, and the smallest dexterity in other branches of disguise would render him completely unrecognisable.

I have been several heights. I have been six-feet-one. And again, in my famous role as ' Ahriman ', the fortune-teller, I was almost a dwarf: with such success as completely to deceive the good Mr Harold Welkyn, when I later appeared before him as Patrick Gore.

Perhaps it would be best to start with the business aboard the *Titanic*. Now, when I returned to claim my inheritance the other day, the story I told to the assembled gapers in the library was true—with one slight distortion and one notable omission.

We changed identities, as I said. The gentle-hearted lad did in reality try to kill me, as I said. But he attempted to do it by strangling, since he was at that time the stronger. This little tragi-comedy was played among the pillars of high tragedy; and you have guessed its background. Its background was one of the great white-painted steel doors, bulkhead doors, which shut a liner into compartments and can swing several hundredweight of ponderous metal against the creeping water. The crumpling and dissolving of its hinges as the ship lurched was, I think, as terrifying a spectacle as I have ever seen; it was like the breaking of all ordered things or the fall of the gates of Gath.

My friend's purpose was of no great complexity. After squeezing my windpipe until I was unconscious, he meant to shut me into the flooding compartment and make his escape. I fought back with anything within reach—in this case, a wooden mallet hanging beside the door. How many times I hit him I cannot remember, but the snake-dancer's son did not even seem to mind it. I was able to dodge, unfortunately for myself, to the outer side of the door; the snake-dancer's son threw himself against it, and, with the settling of the ship, the hinges gave. All of me, I need scarcely say, got out of the way of it except my legs.

It was a time of heroisms, doctor: heroisms never set to music or told afterwards except stammeringly. Who rescued me—whether it was a passenger or one of the crew—I do not know. I recall being picked up like a puppy and carried out to a boat. The snake-dancer's son, with his blood-stained head and wandering eye, I thought had been left behind to die. That I did not die myself I suppose I must attribute to the salt water, but it was not a pleasant time for me and I remember nothing of what happened until a week later.

In my story to the group at Farnleigh Close some nights ago, I told of my reception as 'Patrick Gore' by old Boris Yeldritch, since dead, the proprietor of the circus. I explained something of my state of mind. If I did not explain my entire state of mind, you know the reason. Boris easily found a use for me with the circus, since I was (not to put too fine a point on it) a freak with a knack for telling fortunes gained from my studies back home. It was a painful and humiliating time, especially in learning to 'walk' by using my hands. I do not dwell on this part of it, for I would not have you think I am asking for pity or sympathy: the notion angers me furiously. I feel like the man in the play. Your liking I will have if I can. Your respect I will have or kill you. But your pity? Damn your impudence!

It occurs to me, too, that I have been posturing like a tragedian over something which, after all, I had almost forgotten. Let us take matters more amiably and be amused at what we cannot correct. You know my profession: I have been a fortune-teller, a bogus spiritualist and occultist, and an illusionist. I somewhat imprudently hinted at this when I came to Farnleigh Close the other night. Yet I have been so many different persons, and served under so many different aliases as He Who Knows All, that I did not greatly fear detection.

I cheerfully assure you that the absence of legs has been, in fact, a boon to me in my business. I would not have it otherwise. But the artificial ones always hampered me; and I fear I have never learned to manage them properly. I early learned to move myself about by the use of my hands: with, I venture to think, incredible speed and agility. I need hardly tell you in how many ways this was useful to me in my business as a fraudulent spiritualist medium, and what remarkable effects I was able to produce for my sitters. Reflect on it a while; you will understand.

Whenever I am up to such tricks, I am in the habit of wearing under my artificial limbs and ordinary trousers close-fitting breeches equipped with leather pads, which serve as my limbs and leave no traces on any sort of ground. Since speed in change has often been of the utmost necessity, I have learned to remove or put back my artificial harness in exactly thirty-five seconds.

And this, of course, is the painfully simple secret of how 'I worked the automaton.

A word concerning it, since history has repeated itself. It not only could have happened before; it did happen before. Are you aware, doctor, that this was how the automaton chess-player of Kempelen and Maelzel was run?[1] With the simple assistance of a man like myself inside the box on which the figure sat, they baffled Europe and America for fifty years. When the hoax deceived men of such different temperaments as Napoleon Bonaparte and Phineas Barnum, you need not feel cast down if it deceived you. But it did not, in fact, deceive you; and this you gave me clearly to understand by your hints in the attic.

I have no doubt that this was the original secret of the Golden Hag in the seventeenth century. Do you see now why the automaton fell into such disrepute when my respected ancestor Thomas Farnleigh, after buying it for a whacking price, learned the truth? He had been told the inner mystery; and, like many others who have learned inner mysteries, he was furious. He thought to get a miracle.

[1] Mr Gore is telling the truth. I first came across this explanation in an old edition of the *Encyclopedia Britannica* (ninth edition, published in 1883). The writer, J. A. Clarke, says: 'The first player was a Polish patriot, Worousky, who had lost both legs in a campaign; as he was furnished with artificial limbs when in public, his appearance, together with the fact that no dwarf or child travelled in Kempelen's company, dispelled the suspicion that any person could be employed inside the machine. This automaton, which made more than one tour to the capitals and courts of Europe, was owned for a short time by Napoleon I, was exhibited by Maelzel after the death of Kempelen in 1819, and ultimately perished in a fire at Philadelphia in 1854.'—Vol. XV, p. 210.

Instead he paid for an ingenious trick with which he could not hoax his friends unless he kept a special kind of operator on the premises.

This is how the whole effect was originally managed: The space inside is big enough, as you have observed, for a person like myself. Once you are inside the box or 'couch', and the door closed, the shutting of the door opens a small panel in the top of the box communicating with the works of the figure. Here—worked by simple mechanical weights—are a dozen rods communicating with the hands and body. Concealed holes by the knees of the automaton, which can be opened from inside, allow the operator to see. That was how Maelzel's dummy played chess; and how the Golden Hag played the cittern over a hundred years before.

But, in the case of the hag, one of the best features of the illusion was the device by which the operator was conveyed inside the box unseen. There, I think, is where the inventor of the hag outdid Kempelen. At the beginning of the performance the magician in charge opened the box and let everybody inspect the inside to show that it was empty. How, then, was the operator spirited in?

I don't need to tell *you*. By your remarks in the attic the day after the murder—carefully aimed at me—about the costume worn by the exhibitor, you demonstrated that you knew; and *I* knew that my goose was done to a cinder.

The traditional wizard's costume, as everybody knows, consists of a huge flowing robe covered with hieroglyphics. And the original inventor merely applied a principle later used by the somewhat clumsy Indian fakirs. That is, the robe was used to cover something: in the case of the fakir, a child who climbs into a basket unseen; in the case of the exhibitor of the hag, the operator who slid into the machine while the magician in his great robe fussed with it at the dimming of the lights. I have made use of the trick successfully in many of my own entertainments.

To which history of my life I must return.

My most successful role was in London as 'Ahriman', if you can forgive the name of a Zoroasterian devil as applied to an Egyptian. Poor Welkyn, whom you must not suspect of any part in my dirty work, does not know to this day that I was the bearded dwarf of whom he took such

211

good care. He defended me nobly in that libel suit; he believed in my psychic powers; and, when I reappeared as the missing heir, I thought it only fair to make him my legal representative.

(Magister, that libel suit still tickles my fancy. I hoped fervently that I should be able to give some demonstration of my psychic powers in court. You see, my father had been at school with the judge; and I was prepared to go into a trance in the witness-box and tell his Lordship some realistic things about himself. My father, indeed, had been well known socially in London during the nineties: which fact is less a tribute to Ahriman's awesome insight into his sitters' hearts than to the power of information on which he had to draw. But a weakness for spectacular effect has always been one of my characteristics.)

It is as Ahriman, then, that my story properly begins. I had no notion that 'John Farnleigh' was supposed to be alive, much less that he was now Sir John Farnleigh, baronet—until he walked one day into my consulting-room in Half Moon Street, and told me his troubles. That I did not laugh in the man's face I simply state as a fact. Monte Cristo himself never dreamed of such a situation. But I think, I say I *think*, that in applying balm to his fevered mind I contrived to give him some unpleasant days and nights.

However, the matter of importance is less that I met him than that I met Molly.

On this subject my views are too fervent to be fashioned into smooth prose. Don't you see that we are two of a kind? Don't you see that, once having found each other, Molly and I would have come together from the ends of the earth? It was a love-affair sudden, complete, and blinding; there was burning pitch in it; it was, in the terms of an American pastime called Red Dog, 'high, low, jack, and the goddam game'. I must laugh at this, or I shall find myself fashioning incoherence into poetry and curses into endearments. She did not think (when she learned) my crippled body either funny or repulsive. I had not, before her, to sing the refrain of Quasimodo or He Who Gets Slapped. Do not, I urge you, make light of love-affairs whose inspiration is infernal rather than of celestial gentleness. Pluto was as true a lover as the lord of Olympus,

212

and helped to fertilise the earth; whereas Jove, poor wretch, could go about only as a swan or a shower of gold; and I thank you for your kind attention on this subject.

Molly and I planned the whole thing, of course. (Didn't it strike you that in our thrust-and-parry at the Close we were just a little too much at each other's throats? That she was a little too quick with flat insults and I with elaborate barbs?)

The ironical part was that I was the real heir, yet there was nothing we could do about it except what we did. The swine back there had found out about what you call her private witch-cult; he was using it against her as pure, sharp-clawed blackmail to cling to his place; and if he were dislodged he would dislodge her. If I were to regain the estate—as I was resolved to do—and if I were to regain her for my lawful wife so that we could live without furtiveness in our mutual interests—as I was also resolved to do—I had to kill him and make it look like suicide.

There you have it. Molly could not bring herself to murder: whereas I, with the proper concentration, can bring myself to anything. I say no word of the fact that I owed him something, and when I saw what he had grown into after his pious beginnings I knew what makes Puritans and why they have been wiped from the earth.

The crime was timed to take place at some time on the night it did: I could not lay my plans any more closely than that. It could not take place before then, because I must not *appear* at the Close or risk showing myself prematurely; and the fellow could hardly be expected to commit suicide until he knew the weight of evidence against him. You know the admirable opportunity afforded me when he walked into that garden during the comparison of the finger-prints.

Now, my friend, a word of congratulation to you. You took an impossible crime; and, in order to make Knowles confess, you spun out of sticks and stones and rags and bones a perfectly logical and reasonable explanation of the impossible. Artistically I am glad you did so; your hearers would have felt cheated and outraged without it.

Yet the fact is—as you very well know—that there never was an impossible crime.

I simply went up to the fellow; I pulled him down; I

killed him by the pool with the clasp-knife you later found in the hedge; and that is all.

Knowles, by either bad or good luck, saw the whole affair from the window of the Green Room. Even then, had I not bungled the whole affair with my one great error, the scheme would have been doubly secure. Knowles not only swore to the world that it was suicide: he went out of his way to give me a gratuitous alibi which astonished me not a little. For he, as you have observed, always disliked and distrusted the late incumbent; he never really believed the man was a Farnleigh; and he would have gone to the gallows rather than admit that the real John Farnleigh had killed the fraudulent one who had stolen his patrimony.

I killed the fellow, of course, minus my artificial legs. That was only common sense, since I can move with rapidity and ease only on my leather pads; and in the artificial legs I could not have bent down so as not to be seen by anybody behind those waist-high hedges. The hedges afforded an admirable screen, as well as innumerable alleys of escape in case of danger. In the event that anybody should see me, I took along under my coat the sinister-looking Janus-mask from the attic.

I came on him, actually, from the north side of the house: that is, from the direction of the new wing. I must, I think, have been a sufficiently unnerving sight. It so paralysed our impostor that I pulled him down before he could move or speak. The strength developed in my arms and shoulders through these years, doctor, is not negligible.

Afterwards, regarding this part of it—the attack on him —the testimony of Nathaniel Burrows gave me a few uneasy moments. Burrows was standing at the garden door some thirty-odd feet away; and, as he himself admits, his eyesight is not good in semi-darkness. He saw unusual occurrences which he could not explain even in his own mind. He could not see me, since waist-high hedges intervened; yet the victim's behaviour worried him. Read over his testimony again and you will see what I mean. He concludes: "I cannot give an exact description of the movements he made. It was as though something had got hold of his feet."

And something had.

Nevertheless, this danger was negligible compared to

214

what Welkyn almost saw from the dining-room a few seconds after the killing. Doubtless it has been apparent to you that what Welkyn saw, through one of the lower glass panels of the French window, was your obedient servant. It was foolhardy of me to let anyone get so much as a fleeting glimpse of me, but at that time (as you shall see) I was upset over the ruin of my plan; and, fortunately, I had my mask on.

His actual glimpse of me was not so dangerous as the interpretation of a shade of words—an impression—put on this incident when it came to be discussed next day. Here my old tutor Murray, that eternal trafficker in words, was the offender. In Welkyn's description of the incident Murray caught an echo of what Welkyn was (gropingly and uncertainly) trying to convey. And Murray said to me: 'On your homecoming you are greeted by a scrawling *legless* something in the garden—'

That was disaster fine and full. It was the one thing which nobody must suspect, the one suggestion which must not be implanted. I felt my face contract, and I know that I lost colour like a spilled jug, and I saw you looking at me. I was foolish enough to flare out at poor old Murray and call him names for a reason which must have been inexplicable to everybody but you.

All the same, I feared that by this time I was finished in any case. I have referred to the colossal blunder I made at the outset, which ruined the case I was attempting to build up. It was this:

I used the wrong knife.

What I had intended to use was a common clasp-knife I had bought for the purpose. (I took this one out of my pocket and showed it to you next day, pretending it was my own knife.) I then intended to press his hand on it and leave it by the pool, completing the picture of suicide.

What I actually found in my hand, when it was too late to draw back, was my own clasp-knife—the knife I have owned since I was a boy—the knife a thousand people have seen in my hand in America, with Madeline Dane's name cut into the blade. You remember that your most diligent efforts could not trace that knife to the impostor. But you would have traced it to me fast enough.

It was all the worse because, on the very night of the

murder, I had gone so far as to mention this same knife to the group in the library. In telling my story of the affair aboard the *Titanic*, I told how I had met the real Patrick Gore, how we had fought at sight, and how I had been with difficulty prevented from going for him with my clasp-knife A surer indication of character and weapon it would be difficult to beat. It came of trying to make too artistic a lie, and of telling all the truth except the part you mean to suppress. I warn you against the practice.

So here was I, with the infernal thing in my gloved hand by the pool, after pressing his finger-prints on it; and people running towards me. I was compelled to make a snap-decision. I dared not leave the knife. So I wrapped it in my handkerchief and put it into my pocket.

Welkyn saw me when I went to regain my harness at the north side of the house. I therefore thought it best to say I had been at the south side. I didn't dare carry the knife about with me, so I had to hide it until I could find an opportunity to get it away undetected. And I maintain that, theoretically, I chose an undetectable hiding-place. Your Sergeant Burton acknowledges that except for one chance in a million he would never have found the knife in the hedge without systematically rooting up every foot of hedge in the whole garden.

Were the Parcae, do you say, giving me some particularly nasty breaks? Oh, I don't know. It is true that I was obliged to alter my whole plan at the outset and express a belief in murder. Yet Knowles, with noble instincts of sacrifice, straightway provided me with an alibi; he conveyed a hint before I had left the house that night; and I was ready for you next day.

The rest of it is simply indicated. Molly insisted on trying to make our case better by stealing the Thumbograph, once I had privately made it clear that this must be murder: for, you observe, *I* could not be accused of stealing a Thumbograph with evidence of my own identity. We were going to return it anyway, and with double quickness when it was discovered to be a dummy.

Molly acted well all the way through, don't you think? That little scene in the garden just after the discovery of the body (' Damn him for being right! ') had been carefully rehearsed beforehand. Interpreted, it was meant to convey that I had been right when I said before all the company she had never been really in love with her husband (another rehearsed scene), and that she had always been in love with an image of me. We could not have the widow *too* inconsolable, you know. We could not have her so prostrated with grief that she might be expected to retain an enmity towards me for ever. It was a far-sighted plan, directed towards bringing us together when animosities had been smoothed down in the future—and yet how we wrecked it!

For there was that final unfortunate business next day, when Betty Harbottle caught me tinkering with the automaton in the attic. I must mutter *mea culpa* again. As a matter of strict fact, I had gone up to the attic to get the Thumbograph. But it suddenly occurred to me, when I saw the hag, that I could bring her to life at last. As a boy I knew her secret; but at that time I had not been small enough to get inside the box. So nothing would do but that I must tinker about with it, like a respectable husband with a respectable clock in a respectable attic.

Molly, finding me gone an unconscionable time, came upstairs. She was just in time to find Betty Harbottle investigating the book-closet. And at this time I was actually inside the automaton.

Molly, I honestly believe, thought that I would deal with the little girl as I had dealt with another person. Molly saw that Betty was inside and locked the door. But I had no wish to hurt her. The girl could not, of course, see me: yet I was most badly afraid she would see my harness, propped into the corner behind the machine. I think you know what happened. Fortunately it was not necessary to hurt her; a few movements sufficed; though I could have sworn she saw my eyes through the peep-holes in the automaton. Afterwards Molly and I were in no vast danger. Had you pressed us too hard as to our whereabouts at the time, we should simply have provided each other with a reluctant and grudging alibi. Still, it was a mistake to forget that girl's apron—the hag's claws tore it off as part of the pantomime—and leave it behind when we cleared out.

Well, I had been foolish; and there you are. I saw as soon as the day after the murder that I was, in the simple phrase, for it. You found the knife. Though I made light of it as one the impostor had taken from me years ago, and though Murray assisted me with some unconsciously helpful suggestions designed to make you suspicious of the knife as a real weapon, I was following you and I knew that you had seen through the absence of legs.

You brought up the subject of Ahriman the Egyptian. Inspector Elliot followed with his questioning of Welkyn about the hopping thing in the garden. You returned with some pressing questions on the subject of witchcraft, and neatly brought Molly into it. I questioned in reply; and you conveyed some suggestive hints. Next you stressed the connection between all these points, beginning with Victoria Daly, passing to the late Patrick Gore's behaviour on the night of the murder, and going on to trace Betty Harbottle to the book-closet in the attic.

Your remarks when you saw the automaton were the penultimate give-away. You intimated that the murderer had been doing something here with the automaton which would betray him; and yet at the same time Betty Harbottle had not seen him at all—in the sense that it was not necessary for the murderer to silence her. I then challenged you to show how the automaton worked. You paid little attention, merely remarking that you supposed the original exhibitor wore the traditional magician's costume. And you concluded with a few words designed to show Molly's private witch-cult was about to be discovered if it had not already been discovered. That was when I pushed the automaton downstairs. Believe me, my friend, I had no thought of damage to your person. But I did definitely want to damage the automaton beyond repair, so that one guess as to how it worked would be as good as another.

The inquest showed two more points next day. Knowles was obviously lying, and you knew it. Madeline Dane knew much more about Molly's doings than we could afford.

I am afraid Molly does not like Madeline. Her scheme was to ensure silence on the latter's part by terrorisation, followed by real trouble if it became necessary. Hence Molly's not altogether inspired device of the faked telephone-call purporting to come from Madeline, and asking for the automaton at Monplaisir: she knew Madeline's rooted horror of the machine, and made me promise to bring it to life again for Madeline's edification. I did not do that; I had better fish to fry.

Fortunately for Molly and myself, I was in the garden at Monplaisir when you and the inspector had dinner there with Madeline and Page. I overheard your conversation; and I knew that it was all over as regards your knowing everything—the question was what you could prove. When you and the inspector left the house, I thought it much more profitable to follow you through the wood and listen.

After contenting myself merely with pushing out the harmless old hag by the windows, I, went after you. Your conversation, properly interpreted, showed me that what I had feared about your manner of proceeding was correct. I now know fully what you did, though I had more than a glimmer then. I knew your objective: Knowles. I knew my weak link : Knowles. I knew where there was a witness who could hang me: Knowles. I knew that he would be tortured rather than admit under mere ordinary pressure who had committed the crime. But there was one person he could not see touched or even breathed upon: Molly. There was only one way to make him speak. That was to make a garrotte for her neck and tighten the screw by degrees until he could not stand the sight of it any longer. That was what you were going to do; I was intelligent enough to read evidence as well as you; and it occurred to me with some realism that we were done for.

Only one thing was left to us, which was to get away. Had I been the bowel-less and altogether unbelievable person you will probably hear described, I should without doubt have decided to kill Knowles as casually as paring an onion. But who could kill Knowles? Who could kill Madeline Dane? Who could kill Betty Harbottle? These are real persons I have known, not dummies to pad out a chapter; and they are not to be treated like stuffed cats at a fair. I was tired and a little ill, to tell you the truth, as though I had got into a maze and could not get out again.

Following you and the inspector, I came to the Close and saw Molly. I told her our only course was to get away. Remember, we believed we had ample time; you and the inspector had intended to go to London that night, and we did not fear disclosure for some hours. Molly agreed it was the only thing to do—I am given to understand that you saw her leaving the Close, with a suitcase in her hand, when you looked down from the windows of the Green Room. I think it was unwise, though, deliberately to let us get away so that we should damn ourselves by quick flight. Such a course is wise, doctor, only if you are certain of nailing the quarry when you want him.

In one respect, to conclude this account, I had difficulty with Molly. She did not find it easy to go without a final word to Madeline. When we were driving away in the car she was filled with fantastic notions (I can say this because the lady knows I love her) for getting back at the 'cat' at Monplaisir.

I could not prevent her. We arrived there within a very few minutes, leaving the car in a back lane by Colonel Mardale's old house. We arrived, in short—and stopped to listen. For we were being treated to a very lucid account, heard through the half-open window of the dining-room, of the death of Victoria Daly and the probable character of the witch-mistress responsible for it: it was being delivered by Mr Page. The automaton was still there; and I pushed it back into the coal-house only because Molly wanted to smash it through the windows at Madeline. Such behaviour is childish, no doubt; yet my lady's quarrel with Madeline is of a personal nature—as mine was with the late Patrick Gore; and I tell you that nothing which had occurred so far in the case infuriated her as much as that talk in the dining-room.

I did not know, at the time, that she had brought a pistol with her from Farnleigh Close. I realised this only when she took it out of her handbag and rapped it against the window. Whereupon I realised, doctor, that immediate action was necessary for two reasons: first, that we wanted no women's flaming row at this moment; and, second, that a car (Burrows's) had just stopped at the front of the house. I put Molly under one of my arms and I urged her away with some haste. Fortunately a wireless was going inside and we escaped detection. It was, I am convinced, only a subsequent love-scene of outstanding incoherence—a scene taking place in the window—which caused her to escape my vigilance and fire into the dining-room as we were about to leave. My lady is a good shot and she had no intention whatever of hitting anyone; she wishes me to say that she meant it merely as a comment on poor Madeline's morals, and that she would jolly well do it again.

I stress these unimportant and even ludicrous goings-on, in conclusion, for one very good reason: the reason with which I began. I do not want you to think that we went away in an atmosphere of high tragedy under the dark mutterings of the gods. I do not want you to think that nature held its breath at the evil of our passing. For I think, doctor—I rather think—that in order to make Knowles confess you must have deliberately painted Molly's character as much more stiff with wicked impulse than it really is.

She is not crafty; she is the reverse of crafty. Her private witch-cult was not the coldly intellectual effort of a woman interested in watching minds writhe; she is the reverse of coldly intellectual, and well you know it. She did what she did because she liked it. She will, I trust, continue to like it. To speak of her as though she killed Victoria Daly is nonsense; and anything concerning the woman near Tunbridge Wells is so cloudy as to be beyond proof or even accusation. That she has much of the Lower Plane in her nature I concede, as I have in mine; but what else? Our departure from Kent and from England was not, as I have tried to indicate, a curtain to a Morality Play. It was very much like the jumbled rush of the ordinary family to the seaside, where father cannot remember what he did with the tickets and mother is certain she left the light burning in the bathroom. A similar haste and overset, I suspect, attended the departure of Mr and Mrs Adam from a more spacious garden; and this, the king may say without denial from Alice, is the oldest rule in the book.

Yours sincerely,

JOHN FARNLEIGH (whilom Patrick Gore).